LOVE
LOVE

A NOVEL BY
BETH MICHELE

Dear Alison,

I am so grateful to you.
There is no doubt in my mind
that I would not be where
I am today without all
of your support. Thank you
from the bottom of my
heart. ♡ Beth

Table of Contents

Dedication

For Clara.
Your spirit wraps around my heart,
but I miss your smile every day.

Prologue

This was the moment I'd waited for my entire life, or so I thought. That's if you consider twenty-two years an entire life. It started out as a perfect day, but perfection can be an illusion.

Our blue gowns were fanning the breeze as we made our way up to the podium. The wind blowing through my hair made me feel alive and free. I was inches away from my long awaited independence. All those days I sat on the bleachers, watching UC Berkeley football games and daydreaming about life after college, and it was finally here. My feet were making their way up the stairs quickly. They had a mind of their own and I had difficulty keeping up with them. They obviously knew something I didn't.

Mr. Shorley shook my hand firmly as he happily handed me my degree. The sun's rays bouncing off the paper gave it a rare glow. *This* was my golden ticket. Even better than a lifetime supply of Wonka bars.

As I walked across the stage, I caught a glimpse of Clark and Fran. Clark gave me a wink that made my insides melt, and Fran mooned me. Her heart-shaped ass catching the summer wind was her unusual way of congratulating me. It made me smile. My parents however, didn't have the same reaction; I caught their grimaces, the warm air surrounding me suddenly stale and cold.

♡ ♡ ♡

The graduation party at my house was rip-roaring. The music was blaring, the alcohol flowing, and the hips grinding. The party was a lot more than my parents bargained for when they agreed to it. The adults were outside on the moonlit patio, tossing down hard liquor and blowing smoke rings, while the graduates were inside bringing down the house. I was with my two favorite people. Clark Thompson, my boyfriend since high school, and Fran Heller, my best friend of fifteen years.

Fran and I met in fourth grade. Her mom moved her from the Bronx to California to get away from her physically abusive asshole dad. She's had a tough life, but given the hand she was dealt, she always manages to remain optimistic. I admire that about her. She comes across like she's hard when really, she's anything but. Thinking about Fran always makes me smile. We had an instant connection. They used to call me "Candy Girl" in elementary school because I was always either eating candy or giving it away. From the moment Fran slipped a Hershey's Bar under my desk in fourth grade, she had me, and we had each other.

Clark and I met our sophomore year of high school. I was standing at my locker in between classes and the hallway was packed. My head was buried in books when something crashed hard against my back. Turned out it was Gavin Boone, quarterback of our crappy football team. He wasn't looking where the hell he was going, lucky for me. I was knocked to the ground, and when I looked up, I was met by baby blues and a forehead crinkle. *Clark.*

"You okay?" he asked.

"Never better," I said, rolling my eyes, trickles of pain shooting up my spine.

In the midst of the run in, my bag spilled with all of my personal belongings. I watched in horror as the evidence of my adolescence covered the ground. Clark bent down to help me, and without batting an eye, proceeded to scoop up the Playtex tampons and put them back in the box. He made a beeline right for them. Who does that? When he was done, he bumped my shoulder and shrugged his. "It's just life, right?"

He was the one who embraced my soul in the palm of his hands. The one who lent his ear while I rambled endlessly about my parents and all their bullshit. He was the one who supported me when I fell on my ass and the one whose broad shoulders carried all of my tears.

Clark introduced me to surprises. Bringing me flowers after school just because. Leaving bags of Hershey's Kisses in my locker with little notes like "I love you, sweetness." Even blindfolding me and taking me on little adventures to the beach, my favorite place in the world.

God, I loved Clark. He made me giggle and gave me those crazy butterflies. In high school, we'd make out under the bleachers, in his car, basically anywhere we could get our hands on each other. A single wink from him would cause my heart to explode, and that musky scent of his drove me beyond the borders of desire. I lost my virginity to Clark when we were seventeen. We were so in love, and while it was incredibly romantic, honestly, it hurt like hell. Nothing like you see in the movies. But Clark was gentle and sweet, and never made me feel the least bit embarrassed or uncomfortable, even when he saw spots of blood on the sheet. While Clark had experienced sex before, that was my first time, and it was glaringly obvious. Nonetheless, I'll never forget it. He moved inside of me with such tenderness and cradled me with his touch. Afterwards, he gently touched his lips to mine before walking away and coming back with a warm washcloth. "Let me clean you up Angel." Could he have been any sweeter?

"Gabby." A voice startled me from my nostalgic moment. My beloved mother. It's fascinating that even over the loud music, I could still hear the shrill of her voice. "I'd like to speak with you for a minute."

I cupped my hand to my ear. "What?" I said, pretending I didn't hear her.

"I need to speak with you, dear," she said again, her face set with a frown so deep it was probably where the term frown lines came from.

My mother followed behind me, her heels clicking on the hardwood floor as I walked toward the sliding glass doors leading to the patio. I pulled open the handle, only to be met by a blast of muggy air and the heavy stench of cigarette smoke. She grabbed my hand to stop me.

"No, not outside dear. Let's go in the hallway."

We made our way down the hall and she stopped short, shaking her head as she glanced up and down my body at the white t-shirt, faded blue jeans, and blue Converse sneakers I'd decided to wear.

"Gabby. This is a party. Don't you think you could have chosen something a bit more festive, like a dress perhaps?" She was impeccably dressed, as always, in her emerald green Vera Wang silk dress and her black Manolo Blahnik slingbacks. Her sleek brown hair was pulled up in a perfect bun, complete with diamond clip, and her makeup was flawless, almost as if she'd just left the Chanel counter at the mall.

"Mom," I began, the alcohol causing my words to slur a bit. "When was the last time you saw me in a dress? You know I don't like to wear them. Remember, you're always telling me they make my hips look too curvy and my legs look too thin?"

She fanned her hand in front of her face. "My God, Gabby, you smell like a brewery. I don't think you should have anything else to drink."

I let out an exasperated sigh. "Mom. First of all, this is a graduation party; and secondly, I'm twenty-two years old, how much I drink is currently up to me."

She clenched her fists at her sides and rolled her eyes at me, a look of pure disgust crossing her face. "I also didn't realize Clark's parents were going to be here."

I had to contain myself from hauling back and shaking around any sense that might have been left in my mother's body. "Mom, Clark and I have been together for *seven* years, and this is *our* graduation day; of course his parents are going to be here."

My parents were not fans of Clark's mom and dad. The mail clerk and the bus driver just didn't meet their social status requirements.

I tried my best distraction technique. "Where's Dad?"

My mother sucked her teeth. "He's out back with his latest girlfriend."

"I haven't seen Olivia either. Where is she?"

"Olivia had another party to go to," she said nonchalantly.

"Of course. Another one that was more important than her own sister's." I let out a sarcastic laugh and felt Clark's warm hand on my shoulder.

"Hello, Mrs. Willis," Clark greeted her with a broad smile.

"Hello, Clark," my mother replied, years of disapproval sliding off her tongue.

My parents were never Clark's biggest fans. The fact that he loved me and was so good to me didn't impress them. They wanted me to marry rich and live in the big mansion on a perfect tree-lined street, complete with manicured lawn, fountain, and in-ground pool; perfect replica of our house. Thanks, but no thanks. Granted, they weren't the best role models for long-lasting relationships. My parents were high school sweethearts, but thirty years later they hated each other. That wasn't going to be me and Clark. We could get through anything.

My mom made a tisking sound then skulked away. Clark took my hand and led me into the small den where I used to watch television as a child. The only room that was suitable for us to play in growing up so we didn't destroy the near perfection of the rest of the house. He sat me down on the yellow sofa, stained with years of chocolate milk spills and my favorite purple marker, ran his fingers through my chestnut strands, then tucked my hair behind my ear.

"Talk to me, Angel, what did your mother do now?"

I looked around the room at years of childhood memories. Family photographs from our trip to Disney World, a cuckoo clock that I always got in trouble for playing with, the piano where I learned how to play Chopsticks. "Nothing's ever good enough for her, you know? I don't remember the last time either of them had a kind word to say about me. I'm just one giant disappointment in their eyes." I continued to stare at a spot on the yellow couch.

"Angel, look at me." Clark lifted my chin and stroked his fingers gently across my cheek. "Your mom doesn't define you. *You* define you, and from where I'm standing, you're doing a damn good job." He moved closer and kissed me softly. Taking my hand, he lifted up one finger and kissed it. "Let's see: you're smart." He lifted another one and surrounded it with his lips. "You're funny as hell." Another finger arrived at his mouth for a kiss. "You're caring and kind." He pulled my pinky to his mouth for a final kiss. "You're breathtakingly beautiful. So, screw your mom. I'd say you've defined yourself pretty well." Clark wrapped his comforting arms around me and suddenly all was right with the world. "Come on, let's go back out there and celebrate the beginning of the rest of our lives."

♡ ♡ ♡

The party was rocking. Fran and I continued to get a serious buzz on while Clark eyed us amusingly. For some reason, he decided not to drink tonight, but that never stopped him from having a good time. I was definitely enjoying myself. My new sense of freedom was washing over me like a giant wave crashing on the shore. This was really it. I'd finally be out on my own and out of the grasp of people who I constantly disappointed. I couldn't wait to surround myself with people who would lift me up, not drag me down. I've had way too much of that and it was time to navigate my own future with Clark by my side. Hell, I might even wear a dress.

We were hanging out on the makeshift dance floor. Clark's hands were roaming, our hips were swaying, and we were all dancing our free little hearts out. The fuzzy feeling in my head caused me to react as Clark pressed his firm body against mine. I wrapped my arms around his neck and plunged my tongue into his mouth, relishing the familiar taste of him. When I pulled back, I could see Fran staring at us, probably because we were practically making out in public. I didn't care, Clark turned me on in ways I never imagined, and there wasn't a moment that went by that I didn't crave his touch, his lips, his everything.

He leaned in close to my ear and his warm breath blew a breeze my way, causing me to shiver. "Angel, let's get out of here. I need to be alone with you." The look in his eyes told me he wanted me, not to mention the stiffness I felt pressing against my thigh. I wanted him, too. "There's somewhere I want to take you," his hot breath whispered and his musky scent overtook my senses. When he looked at me with those persuasive baby blues, it was hard to say no.

"Okay, babe. Let me just tell Fran we're leaving, and then I'm all yours." I pulled him to me and planted a large, wet kiss on his soft lips; he grabbed me and deepened it. His tongue explored mine tenderly, sucking gently, while his arms brought me in to him. When I broke the kiss, I heard him exhale with a sigh.

I walked up to Fran, who was doing the bump and grind with our friend Ashley. She was seriously plastered. "Fran, Clark and I are going out for a bit. We'll be back."

Fran gave me a big smacker right on the lips. Yup, she was hammered all right. "Okay sweetie. Don't do anything I wouldn't do." She cackled relentlessly and continued her drunken dance.

Clark interlaced his fingers through mine as we walked out to the car.

"So where are we going, babe?" I asked, my mind open to all possibilities.

"It's a surprise, Angel. You'll just have to wait and see."

We drove for less than a mile before I realized exactly where we were headed. Clark's house. His empty house. That made me smile. There's only one thing I wanted right now, and that was Clark...inside of me.

When we pulled in the driveway, Clark cut the engine. The look that crossed his face wasn't one I'd seen before, so I wasn't sure what to make of it.

"Angel, I need you to stay here for just a minute, okay?"

"What's going on?"

"Just wait here a minute and then I'll be back to get you."

"Okay."

He gave me a quick kiss and then slammed the door shut behind him. My mind was working overtime. He seemed nervous. What on earth was he doing? It felt like forever before he returned to the car. Coming around to the passenger side, he opened my door and helped me out. Immediately, I grabbed him and pressed my breasts against his tight chest, giving him a sneak preview of what was to come.

"Come on, hot stuff," he said, tangling his fingers with mine and leading me around to the backyard.

As we rounded the corner, I stopped in my tracks and my heart started racing. My eyes were taking in everything all at once. The deck was covered in little white Christmas tree lights. A table sat in the center with a crisp white tablecloth and a vase of crimson red roses in the middle; it was set for two. I heard Train playing softly on the CD player sitting next to the weathered charcoal grill. My feet were frozen, my insides tingled, and my brain was running at mach speed. I spun around and looked at Clark.

"What is all this?"

He shrugged his shoulders. "Happy graduation, Angel."

Wrapping my arms around his waist, I leaned forward until our foreheads were touching. "I love you so much," I said as our noses rubbed together and our lips melted into one another.

Clark settled me in my chair and walked back into the house. I suddenly felt very sober, keenly aware of everything that was happening in that moment. It seemed impossible that I could love Clark any more than I already did, yet every day he did something to make my heart fuller. I sat there with a goofy grin plastered on my face, awaiting his return. He came out moments later with two white plates holding dark chocolate lava cake surrounded by two Twizzlers forming a heart, with whipped cream on the side. My absolute favorite.

"Thank you, babe," I said, my heart so full and my body so damned turned on by his kindness. "I'm not really hungry though. Well...I am...but only for one thing."

Clark let out a hearty, sexy laugh, and licked his lips. "Eat, Angel. You're going to need your strength."

Oh.

He didn't say much while we were eating, but I felt his eyes on me. When we were done, he took my hand and led me to the brown wicker couch that sat facing his mother's plentiful garden. He sweetly took my face in his hands and I relaxed into him. His thumb caressed my cheekbone and my eyelids fluttered closed. His touch always did that to me. When I opened my eyes, he was staring deeply into them.

"I love you, Gabrielle Willis. I've loved you from the moment I laid eyes on you, the moment I bumped your shoulder in that crowded hallway of our high school. I love everything about you...the way your lips turn up when you smile, your generous heart, your flowery spirit, your two left feet, and of course, your love of all things sweet." He smiled widely, then brushed his lips ever so softly against mine before he pulled back. "You're it for me, Gabby. There will never be anyone else. I don't want anyone else. I want to wake up to every single sunrise with you, and at the end of my day, I want you to be my sunset."

Clark left me, but only for the briefest of seconds, to slide off the couch and get down on one knee. He placed my hand in his, brought it to his mouth for a kiss, and then with the most sincere blue eyes I'd ever known, looked into mine.

"Gabrielle Christina Willis," his voice shook, "will you make me the happiest damn man alive and marry me?"

My eyes grew wide and my lips suddenly felt dry. I watched as Clark pulled a burgundy velvet ring box from his pocket, my mouth dropped open at the sight of a gorgeous, emerald-cut diamond sparkling brilliantly in the moonlight.

He smiled nervously before he spoke. "I like your mouth hanging open like that, Angel, but in this particular case, it's because I'm waiting on an answer."

His words seemed to unfreeze my lips and I began to laugh, something only Clark could make me do. I cupped his face in my hands and leaned in close, teardrops falling rapidly from my eyes. Moving in close so that our lips were touching, I breathed, "Yes, I will marry you, Clark Thompson."

He locked his lips with mine, wrapping his arms around me and kissing me like I was the air he needed to breathe. When he pulled back, he took the ring from the plush velvet and placed it on my finger, tears forming in the creases of his eyes. "Do you have any freaking idea how happy you've just made me? I love you so much, Angel, with every ounce of my heart. You are my only."

"I love you too, Clark...forever." His head fell against mine, and I swore time stood still. Everything about that moment was perfect. Clark was perfect...perfect for me. I tangled my hands in his hair and sucked on his bottom lip. "So can we have engagement sex now? Because I've heard engagement sex is hot."

Clark leaned in close to my ear, his warm breath making my skin sizzle. "Angel, anything with you is hot." He scooped me up under my knees and I kicked my legs in the air, giggling ferociously. Draping my arms around him, I played with the wisps of his hair and buried my face in his warmth. His musky scent and the perfection of the moment made my heart pound rapidly against my chest.

He set me down on the floor of his room. The familiar room was filled with his delicious smell, hockey trophies aligning the shelves, rumpled sheets, and piles of clothes. I let out a deep breath and my whole body relaxed, recognizing this as home. Smiling, I recalled all the times I snuck into this room through the side window once Clark's parents fell asleep. It always felt like forbidden fruit and I was a health nut. Glancing down at the giant sparkle on my finger, I looked over at Clark.

"You do know what this means, don't you? No more sneaking around! We can be together whenever we like, and however..."

Clark dropped a wet kiss behind my ear that made me shiver. "Get naked, wife-to-be. I want you in my bed right now."

I didn't need to hear anything else. I jumped on his bed and proceeded to do my best striptease, casually sliding my t-shirt over my head and tossing it at him. It landed on his face, and when he removed it, the sexy grin I received spurred me on. I ran my hands down my body slowly, brushing the curves of my breasts and leading to the zipper of my jeans, slowly unzipping and shimmying them off, revealing my peppermint pink lace panties. Clark's eyes grew wide as he tore his polo shirt over his head and stepped out of his pants. I brought my hands behind my back and unclasped my satin bra, seductively trailing the straps down my arms until I fell back and hit my head on the wall. So much for my seduction.

He lunged for me. "You okay, Angel?"

I rubbed the back of my head. "Yup...so much for my seduction."

He licked my bottom lip. "Oh, I quite liked your seduction." His eyes moved over his erection. "Can't you tell?"

I eyed the bulge in his boxers and licked my lips, then chuckled. "I need something sweet. Bring me that honey stick right now."

Clark smirked and tore off his boxers. "Is this what I have to look forward to after we're married?"

As he climbed over me I said, "Uh huh...and so much more." I could picture Clark and I in our house together, sitting side by side at the kitchen table eating pancakes and bacon, planting flowers in the yard, brushing our teeth in the same bathroom, snuggling together on the sofa for Friday movie nights, and doing all of the things that married people do. The thought of him being the last person I saw at the end of my day and the first one I'd wake up to made my insides twist with happiness. I could visualize a giggling shaggy-haired, blue-eyed mini version of Clark running around barefoot in the backyard being chased by his adoring father. Sigh. All of the things that people so easily took for granted. I wouldn't ever do that with Clark.

He settled between my thighs and captured my mouth, delicately tracing my plump lips before slipping inside and stroking my tongue with his. Breaking the kiss, his head lowered until I felt his lips and tongue surround my nipple and desire exploded between my legs. Clark's cell phone rang and he let out a groan.

"Don't answer it," I moaned, and he didn't, until whoever it was kept calling back and the ringing in our ears wouldn't stop. I let out a frustrated sigh. "I guess you better answer it, babe, it's obviously important."

He reached for his cell phone on the side table without straying from my body. "Hello?"

"Clark, it's...Su...si...e..."

"Susie, you sound like you're wasted. What's up? I'm kind of busy." He stuck his tongue out at me and I wanted to bite it.

"I'm at Naomi's hou ... se ... and ... everyone is ... drun ... k ... I ... need ... a ride home ..."

A huge puff of air left Clark's chest. "Alright, I'll be there in a few minutes."

"Is Susie okay, babe?"

"Well, my sister's completely drunk again, and so is everyone else, so I have to pick her up. I'm sorry, Angel."

I met his lips with mine. "Don't be, babe. I'm not going anywhere. I'll be right here when you get back, naked and ready."

He kissed me again and reluctantly dragged his body off of mine. He sighed deeply. "I like the sound of that."

Clark pulled on his stonewashed jeans and blue polo and grabbed his keys. He walked over to me and held on tight, moving his lips over mine tenderly. "God, I love you, Angel. I can't wait for you to be my wife."

"Me too. Now hurry back." I swatted his ass.

He turned around and gave me one more peek into those fields of blue before he headed out.

That was the last time I ever saw him.

Chapter One

*"If there ever comes a day when we cant
be together, keep me in your heart,
I'll stay there forever." - A.A. Milne*

Three Years Later

I startle awake out of a dream to the buzzing of my annoying alarm clock. Why I don't set it to the radio is beyond me. Maybe I like the shock value. Rubbing my crusty, sleep-filled eyes, I drag my legs over the side of the bed and try and get my bearings before stumbling into the bathroom. I pause for a second to look in the mirror. Yes, this is my life. Every day is the same. My hour and a half morning routine consists of getting dressed, a not-so-pleasant ride on the subway to 62nd and Broadway, a caffeine stopover at Starbucks, and finally, my arrival at Landon & Castell Interior Design by nine a.m. That's the time Robby Mathers, my boss, likes me to be there, and he likes me prompt. I've been working there for almost three years since I received my Business Degree, and it's a job for which I actually have my dad to thank. He used his connections, but not before emphasizing how many strings he had to pull and reading me the riot act about working hard and proving myself. I guess I owe him for this one. Yeah, maybe.

Stepping in the shower, I'm quickly shocked awake by a blast of cold water. As I let the stream pour over my face, I can't help thinking to myself that all this monotony is getting to me and I'm in desperate need of a spark. Maybe I should bungee jump off of the Empire State Building or run naked in Central Park. Nah, that would just be plain crazy, plus I'd get arrested. That wouldn't end well. Unless there was a hot guy dressed in a uniform fingerprinting me. Then it might just be worth it. After all, there's really nothing like a man in uniform. I know it sounds like I have sex on the brain. I really don't.

Let's be real. I've always liked guys. Even when they were boys. I remember chasing Michael Bagley around the kindergarten playground, trying to get him to kiss me. Then there was Jason Rasmussen in fourth grade. He played the Tin Man in the school production of *The Wizard of Oz*, while I played a short, chubby munchkin. God, he was cute. He had the sweetest dimple on his left cheek and a birthmark just above his perfectly shaped lips. Even now, thinking about him makes me smile. I never managed to get much of his attention, but it certainly wasn't from a lack of trying.

So here I am. Twenty-five years old and living in New York; The City That Never Sleeps. Of course, it's impossible to sleep when someone's banging tin cans outside your window. Nonetheless, New York is truly awesome. I mean, I loved California; the palm trees, the beaches, the hot guys on the boardwalk. Yeah, all of that was good. But New York City, that's a whole other ball game. You can find anything here, and I mean *anything*. A vendor selling hot dogs on the street, a guy playing guitar in the subway, or a naked cowboy in Times Square. It's all here. And the energy wow! It electrifies me. Sets me on fire. Makes me smile.

I make my way up the stairs of the subway platform until I'm finally greeted by a patch of clear blue sky. My heels click against the pavement while I stare up to the heavens, thinking I might find the answer to what I'm searching for. When there's no response, I decide on my usual. An iced vanilla latte from Starbucks. I've been drinking coffee since I was a kid, back in the day when no one was looking and I'd put four teaspoonfuls of sugar in it. Now, I'm onto the fancy stuff; the lattes, the espressos, the mochaccinos...I can't get through the day without my caffeine fix. It's my only addiction. Well, that and candy...and chocolate. That's it, though.

Standing in front of the Starbucks sign, I hesitate. I'm so freaking predictable and need a change. I've heard some friends of mine talk about this new gourmet coffee shop around the corner that's supposed to be mind-blowing. How can coffee be mind-blowing? That might be a bit extreme. Regardless, I need something different, so I keep walking until I reach The Brew House. It seems like a regular coffee shop; lots of people chatting away in cozy velvet booths and sitting on plush couches, drinking coffee. Although I do like the colors more than Starbucks; olive greens, splashes of burgundy, and desert creams, while local artwork aligns the walls. There are various pieces of mismatched furniture in a variety of fabrics. It's eclectic and definitely my style.

I see a couple with their tongues down each other's throats. Talk about a public display of affection. Holy cow. I try to walk in further and notice my heels are sticking to the floor. Yuck. I look down into the giant blue eyes of a little blonde boy who's blowing raspberries at me and crushing his sugary doughnut into the ground, and at the same time pouring his apple juice on my shoe.

His mother, of course, doesn't notice. I smile and blow one back at him and he runs and hides behind his mother's leg. I didn't realize I was that scary.

When I look up, I see the other not-so-lovely thing. A line that's almost out the door. The coffee must be really good here. As I wait, I glance up at the menu on the wall. There are a multitude of drinks to choose from. The line actually moves quickly and when I reach the counter, I'm greeted by a guy who looks around my age standing about six feet tall with blue jeans, white fitted t-shirt, a lopsided grin and a dimple.

"Hi, can I help you?"

I hesitate because I still don't know what I want, even though I had a whole ten minutes to decide. Making a decision isn't my strong suit; I excel at indecisiveness. I think I hear sighs and groans coming from behind me. I'm holding up the line, a big faux pas in a coffee shop. As the line builds and the whines grow louder, the guy behind the counter speaks again.

"Do you know what do you want?"

"Ummm...I..."

He leans over the counter. His shaggy light brown hair falls over his face and covers his eyes. I can't make out what color they are. Maybe brown. "What do you like?"

I'm on my tippy toes a bit distracted by the glass case of doughnuts. "I don't know," I whisper, embarrassed that I'm holding up the line.

"Do you like chocolate?"

Ding, ding, ding. "Yes!"

"Good, what else?"

"Umm...I like caramel."

A small smile tugs at his lips. "Okay, we're getting somewhere. Do you like whipped cream?"

"Love it," I say excitedly.

"Excellent."

"Ice cream?" he asks with hopeful eyes.

"Ew. Not in my coffee."

He laughs, then says, "okay, I think you'll like the Salted Caramel Mocha."

"Sounds good." Anything to rid myself of the annoying whines behind me. I'm tapping my fingers on the counter as he makes my drink. "Sorry about the holdup. I usually just go to Starbucks."

"Starbucks, huh? So, you decided it was time to cross over to the dark side?" he remarks with a raised eyebrow.

Humor laces my lips. "Yes, the force was very strong."

He cracks a smile and sets my drink down. "I'm Brad Dixon, by the way."

"Gabby Indecisive Willis, and thanks for the help."

"Don't mention it," he says, airing me another quirky grin.

I go to pay him; my purse is a mess and it's like playing hide and seek to find my money. While digging, I inadvertently knock the entire fancy whatever mocha all over the counter and watch as the warm liquid seeps under the cash register. Fabulous. My cheeks heat and I squeeze my eyes shut, wishing I could click my heels three times and be anywhere but here.

When my eyes finally open, Brad appears to be counting to ten, and I can't blame him. Grabbing napkins from a nearby table, I try to help with this wonderful mess that is my creation. By the time I return, Brad has it completely under control.

"I'm really sorry," leaves my mouth before I can stop it, and I stand there like an idiot trying to escape the red tint engulfing my face.

His sincere, caring brown eyes peek out from under his hair and meet mine. "Don't worry about it. It happens all the time." He smirks. "I'm gonna make you another one. On the house."

"Thanks, Brad, but you don't have to do that."

"I can't very well let one of our new customers leave unhappy her very first visit."

My hand dives into my purse. "Let me pay you for it. It's the least I can do."

"Nah. Take it. Just bring an extra roll of Bounty next time you come in." I hear a rich, throaty laugh as he walks away.

Salted Caramel Mocha in hand, I make my way out to the street and head towards work. It's a beautiful day in Manhattan. The sun is shining brilliantly and there's not a cloud in the powder blue sky. The skyline looks just like a postcard today, and the energy, as always, is infectious. The constant hustle and bustle is one of the reasons I love the city so much. The intensity of the city manages to take my rather monotonous routine and breathe life into it. It's nice knowing that my daily commute will always have something different to offer, whether it's a guy singing acapella in the subway or someone playing bongo drums. It always manages to elicit a smile.

Since I'm early today, I sip my mocha and casually make my way to work. I hear the taxi cabs honking, feel the smell of rotting food invading my nose, and notice the chatter of strangers. A guy spits on the ground and I almost step in it. Why do people spit? It's the most disgusting habit, and should probably be illegal. Oh God, not to mention the woman trying to shove an entire egg sandwich in her mouth. I see an elderly woman with a cane stumble over a crack in the sidewalk and several people run over at once to help her, including myself. When I reach her, I lift her cane off the ground and hand it to her. She looks up at me with worldly eyes and a fragile voice. "God bless you, dear." My returning smile says *you're welcome*. As crazy as the city gets, people here really do care.

My walk takes me past Bloomingdale's, and I stop to admire a dress in the window. They must have changed out the dresses this week because I haven't noticed it before. It's royal blue satin with cap sleeves and a high boat neck. We have a formal company party next week and this dress looks perfect. Too bad it's only 8:45; Bloomies doesn't open until ten. I make a mental note to stop by after work to try it on. I'll definitely bring Fran with me. She'll tell me if it's too conservative, too slutty, or doesn't show enough cleavage...because she always thinks I need to show more.

A couple of relaxing, mocha-sipping blocks later I'm suddenly frozen to the spot, my coffee almost spilling on my blouse. I check my pulse. I'm still alive. Good. Whoa. This guy is hot. Smooth jet black hair, beautiful emerald green eyes, broad shoulders, and a body built for sin strolls toward me, one sculptured arm dangling a suit jacket over his shoulder, his body donned by a finely tailored black suit. I think I just had an orgasm. He's freaking beautiful. I close my eyes and I'm immediately locked on a visual. Yup, I've got it. My fingernails digging into his back while he hovers over me, screaming my name, sweat dripping from his chest and landing on my breasts. Okay, close your mouth, Gabby. The drool is pooling at your feet. Shit. He must have noticed me staring. When I pass by him, I see the corner of his lips curl into an alluring smile.

He makes his way past me and I turn back for one last look. Jesus. I see his head whip around for a split second and glance in my direction. I can't believe he's actually looking at me. Then I notice that the lovely breeze has blown my skirt up to declare my ass available for public viewing. Great. Not only that, but I just tripped over a little brown and black rat dog and am getting dirty looks from its disgruntled owner as she pulls his leash and yanks him away from my clumsy left foot.

I try to regain my weakened composure and head into work. I literally have to shake myself to erase the erotic images from my mind. Two thoughts occur to me as I enter the double doors of Landon & Castell. First, I need to find out who the hell those green eyes belong to; and second, I need a cold shower.

I see the red light on my phone blinking from what seems like a mile away. I plunk down on my chair, throw my purse in my desk drawer, and take the deep breath that I need to run through all my messages and the overwhelming amount of post-it notes Robby always leaves for me. They're everywhere. On my computer, my desk, the wall of my cubicle, and he even stuck one on the picture of Fran and me at Fisherman's Wharf. I think he just likes the idea of sticking them to something. I've got thirty messages. Shit. As I scroll through them, I find that half of them are garbage and just leave my finger on the delete button.

My electronic schedule says Robby and I have to visit three clients, and the fifteen "urgent" messages indicate that there are various issues with furniture orders to sort out. I'm really not complaining. This is a very cool job. It gets me closer to my dream of being an interior designer, which is something I've wanted to do since I was a kid. Memories flood my mind of buying stacks and stacks of *Architectural Digest* and *Better Homes & Gardens* magazines, wanting to absorb the color palettes and furniture choices while I played out the fantasy in my head. I'd sit there for hours, tearing out pictures I liked and making collages, only to end up annoying my mother by leaving paper scraps all over the floor. I'd smile though, when I'd look up at the fairy pink walls covered with my childhood dreams filling up every open space of my room. It was something my parents couldn't touch or crush within me.

The day drags at a snail's pace. I'm getting ready to leave when my cell phone vibrates. I let it go because, admittedly, I like the sensation. When the buzzing continues, I finally check and see that it's Fran. I pick up the phone with excitement for the first time all day. "Hey!"

"Hey," she replies. Her voice lacks her usual burst of enthusiasm.

"What's wrong?" Did you have a bad day?" It's unusual for Fran to let things get to her, so I know it can't be good.

She groans. "Yeah. It was shitty. I had a client want me to redesign a brochure six times before they were happy, my boss got on my ass about being late because I missed an important client meeting, and my heel broke while I was out getting lunch. All in all it was a banner day. Yours?"

"It was long, and very busy." Knowing my day is coming to an end puts a smile on my face for the first time, and I relax. "So, I'm assuming you want to go out? How about a movie with a giant tub of buttered popcorn and a jumbo pack of Twizzlers? We can get lost for a little while."

"Yes, I want to go out, but not to a movie. I need a drink, or a few drinks. There's a new bar that opened up on Amsterdam Avenue and I want to check it out."

"Oh." I hesitate before answering her. My first thought is she's going to try and set me up like she usually does, and I'm not in the mood.

"So, are you in?" she asks, her voice raising an octave.

"On one condition," I add reluctantly. I have to be honest, right?

She chuckles. "And that would be…"

"It's just been a long day, Fran. I don't want you trying to work your love magic on me tonight. Also, before I forget, I need to stop by Bloomingdale's first."

"Alright, deal," she asserts a little too quickly. "Why do we need to stop at Bloomies?"

"There's a dress I want to try on for our company party. I want to see what you think."

"Great. Oh, and by the way, someone is coming by the apartment tomorrow to exterminate. I found a lovely little cockroach behind the fridge this morning."

"Ew!" I can't stand those pesky little things. Fran and I have lived for almost three years in an extremely small two bedroom apartment in Washington Heights. It's actually a pre-war walk up, tastefully decorated with very special discount and consignment store items and a couple sale items from IKEA. The only thing not-so-charming about it is the little roach problem, which has taken some getting used to. "Gee, thanks for that."

"Anytime. See you soon."

Fifteen minutes later, Fran is waiting for me outside of Landon & Castell, looking stunning, as always. With wavy, shoulder length ebony hair, bright green eyes, a fair complexion with a hint of pink, and curves that make men swoon, Fran oozes sex appeal. Her tight white tank accentuates her breasts, while her short black skirt shows off her long, shapely legs. Her feet are covered by Jimmy Choo heels in the same color. "You look hot, Fran!" I look down at my gray pencil skirt and white blouse and suddenly feel very undressed.

She lets out a sexy laugh. "I'm on fire every night. Now if I could only find someone to put out that fire, my world would be complete. By the way, notice the new pumps? Breaking a heel is a great excuse to buy a new pair of shoes...not that I ever need an excuse to shop!"

My mind drifts from Fran to the hotness on the street this morning. It's hard to shake *that* visual.

Fran waves her hand in front of my face. "Hello? Earth to Gabby, where'd you go?"

"I'm here," I murmur as I float back down to earth. "Now, let's go see about that dress."

We're making our way over to Bloomingdale's, and I can't help but notice people staring at me. It's really starting to piss me off. "Fran, do I have something on my face?"

She looks at me with a confused smile. "What the hell are you talking about?"

"Well, it's just that I feel like everyone's looking at me, and it's getting annoying."

"Oh my God, Gabby. When are you going to get a clue? You're beautiful! That's why everyone is staring. Do you know how many women would kill to look like you without having to slather shitloads of makeup on their face? You don't even have to try and you're gorgeous. Hell, you get out of bed in the morning and you're a guy's wet dream. That's just sickening, even to me."

I let out a frustrated groan. That's the total opposite of everything my parents said when I was growing up. It was always about them not liking the clothes I picked out, or wanting me to cut my hair a different way, or how I'd look prettier with makeup. I remember my mom taking me to Macy's and making me sit through one of those complimentary makeup sessions at the Clinique counter. Afterwards she always bubbled, *see how much prettier you look now*? Isn't every parent supposed to think their child is beautiful? That their child is smart? That their child is worthy? She'll never know how deeply her comments hurt me.

A huge sigh leaves my chest. "Can we just go check out my dress please?"

When we get to the store, I eye the dress again in the window, and know it's perfect. Fran waits outside the dressing room while I try it on. The dress moves over my body and once it's in place I realize why it caught my eye. It's just like everything else in my closet. The blue satin looks even prettier up close, it has a high neckline so it's not too revealing, and it falls below my knee. It doesn't really accentuate anything, which is why it works for me. I tend to pick the boring, traditional clothes lacking pizzazz, while Fran's choices are always funky and accentuate what she's got. She won't like this dress because it's too conservative.

I walk out of the dressing room and Fran's mouth hangs open. I guess she feels the same way. "Gabby...that's the dress you were dying to show me?"

"Yes, why?" I try to act innocent, but even I know this dress is boring with a capital B.

"Honey, it's too conservative. There's not an ounce of skin showing. We need to find you another dress."

I certainly know my best friend and that alone is a good feeling. Predictability wins out, however, and my mouth turns down in a pout. Suddenly I'm eight years old, standing in front of my mom, trying to convince her to let me choose my own clothes for school. "But I like this one, Fran," I whine.

"Sweetie. I know you have a tendency toward the conservative, but come on, you have to let loose a little. Show a little morsel. You have an amazing figure, but you hide it under all those clothes."

"I don't want to look like a slut, Fran!" I practically shout and see a woman whip her head around and peek at us through a rack of clothes.

"Gabby, showing a little cleavage isn't going to make you a slut. Sleeping around is the only thing that will grant you that very special title, so you're in the clear."

Fran starts rifling through racks looking for the perfect dress for me, which, quite frankly, makes me nervous. Our sense of style is just so completely different. After an hour of trying dresses on, I'm about ready to throw in the towel. Then I see her eyes light up. "That's the one!"

It's an olive green satin dress with a low cut scoop in the front and a V in the back, cut slightly above the knee. Something I would never wear. "Fran, that's way too revealing. I can't wear it!"

"Try it on, for heaven's sake. Can you just do that for me?" She gives me her best puppy dog eyes, and I have no choice but to concede.

I don't look in the mirror until I'm zipped. At first glance the fabric and cut seem to show way too much skin, but if I'm honest with myself, it makes me feel sexy.

Fran eyes me appreciatively, a satisfied smirk on her face. "Am I good, or am I good? That dress is perfect!"

I stare blankly at Fran. "I don't know, Fran."

"Gabby, you look beautiful. Really, honey. I mean, come on, you're five foot seven, with beautiful chestnut hair, gorgeous blue eyes, and a great figure! When are you going to start realizing this?"

My mother's voice plays like a record in my head. *Gabby, dear. That dress shows too much of that curvy figure and it makes your legs look skinny. It's not flattering at all. In fact, it's an unattractive look for you.*

Fran's eyes meet mine. "Well, we both know your mother's like the scarecrow from your favorite movie...you know, the one that doesn't have a brain."

$$\heartsuit \; \heartsuit \; \heartsuit$$

Excitement builds as we make our way over to the Sky Bar, the new lounge on the Upper West Side. After my new dress and Fran's pep talk, I'm definitely up for some fun; maybe a little harmless flirting. Maybe more. Who knows. Maybe I should let Fran set me up. Or maybe this is my sexual frustration talking. It's been a while.

We enter the bar and it's wall to wall people. Ugh. Sweaty bodies are rubbing up against me and the body odor is offensive. Someone just grabbed my ass. Gah! A shattering sound catches my attention and I look over to see a nervous waitress anxiously scooping up glass from the floor, trying to hide the red consuming her pretty face. I scan the room. Everyone here seems to be looking for something. A good time, a few drinks, an escape from their day, a sexual encounter, or even love, I suppose. As that last thought hits me, I wonder why anyone would go looking for love in a bar. I mean, let's be real, this isn't the place to find the key to your heart. The key to your vagina, maybe.

As I ponder my thoughts on the philosophy of life, Fran taps me on the shoulder. "What do you want to drink? The usual?"

"No way, Fran. Screw that. Tonight I'm living on the edge. I'll have a lemon drop."

"Wow, Gabby." She swipes the back of her hand across her forehead, feigning surprise. "That's your idea of living on the edge?"

I cross my arms over my chest. "Why, what's wrong with a lemon drop?"

"Sweetie. Lemon drops are for college girls, not a gorgeous, sophisticated woman like yourself. You really want to take a walk on the wild side? I'm ordering you a martini with an olive."

I let out a frustrated groan. "Okay, Fran, whatever."

Fran and I take a seat at the bar and wait for our drinks. My eyes wander and I scope out the crowd, hoping to find someone that might be worth a second look. Anyone with emerald eyes. Realizing I forgot to tell Fran about my encounter, if you could even call it that, I start to tell her when she cuts me off. "Fran, you'll never believe what happen—"

"Please tell me you took that guy Scott you work with right across your desk and had your wicked way with him!" Leave it to Fran to think it was about hot sex. She's always having hot sex, or thinking about it. God, I do envy her sometimes.

"As appealing as that sounds, no. I was on my way to work this morning when I saw the hottest freaking guy in creation."

Fran waits expectantly for me to elaborate and is disappointed, as usual. "That's it? *That* was your interesting morning?! I hope there's more to tell that makes it *interesting*."

"Well, there isn't really. Except that he was hot and seriously sexy. Tall, with shiny black hair, sparkling emerald green eyes, golden brown skin, and a rock hard body." I didn't tell her about the orgasm I practically had right on the street, or that my panties almost disintegrated the moment I saw him.

"Please tell me you tackled him and ripped his clothes off. Or, at least got his phone number."

That does sound appealing. The idea of hot sex with no commitment might be the way to go. At least it would be a great distraction. "Fran, as much as the idea of that turns me on, all I did was embarrass myself when he caught me staring. I'm sure he didn't think twice about it. He probably gets it all the time."

Fran waggles her eyebrows. "Oh, I'm *sure* he gets it all the time."

I smack her shoulder. "Do you ever think about anything besides sex? Nevermind, don't answer that."

"Hmmm...well, no, and why would I want to? Gabby, let's be honest, you need to get laid. It's been a while, and you've been very cranky lately, not to mention the fact that I found an excessive amount of empty Swedish Fish bags and Hershey's Kiss wrappers when I was taking out the garbage...a telltale sign. We need to remedy this situation and fast. You're not yourself, but I'm sure it's nothing a good, hot piece of ass can't take care of."

I crinkle my nose. "Oh my God, Fran, you're incorrigible!" She's not paying attention to me anymore, but looking toward the end of the bar. "What are you staring at?"

Her hand fans her face. "Check out those two hotties over there!"

I see two tall, honey blondes in very expensive-looking gray suits, one with blue eyes, the other with brown, both with muscular physiques. Blonde isn't really my preference. They make their way over after they catch us staring. The one with blue eyes speaks first.

"Hi, what are you two ladies drinking?"

Fran immediately pipes up. "Vodka tonic, and a martini." Then she moves closer to me and whispers "I'll take the one with the sexy birthmark."

I smirk and look over at her. "Don't worry about me. I'll just take whatever's left."

Blue eyes leans in and extends his hand. He's handsome, I guess, with a broad smile and a cleft in his chin. "I'm Blaine, and this is my friend, Kyle." Kyle's birthmark accentuates his full lips and he looks a bit like a Calvin Klein model, except with a suit as opposed to the fabulous tight-fitting underwear. Judging by the way he fills out his suit, I imagine he looks great in his underwear, too. Both of them.

Fran, of course, starts. "I'm Fran, and this is Gabby."

"Pleasure to meet you," they both say at the same time.

We all giggle a little nervously. Fran's making eyes at Kyle and I'm hoping the floor will open and swallow me.

"This is the first time we've been here," Kyle says. "What about you?"

"Yes, this is our first time, too," I agree, trying to make sure they're aware I can actually speak. "So, what do you both do?"

"We work at a hedge fund on Wall Street." Of course.

"What about you two?" Kyle asks, and I notice he moves closer to Fran.

"I work at an interior design firm," I respond. I keep my answers short in hopes that they'll tire of us, or at least me, and move along.

"Graphic design studio," Fran says, polishing off her second vodka tonic.

As we continue to make what I feel is boring conversation with Blaine and Kyle, the drinks keep coming, and the martinis are giving me a good buzz. After drink number three, I notice Blaine's arm sneak around and massage my waist. Needless to say, I'm not *that* buzzed. I immediately move his hand away and see the smile on his face turn into a frown. No matter how fuzzy the alcohol is making me feel, it's not enough to want a one night stand right now; not with this guy anyway.

Nothing about Blaine interests me and I find myself tuning him out and checking out the other guys at the bar. A warm body finds the seat next to me and a musky aroma floats in my direction. It smells familiar and I suddenly feel nauseous.

I anxiously turn to Fran. "I've got to get out of here." The smell is invading the void in my heart and a longing is taking over, one that I can't cope with because it just hurts too much.

"What's wrong?" A look of concern crosses her face.

What am I supposed to tell her? She's heard it all before...that every night when I close my eyes I see Clark's face, his smile, hear his voice...that I still smell his musky scent...that sometimes I try with every bone in my body to remember what it felt like to have his arms around me. She knows I end up sobbing some nights because it's getting harder and harder to remember. I don't want the memory; I want Clark. "I just need to go, Fran."

"Okay, then I'm coming with you."

"No, you stay and have fun. I'll see you at home later."

Fran puts her hands on her hips. "No way. I'm coming, too."

"Okay."

We say hurried goodbyes to Blaine and Kyle and stumble towards the subway. Fran puts her arm around my shoulder. "So, what happened in there?"

I stop walking and look up to meet her eyes, recognition hitting her immediately.

"Oh God, Gabby...Clark? Again?"

The combination of booze, anger, and sadness slurs my speech, and I come back practically spitting on her. "What the hhelll is that ssupposed to mean?!"

"You know what it fucking means, Gabby. It's been three years, and we've had this conversation over two hundred times. You need to move on!"

"I can't help it! I loved him so much, and I miss him. Every damn day...I miss him. I fffucking hate love Fran, I just fffucking hate it. I hate the way it smells, the way it tastes, the way it gives you those itchy little goosebumps, the way people walk around with those ridiculous happy smiles." Falling to the ground, my knees scraping the pavement, I wrap my arms around myself as new tears trickle down my mascara-stained face. "You just don't understand, Fran, it's not that easy!"

"The hell it isn't!" Fran bites back. "I was having a good time in there. I actually liked Kyle and didn't want to leave." Her hands go to her hips, her jaw working itself back and forth, face tense with anger. "You know what, Gabby?! I'm getting tired of you acting like you're the only one who lost Clark. I lost him, too! I loved him, too!" A heavy sob escapes her chest. "He was like a brother to me..." She looks down at the ground for a minute before she makes her way back up to me. Her eyes soften and her voice is raw with emotion. "I miss him, too, Gabby...I miss him, too."

"I'm sorry, Fran," I whisper. "I'm sorry for being so selfish."

Fran lowers herself to the pavement next to me, taking a deep breath and bumping my shoulder hard. She reaches under my arms and lifts me off the cement. "Come on, you pain in my ass, let's go home."

Chapter Two

The next morning I wake up with what feels like a hammer to the side of my head. Remind me never to take Fran's advice again. I practically fall out of bed, holding my pounding brain in place, and make my way to the bathroom to grab some Advil. I crack open the medicine cabinet, take out what I hope will be my instant relief, then pull apart an animal-themed Dixie Cup from the stack on the counter. I fill it with tap water three times and down it quickly, grabbing onto the sink to steady myself from this dizzying whirl. I'm surprised I can even put an outfit together this morning, but when I finally do and am getting ready to leave, Fran stumbles out of her bedroom, holding her head.

"Bad hangover, huh?" I laugh.

With a throaty voice, she replies, "yeah, you could say that."

I walk over to the kitchen, find a clean glass, quickly pull a bottle of Poland Spring from the fridge, then pour it for her before grabbing my coat and purse. "Better drink a couple of those so you can make it through the day. There's also some Advil in the bathroom cabinet. I'm off to work; I'll see you later."

"Gabby, wait," Fran says, slowly making her way to me.

"What?" I don't know if it's the headache or last night's argument that makes me want to run away.

"I just wanted to apologize for what I said last night. I mean, I meant what I said, but it just came out wrong. I don't know, Gabby...I just want you to be happy, you know, and I haven't seen you happy in a long time. It's just time, that's all." She pauses. "You know, remember when we were growing up and I had issues with friends, boyfriends, and my stupid dad? All those days I just wanted to disappear, to crawl into a hole and just stay there. Gabby, you wouldn't let me. You were always the one who was there for me and who lifted me up from my well of despair. You made me see that things would get better. In many ways, you helped me to believe in myself; you helped me to realize my own strength. Well, now it's my turn, Gabby. I want to do that for you."

I don't know what to say. Fran and I don't usually talk about these touchy-feely things. "Thanks." Then I turn and walk out the door.

Someone is smoking a cigarette in the entranceway of our building. I guess the *No Smoking* sign on the wall means nothing. I fan away the smoke, which only makes my head hurt more, and head toward the subway. Every sound, every movement, is intensified this morning. The screeching of tires, heels making their way across the sidewalk, taxi drivers screaming at each other. Why do they have to scream?

By the time I step off the platform and onto the street, I'm suddenly aware of an urgent need to pee. I have to go, and desperately. I pressure my feet to carry me faster, but they're less than cooperative. When I finally get to The Brew House, I head straight for the bathroom, rushing so I don't have accident number two here.

I'm greeted by a delightful bathroom, if there is such a thing. One wall is purple and the other yellow, covered with what looks like graffiti art, while the third is covered in a giant chalkboard. How cool. I quickly pee, trying to translate the graffiti words into English, then put my purple lace undies back in place and smooth my skirt. When I go to flush, I notice the gifts in the toilet that were left for me. Gross. Grabbing the handle, I try to flush it. Nothing happens. You've got to be kidding me! Shit. The toilet is backed up!

Now what? Pacing the floor, trying to come up with some wondrous plan of how to make this all go away. My mind's blank. Maybe I'll kill some time and try again. I wash my hands slowly. Hmmm...better wash them again. There's hand lotion on a funky café table, so I put that on and rub it in thoroughly. I think I need some lip gloss. Pulling it out of my purse, I stare in the mirror a bit too long until my lips are glowing. Then I hear a knock on the door. Great! Now the next person is going to think I left this shit in the toilet. "Just one second," I call out. I try to flush again with no luck, so I snatch a couple of pieces of toilet paper and throw them over the crap in the toilet. That'll have to do. Grabbing a piece of chalk, I write the words "it wasn't me" on the chalkboard and draw an arrow to the toilet. Yeah, real believable.

When I leave the bathroom, the next person is practically standing on top of the door. I guess she really has to go, too. Chewing on my lip, I walk slowly over to the counter. It's the same cutie from yesterday. His hair looks a little different; maybe shorter. I can see his eyes today. They're a warm, welcoming brown. "Hey, Brad."

A smile turns up his mouth, forcing out that adorable dimple. "Hey, Gabby. What can I get you?"

Well, here goes nothing. My cheeks are burning and my foot taps nervously on the floor. "I'm not sure how to tell you this, but there's a problem in the bathroom, and I swear I had nothing to do with it. I did go, because I just couldn't wait, but I didn't leave the crap in there." I hold up two fingers. "Scout's Honor."

Brad raises his eyebrows and cocks his head to the side. "Did you just say Scout's Honor?"

I nod my head because, at this point, I shouldn't be speaking at all.

The left corner of his mouth curls up. "Is the toilet clogged?"

I bite my lip so hard I think I taste blood. "Kind of."

He makes his way over to the bathroom and disappears for what seems like an eternity. While he's gone, I order the biggest sticky doughnut they have and scarf it down. Then I order another one. By the time I'm finished eating, I've added a serious sugar high to my hangover. I start humming Eliza DeAngeles's song "Clumsy Girl" to myself...my theme song. Brad finally emerges and his eyes meet mine. I wonder what he's thinking. Does he believe me, or is he thinking that was my crap in the toilet? Ugh.

Shaking his head and smirking, he walks straight over to me. "All taken care of."

I hope that by now the pink has left my cheeks and taken the embarrassment with it.

"I like your note, by the way. The arrow was a nice touch."

I can't help but smile. "Thanks. I'm kind of creative that way."

"So, do you want a coffee?"

"Well, I'm not sure my stomach can handle coffee after that. Plus, I just ate two sticky doughnuts. Do you have any Tums?"

Laughter coats his eyes. "Come on, I'll make you another Salted Caramel Mocha on the house. I mean, you don't want that shit on your mind when you leave here...no pun intended."

"Yeah, real funny. Okay, I'll take one, but I'm paying you for it, and I won't take no for an answer this time."

"You got it."

While he's making my drink, I check out more of the sweets in the display case. I'm wondering if I should grab something else for work when I glance down at my watch and notice it's 9:15. Shit, I'm late! Robby hates tardiness!

Thankfully Brad hands me my coffee and I manage not to spill it all over. "Thanks, Brad. I gotta run, I'm seriously late." I start heading for the exit when I feel a hand at my shoulder. Flipping around, I see Brad.

He bends down and grabs something from the floor, then pushes back up to his feet. A smile tugs at his lips. "You had a piece of soggy toilet paper stuck to your shoe."

"Thanks." The hits just keep coming.

I hurry down the street, weaving through the maze of body odor crowding the sidewalks. Everyone is a blur today, literally, and I just realized I left my sunglasses at The Brew House. Unbelievable. Robby's going to kill me. I rush back in the other direction and as soon as I walk in, Brad waves my glasses at me.

"I figured you'd be back for these," he says with a small smile.

"Thanks. See ya."

"See you around, Gabby."

I grab my sunglasses and my now lukewarm mocha and head for the door, again. I'm almost free and clear when I hear the door jingle and instinctively look up. My blue eyes are met by a forest of green sparkles, and that's all I see. I don't need to see anything else, recognizing those eyes immediately and knowing who they belong to. My heart pounds in my chest. I move forward and clumsily trip over one of the chair legs, dropping the contents of my purse on the floor and my drink along with it. "Shit," I mumble to myself. Let's look at my list of infractions. First, caught gawking, and second, spilling my drink. And I can't forget dumping out my purse. Geez, I shouldn't even be allowed to walk around by myself.

All at once, everything goes into slow motion. Dark and Sexy moves toward me; at the same time I hear Brad say, "are you okay?" No, actually, I'm not. I want to crawl into a deep hole and start this day all over again.

Dark and Sexy eyes me amusingly, and again I'm embarrassed. God, I'm so transparent it's ridiculous. Could I be any more flustered? Or klutzy, for that matter? I don't think so. When he reaches down to help me pick up the contents of my purse, I'm suddenly eternally grateful there aren't any tampons in there. All at once, my muscles tense up and I dig my fingernails into my palm as I stare blankly over his shoulder.

He continues in silence, then looks up at me, waving my wallet in front of my face. "Hey, are you alright?"

And I'm immediately snapped back to the now.

Somehow I manage to find my voice. "Yes, I'm fine. I wasn't looking where I was going."

He gives me a dubious grin. I'm sure he's thinking my excuse has *bullshit* written all over it. He finishes helping me with my purse and pulls me to my feet. When our fingers touch, I immediately feel a shudder move through my entire body.

"Let me at least buy you another drink. What was it you were drinking?"

At the moment, I can't even remember my own name, let alone what I was drinking. Brad returns with more towels. I see him shake his head back and forth but I'm too preoccupied to give it a second thought.

After hearing the question, Brad replies for me, "she was drinking a Salted Caramel Mocha."

Dark and Sexy immediately requests another one and I stand there like a fool, tapping my hand against my thigh, while his eyes feel up my entire body. Thankfully, Brad saves the day and returns with my drink.

"Thank you, " I say, still a little taken aback by this whole fiasco.

Dark and Sexy pays for my drink and gives me a wink, says "anytime," and heads out the door. No name, no introduction, and he didn't even get a drink for himself. What the hell?

By the time I arrive at work, it's ten o'clock, and I know Robby's going to give me hell for being late. I sneak into my cubicle, shove my purse in the drawer, flip on my computer, and take note of the demonic red light on my phone blinking at top speed. I sigh loudly, so much so, that when I look behind me, Robby is standing there. His dirty blonde hair is perfectly coiffed and he's wearing one of his signature silk shirts, this one hunter green, black pants, and loafers. His arms are crossed over his chest, his foot tapping, and his lips form an annoying grin when I make eye contact.

Busted.

"Gabby, dahling. Do you realize what time it is?"

I swallow hard. "Yes, Robby. I'm really sorry. I had a bit of a difficult morning."

"Well, difficult morning or not, there's work to be done. As it is, I had to deal with the calls you were supposed to be taking, and you know how much that pains me."

"I know. It won't happen again."

"Good, now let's get to work. Have a look at your latest sticky notes. I couldn't sleep last night so I started then."

Lovely. "Okay, Robby, thanks." When Robby leaves, I put my head on my desk. Could this day get any worse?

♡ ♡ ♡

"Are you fucking serious?" Fran asks me when I get back to our apartment.

"I know. This is the second time he's made me crazy with lust, and he hasn't even touched me."

"So let me get this straight, you saw the hot guy at the coffee shop and dropped your drink and your purse...geez, that must have really turned him on," she deadpans.

"Very funny. I don't know what the hell happened. I never thought I'd see him again, so when I did, it caught me completely off guard."

Fran's eyebrows crease and her lips press together. "So no name, no introduction, no drink, and he just left."

"Yup, that about sums it up."

"What the hell?"

"Exactly. It was very odd. But, if I thought he was hot from a distance, you should have seen him up close. Dear Lord. Those green eyes were mesmerizing, that mouth was intoxicating, and his body...well, it screamed sheet-clawing sex." A light bulb immediately goes off in my head. "Not to change this hot topic, but do you want to be my date for the company party next Monday? It's actually going to be pretty cool. There'll be food, drink, and lots of hot guys."

That last comment clinches it. Fran looks excited. "Well, that's an offer I can't refuse. I even have the perfect dress to wear! I'll be right back. I want to try it on for you." She disappears down the hallway excitedly.

I open the fridge and pull out the leftover pad thai, pop it in the microwave for two minutes, grab a fork from the drawer, and dig in. After five minutes, Fran still hasn't come out of her room. "Hey, hot stuff! Let's see that dress!" I call out, but she doesn't respond. I put down my fork, chomp on the last bit of pad thai, and walk down the non-existent hallway to her bedroom.

When I step in, her black dress is laid out neatly on the bed and she's standing in front of the full-length mirror wearing nothing but her bra and panties, clutching her belly, and staring at herself. "Are you going to put that sexy dress on, or what?" I ask, but she doesn't answer.

I walk up behind her and put my hand on her shoulder. "Fran, what is it?"

She continues to stare in the mirror. Her eyes are glazed over and her hand passes across her stomach again and again, tracing hundreds of tiny scars. "I remember the first time my dad cut me. I was five years old. My mom had gone back out to the grocery store after he pushed her into the wall because she forgot his favorite cereal. He came into my room...holding it...the small paring knife...the one my mom cut fruits and vegetables with..."

I can see in her eyes that she's there, back in her memories, so I squeeze her shoulders, put my arm around her chest, and pull her back against me.

"He told me he was doing it on my belly because no one could see it. He said it would be our special place...that after, he would put my favorite Dora Band-aids on for me. He always gave me a kiss on the cheek and told me he was doing it because he loved me." Tears roll down her cheeks. "I was so scared. I kept praying my mom would come home and save me, but she never did. She couldn't even save herself, Gabby. How was she going to save me?

Now I have all these horrible scars, and I wonder if I'll ever find anyone who isn't silently disgusted by the way I look once my shirt comes off."

A tear tumbles down my cheek. I turn her around and take her precious face in my hands. "Fran, you're beautiful and anyone who can't see that doesn't deserve you." I wipe the tears from her eyes. "What brought all this on?"

She tears her gaze from mine and stares at the carpet. "My mom called me today. My dad got in contact with her...he wants to know where I am. He wants to see me."

Fran hasn't seen her dad since she was ten years old, the exact time when the desire to ever see him again disappeared. His abuse of both her and her mom left permanent scars not only on her body, but on her heart. The thought of seeing him again terrifies her. I didn't meet Fran until after the horrors of her childhood, but the damage remains. The cigarette burns on her thighs and small cuts on her stomach are only the physical reminders. The thought of anyone ever hurting her again makes me sick to my stomach. I would go to the ends of the earth to protect her.

My jaw clenches and my shoulders tense up. "And your mom said no way in hell, right?"

Fran exhales a harsh breath. "Yeah, she didn't tell him, but I'm worried because you know how persistent and resourceful he can be when he wants something. I don't want anything to do with him. Do you remember how many years of therapy I went through to try to heal from his bullshit? The emotional scars are fading, I guess." She runs her hand along her belly and across her thighs. "But these? These will never go away."

What could I say? Words seem pointless. There are no words to heal. Only time and love can do that. So I just hold her.

Chapter Three

The week flew by and it's already Monday. I wish the company party were on a Friday, but what can you do? This is the first year I'm attending and I hear it's awesome. It feels like a bit of a privilege, especially given the value I place on my importance at the firm; very little. Colleagues, clients, and even celebrities attend; it's pretty extravagant. A colleague told me that last year she saw Brad Pitt, which is wild. She stared at him the entire night, but I'm pretty sure he's used to it.

It's my first work party and I don't have a date. Well, I do, and it's Fran, which is okay. We get to dress up, drink champagne, and drool over hot guys. I can't think of anything better to do with my best friend. And I get to wear the dress Fran coerced me into buying at Bloomingdale's.

After I'm dressed, I glance at myself in the full-length mirror. My nerves are on end because I'm not used to wearing clothes this revealing. I practically feel naked. My only saving grace is that I leave my hair down so it's sleek, shiny and straight. It lands on my breasts and covers up some skin. The silky fabric of the dress falls just past my clean-shaven thighs; shorter than I normally wear, but not so short that someone will have a heart attack if I bend over.

I hear my mother and father in my head. *Dear, your private parts should not be on public display like that, it will attract the wrong type of person; like Clark.* Sitting down on my bed, I put my head in my hands. My mother's an idiot. She couldn't have been more wrong. Clark was exactly the right type of person.

I try to gather my thoughts and rekindle my excitement for the night. Maybe I'll get lucky. Fran obviously thinks I need it and maybe she's right. When I walk out of my room, the sight of her jars me from any wayward thoughts. She looks absolutely stunning in a short, black, fitted, off-the-shoulder dress, complemented by red stilettos. Her black hair is pinned up in a messy bun and her makeup dramatic.

"Fran, you look gorgeous." I'm consistently blown away by her beauty.

She gives me the once over and it appears she approves. "You look beautiful, Gabby! Really sexy! In fact, you might even get yourself laid tonight."

Fran and her one track mind.

The party is being held at the gorgeous W Hotel in Union Square. The event is attended by about two hundred people. Clients, employees, and local celebrities flock to the party every year. As we arrive at the W, I'm instantly pleased that Fran suckered me into buying this dress. The women look stunning, and the guys, well, they're seriously mouth-watering. Photographers are snapping pictures left and right. If there was a red carpet, I'd think we were at The Oscars.

Fran looks over at me with a wide smile. "Let's rock this joint."

We wave to cameras and keep an eye peeled for celebrities as we walk into the party and check in. The Landon & Castell party is nothing if not exclusive.

We're immediately blown away by the ballroom. It's decorated in blues and silvers, with sparkly crystal chandeliers over each table and overflowing vases of lilies and irises in the center. Ice sculptures surround the room, the lighting is dim, and there are several small circular candle holders on each table, adding to the ambience. Soft jazz plays in the background; it's actually quite romantic and makes me feel a bit melancholy.

Fran grabs us champagne and hors d'oeuvres and I introduce her to several of my colleagues and a couple of our clients. She's a bit disappointed that none of them are single, as her main goal of every outing is to find a man.

When we move away to find our table assignment, I fix her with a stern look and raise a finger. "Fran, you can't, and I repeat *can not,* flirt with any of my clients." That could get me in trouble. Trouble is Fran's middle name.

She grins. "Who, me? I wouldn't do anything like that."

Soon I'm feeling good and slightly buzzed. The guys are making the rounds to see my cleavage tonight, so I must've done something right. It's nice for a change, and boy, would it piss off my mom. I can't help but smile at the thought.

There are some pretty cute guys at work, but I remember Fran telling me she got involved with someone in her office and it ended terribly. That's a whole ball of shit I'm not interested in rolling in.

We're having a great time, eating lobster stuffed pastries, sautéed mushrooms, and other delights that waiters are bringing around on silver trays. The champagne is flowing freely. Fran hands me a glass and we link arms to begin our first round of the room. I trip over something invisible and nearly spill my drink all over my new dress. My face pales, my heart rate spikes, and my legs suddenly feel like jello. There he is again.

Fran looks worried. "Gabby, what is it?"

"Well...oh shit." It's pointless. My mouth goes limp as I watch him move gracefully towards us.

Fran scans the room frantically to find the source of my unease. It doesn't take her long to find the long legs, attached to the broad shoulders, attached to the fine hips, attached to the gorgeous face with the emerald green eyes.

"Holy crap! You weren't kidding. He is super hot! Gabby, he's headed this way."

Just great. Unable to speak, I can only pray that drool isn't running down the corners of my painted lips.

He reaches us in long, quick strides. "I thought I recognized you from across the room, and I realized we were never formally introduced the other day. I'm Dane Rhodes."

His voice is smooth, like the finest of silks. After nothing but silence for several seconds, Fran elbows me and I realize I'd better open my mouth and say something. Like maybe proposition him for sex.

"I'm Gabrielle Willis, and this is my friend, Fran Heller." I feel his eyes cut through me like shards of glass and a thrill courses through my body. Suddenly, I'm grateful for Fran's sense of style. A definite improvement over the yellow sundress and bushy ponytail he caught me in during our awkward encounter at The Brew House.

After endless mutual staring, the smooth voice speaks. "So, what brings you two here?"

"I work for Landon & Castell, and Fran is my date for the evening." Oh my God, did I seriously just say that?

"That's hard to believe. I can't imagine a gorgeous woman like you wouldn't be able to find a date." Okay, so he's definitely flirting.

Fran saves the moment and finally says, "So Dane, what brings you to this event?"

"I've just signed on as a client with Landon & Castell. They're going to be decorating my apartment on the Upper East Side. Now that I know you work for them, I'll know where to find you." Then, with a cock of his eyebrow, he says, "well, I'm going to mingle a bit. Nice meeting you both."

When he walks away, Fran and I use the moment to admire his extraordinary ass. I don't know that I've ever called an ass extraordinary before, but well, it just is.

Fran can hardly contain herself. "Gabby, he's...he's...well, he's amazing! You weren't exaggerating one bit. The images my mind is conjuring up right now. Oh, the things I'd like him to do to me..."

"Okay, Fran. I get it. But remember, I saw him first."

Fran shakes her head and wrinkles her nose. "Screw you. What are we, in high school?"

My mind drifts from Fran over to Dane for a moment. He's a client with the firm. What are the chances of that? Does this mean I can't go for him? I certainly didn't pay enough attention in our employee orientation to know if this kind of thing would be against company rules.

Fran and I make our way across the crowded room to one of the buffet tables and grab some more champagne. "Fran, don't you think it's odd that Dane was here? I mean, especially after our run in at the coffee shop. Doesn't that seem a bit too coincidental?"

She stops slurping and her eyes meet mine. "Does it really matter, Gabby? This is your chance. Look at it as a gift."

We're having a great time laughing, drinking, and ogling. I'm so glad I brought Fran. When I look over at her, she tosses her hair back.

"Check out our man at three o'clock. Plaid tie, checkered pants, hungry look. He wants you."

I howl with laughter. "Fran, in this case, you can have first dibs. He's all yours."

Chapter Four

For some reason, I wake up very early the next day. In fact, when I look at the clock it's only five a.m., which means I have two extra hours to stay in bed and daydream. Hmmm…a Dane Rhodes daydream perhaps. I wonder when I'll see him again. Now that I know he's a client of the firm, maybe I can make it happen. Determination is one quality I'm not lacking.

I don't realize I've fallen back asleep until I hear the annoying buzzer go off on my alarm clock. Pushing the hair out of my face, I will my legs over the side of the bed and take a moment to fully wake up. My head doesn't feel too bad, given the amount Fran and I had to drink last night. Making my way out to the kitchen, I pull out a jug of Poland Spring, reach up for a glass from the cabinet, then listen to the glug, glug, glug of the water filling the glass. Maybe I am still a little drunk. I gulp it down and set the glass in the sink, dragging my ass to the bathroom and into a hot shower. My thoughts wander to Dane and I suds my body a little bit too much.

When I get in the subway car, my mind continues to be consumed with all thoughts Dane. That is, until the wonderful odor of sweaty human bodies flies under my nose. Ugh. I take a seat, try not to touch anything, and basically shrink into myself to make sure no one comes near me. This is the only thing I don't like about Manhattan. The daily dose of railings that are laden with fresh boogers, seats stained with God knows what, and strangers with bad breath hovering over me. Crap, I forgot my Purell!

Arriving at the coffee shop for my much needed caffeine, Brad smiles at me from behind the counter. "Good morning, Gabby. Are you here to use the bathroom, or did you want coffee?"

I can't help but smile. "I didn't realize you also moonlighted as a comedian. No to the first question, and yes to the second." Since I've got some time this morning, I take a seat at one of the tables to review my to-do list for Robby.

Brad brings my coffee over to the table. "You look especially cheerful this morning, Gabby. Does it have anything to do with that guy from the other day? Are you dating him or something?"

"What makes you think my mood has anything to do with that?"

"Just an educated guess."

"Okay, this is incredibly scary. Are you doing a mind meld on me?"

"A mind meld? No, but the way you were looking at him the other day like you wanted to..." He stops and a tiny smile turns up one corner of his mouth. "Lick chocolate off his stomach or something. It was a dead giveaway."

"Like I wanted to do what?"

"You know...lick..."

"Yeah, I heard you, no need for an echo."

He stands up straighter and looks me square in the eye. "Well, I know how much you love chocolate."

"And how did your brain conjure up that little deduction?"

"You told me the first day I met you. Remember, when you were racked with indecision and clumsily spilled coffee all over my new cash register." He's trying to hide his smile.

The red creeps from my ears to my cheeks. "Thank you for the reminder of my most embarrassing moment. Oh wait, I forgot about the clogged toilet. That trumps it."

"Well, if that's your most embarrassing moment, I'd say you're doing pretty well."

My eyebrows perk up. "Why, what's your most embarrassing moment?"

"I'm not sure I can trust you with that information."

A giant puff of air leaves my mouth. "Why not? I'm extremely trustworthy."

He taps his long index finger against his full lips; a detail I just noticed. "Hmmm...I don't know, actually. This is pretty serious stuff. If anyone ever found out..."

"Okay, you're killing me here, Brad...just spill it." I wave him into the chair across from me. "I won't tell anyone. Cross my heart."

He shrugs his shoulders and sits down before continuing. "Okay...so I was about twelve at the time and waiting for my brother, Matt, to get home from school to go play basketball. I was pretty bored so I turned on the radio and the sound of Bob Seger's "Old Time Rock n Roll" filled the living room speakers. Something in me came alive, and I couldn't resist the temptation to strip down to my underwear and do my best Tom Cruise impression. Just when I started getting into it with the pretzel rod that came to life as my microphone, the door burst open and in walked my brother with his girlfriend, two of his friends, and a girl from school that I had a crush on at the time. Needless to say, hysterical laughter ensued and I ran up to my room, never to be heard from again."

Laughter bubbles up to the surface, but I try and force it down.

"You can laugh. It's okay. Even though it was the most humiliating experience in my life, there's no disputing the humor in it."

My face crinkles in laughter. "Okay, Brad, you got me. That totally beats the toilet incident. By a long shot."

His eyes shine and that dimple pops right out. "Yup, it's hard to top that one." He laughs with me for a moment. He sounds even more relaxed and carefree when he does. "My brother reminds me of it. Often."

"What happened with that girl you liked?"

"Absolutely nothing. It was a wash after that. Every time she saw me she broke into fits of laughter, and all her friends starting calling me Tommy."

My lips turn down in a pout. "Oh, that's awful. Well, if it's any consolation, I would've thought you were cute. Definitely strange, but cute."

His face breaks out into a huge smile. Holy cow, he's got a great one. Right out of a freaking Colgate commercial.

Chapter Five

Wednesdays are always ridiculously crazy. Happy Hump Day to me! Well, now that I think about it, it's hump day for everyone else...except me. I definitely need to work on that. In addition to my regular assistant responsibilities, Robby has me picking up design plans and going out on a couple of client visits with him. This is one of the great things about my job. It gives me a change of pace from sitting in my creaky desk chair all day staring at the lovely four walls of my cubicle.

I manage to make it to my desk without being too overwhelmed by yellow sticky notes, and I only have ten voicemail messages. It's a banner day. Settling in, I manage to take one blissful sip of my Salted Caramel Mocha before Robby calls to me.

"Gabby, dahling. Come in here a minute."

I hesitantly get up from my not-so-comfortable chair and make my way over to his office. The sun is shining through the windows casting a warm glow on his face that almost matches his orange silk shirt. A pencil sits atop his ear and he has his feet up on his desk per usual, looking very relaxed.

"Good morning, Robby."

"Good morning, sweetie. So I hope all the sticky notes didn't scare you." He waves his hands in the air. "But you know me, whenever a thought pops into my head, I have to write it down."

I chuckle softly. "No problem. I'm good."

"Great! So we have a couple of clients to see today, and I believe there's a new one on the schedule as well. Busy, Busy, Busy. Design, Design, Design." He claps his hands. "Let's get on with it."

I like Robby. He never makes me feel like a peon and always makes me laugh. My desk is piled with paperwork, and prioritizing is number one on my list today. We have about thirty minutes before our first meeting and I'm in the organizing zone. The stack of papers filled with design sketches Robby drew are piling up and filing them is essential. My phone rings, startling me, and I quickly answer it, almost dropping the receiver to the floor. "Gabrielle Willis."

On the other end I hear, "Hello, Gabrielle Willis, this is Dane Rhodes." Then silence.

I can't seem to talk, but my body is responding to his silky voice. After a pause, I offer, "Hello."

"I just spoke with Robby, and apparently you're supposed to pick up some design plans at my apartment today. I just wanted to find out what time you'd be here."

I am? I'm glad someone decided to tell me that. "I'll see you at two o' clock." Click. I hang up. I didn't even give him a chance to say anything else. At this point, my name can be found right next to the word idiot in the dictionary.

I can't pay attention to anything Robby or the clients are saying, as I'm anxiously glancing at the clock non-stop. It's like watching molasses drip from a spoon. It's only noon. The lunch meeting is dragging and I can't even think about food. It's also not very appealing to listen to people talk as they're chewing. Two more hours to go. I'm nervous and my mind is doing crazy Dane somersaults. All kinds of thoughts are going through my head. Dane obviously called and asked for me specifically. He must've been thinking about me, right? Must've wanted to see me again, or perhaps he just heard I'm a skilled assistant? I giggle. Perhaps he's hoping I'm skilled in other ways, too.

Robby glares at me. I guess my giggle was a little too loud. "Gabby, do you have anything you'd like to add?"

My smile suddenly disappears and I put on my serious meeting face. "No."

Finally it's 1:30. I gather my scattered wits and make my way to the ladies' room for one last check. I've been in here four times in the past hour; I'm sure nothing has changed. I smooth my dress, brush my hair and tuck one side behind my ear, and reapply blush and a bit of lip gloss. That's it. This is as good as it gets.

As I make my way to Dane's Upper East Side apartment, my heart is drumming against my chest. I haven't been this nervous about anything in a long time. I'm not sure what's happening to me, but whatever it is, I don't want it to stop. I wonder what he wants from me. I know what I want from him. Sex, with a capital S.

Sweat is clinging to my palms, my pulse visibly racing through my heated skin. I'm having a hard time controlling my breathing as the elevator ascends to the twenty-seventh floor. So much for the time I spent in yoga class. I wring my hands repeatedly and slowly count to ten. When I finally get to ten, the elevator pings. Steadying my wobbly legs and wiping away the moisture trickling down my forehead, I head down the hall to apartment 27-F, attempting one last deep, calming breath before I ring the doorbell.

The door opens almost instantly and I freeze at the sight of Dane. I've obviously never walked through a door before, because when he ushers me in, the feet that I so often rely on have no idea what to do. I look down at my awkwardness telepathically expecting a response, and wait. Still nothing, so I look up. My eyes sweep the length of his body. The natural inclination would be to stare into his green emeralds, but it's impossible not to move lower; a lot lower. I can almost trace a line through the bunched cream fabric of his pants. Is it even real? It should be illegal to walk around with that thing. Dane's lips part, forming a perfect O, for orgasm, I believe. The one I'm about to have all over his brand new hardwood floors.

His lips curve up in a mouthwatering smile. "See anything you like?"

My blue eyes manage to crawl back up to his. "Nah, not really."

His lips twitch, while the green in his eyes sparkles. "So, shall we sit?"

That's not exactly what I had in mind. Geez, when did I turn into a sex fiend? After a second or two, I find my voice. "Sure, let's." I try to calm my nerves and the excitement I feel building in my body with a distraction. The view seems to work. It's actually pretty magnificent. Every facet, every curve, every color, every inch of blue sky is visible from his floor-to-ceiling windows. Wow. My view of the back alley pales in comparison. "What a stunning view."

I see Dane staring at me from the corner of my eye. "I was thinking the exact same thing."

Shit, he's flirting with me again. My cheeks warm and I quickly make an attempt to divert the conversation. "So, when did you buy this place?"

He stalks closer to me. "I just closed last month. I told Robby I want to move forward quickly, so I can move in within the next three months."

"That's a pretty aggressive timeline."

"Well, I'm a pretty aggressive guy." Gulp. "Let me get the design plans." He strides out of the room, a walking billboard for sex. The temperature in here is rising quickly.

I immediately become aware that there are only two pieces of furniture in the apartment, a sofa and a coffee table. Dane motions for me to have a seat beside him on the couch. Taking out my notepad, I lay it on the table.

"Come, have a seat next to me."

Cautiously, I make my way over and sit down, but not too close. Dane smirks. He's obviously enjoying my uneasiness.

"So, what did you have in mind?" Could I be any more suggestive?

I see a hint of wickedness cross his face. "Well, Gabrielle, that appears to be a very loaded question."

As if I couldn't embarrass myself any more with this guy. I attempt to clear my throat and speak. "So, furniture and color, let's start there."

"I'm thinking burgundy and creams. In terms of furniture, I'm clueless, so that's where I'll look to Robby for his expertise."

"Well, the space is vast, so it can accommodate larger pieces of furniture. Because of the expansive open floor plan, you'll need to decide how you want to break up the space – kitchen, living room, dining room, etc."

"You certainly seem to know a lot about design," he says, "and I'm excited about seeing what Robby can do with this place."

Dane continues to talk, but I'm not even listening. Some assistant I am. I'm busy admiring the view. Contoured lips, sculptured shoulders...Fran's right, I do need to get laid. And he may be just the man for the job.

"So what do you think, Gabrielle? Or is it okay if I call you Gabby?"

"Huh, yes, what was that?"

A devilish grin passes over Dane's face. I've been caught red handed. I play it cool. "Yes, you can call me Gabby. And I think I've got enough information for Robby. He and I will put together some color swatches and when we meet again you can decide what you like best."

Gathering up my notepad, I make my way to the door. Dane saunters forward three steps, while I clumsily take three steps back until I feel a cold surface seeping through the thin cotton of my blouse. His arms outstretch to the wall behind me, surrounding me with muscle and virility, and I'm trapped. I feel like a caged animal; one that's in heat. My face is burning from his proximity. His warm breath is inches from my mouth.

"When can I see you again, Gabby?"

Those lips are so close now, and they look so incredibly soft and delicious that I can practically feel them on mine. He runs his tongue along the contour of his lips and words escape me, and I press my legs together in hopes that I don't come all over his floor.

My mouth goes dry as I attempt to swallow the giant lump that's taken up residence in my throat. "When...would you like to? See me that is?"

His eyes never leave my lips. "I'd like to...see you on Friday. How about dinner?"

"Sure. We can do dinner." Then, maybe we can do something else.

I turn to leave. Places to go, messages to answer.

"So, do you have time to grab a coffee before you go back to your office? Perhaps at that shop you frequent?"

Now? How the hell does he know I frequent there? Has he been stalking me? "How do you know I frequent there?"

"I don't know, I just assumed." Yeah, well don't.

During our walk to the coffee shop, Dane tells me about his job as an associate creative director at an advertising agency. "It's a fascinating job, really. I love the creative freedom it gives me, and the ability to develop a design based on an overall marketing strategy is really exciting."

"It does sound interesting." Creative minds need creative jobs. That's the one thing my mom used to say that made any sense to me.

Dane's job sounds sexy and seems to fit his persona perfectly. He'd actually have a lot to talk about with Fran. I'm trying to figure out how old he is. From what he's told me, coupled with his confident swagger, I'm thinking he has to be about six years older than me, so maybe around thirty-one. Perhaps I can learn something from him. The thought makes my insides churn.

He puts his hand at the small of my back and ushers me into The Brew House. I flinch, but don't think he notices. His touch does strange things to me. I feel needy and achy in all the right places, and I like it. Brad sees me and I'm on the receiving end of that killer smile. Wow.

"Hi, Gabby."

"Hey, Brad. Brad, this is Dane. Dane, this is my friend, Brad."

Brad looks Dane over, eyeing his expensive suit and manicured nails. "What's up?"

"Pleasure to meet you, Brad."

I order drinks for both Dane and myself. Standing there, playing with the fabric of my blouse, I watch Brad make our lattes and notice a tattoo peeking out from his short-sleeved shirt, surrounding his bicep. I squint to make out what it is, but we're too far away. I grab our drinks and make our way over to a corner table.

Dane speaks first. "So, you like this place, huh?"

"Well, obviously so if I 'frequent it.'"

A smile plays on his lips. "Touché."

"Actually, I like the cozy atmosphere, and after going to Starbucks for such a long time, it's a welcome change."

"So, how long have you lived in New York City?"

"Three years now." There's no way I'm telling him about all of my baggage. "Don't get me wrong, I loved California, but there's something about New York that excites me."

Dane's eyes twinkle. "I would say there's a lot about New York that excites me."

Okay, he's seriously flirting with me. I turn my head to hide my face because it's turning three different shades of red right now. When I do, I happen to catch a glimpse of Brad staring at me from behind the cappuccino maker. For some reason, it makes me a bit uncomfortable and I start nervously twirling the ends of my hair.

We sit and chat for another few minutes. Dane tells me about his rather large family. "I have three brothers and two sisters, all located in different parts of the country. We're all spread out, including my parents, which is hard sometimes."

As Dane is talking, I'm swinging my leg under the table, my stiletto heel bouncing wildly. Suddenly, it flies off my foot and across the tile floor of the coffee shop. How Dane doesn't notice the flying shoe is beyond me, but when I look up, someone else certainly has. Brad has an enormous grin plastered on his face, and I have a mask of red stuck to mine. I look back down quickly and continue talking with Dane. How the hell am I supposed to get my shoe back?

Shoe loss notwithstanding, I act like I'm completely involved in this conversation. I don't miss a beat. "Do you still manage to see each other?"

"Yes, we always make an effort to get together a couple of times a year."

"I'm a bit jealous. It's just my mom and dad, and my sister." Scratch that, it's really just me.

He rambles a bit about how important his family is to him, how lucky he is to have so many siblings, and how he has a new niece on the way. My foot is starting to get cold when he finally includes me in the conversation. "So, Gabby, what made you decide to go into interior design?" I get the sense that he's just being polite. He seems much more at ease talking about himself.

"It's something that has fascinated me since I was a kid. I always took note of furniture and layout, as well as color. I'm a very visual person."

Dane raises an eyebrow. "Really?"

I realize what I just implied and start fidgeting with my napkin.

He looks at his watch and then back to me. "Listen, I really need to get back to work, but I'm looking forward to seeing you on Friday. I'm staying at the W Hotel on Broadway until the apartment is finished, so we can have dinner there, if that's okay with you."

"Yeah, that'd be great." I certainly hope the conversation is more interesting at dinner. Or perhaps, we won't talk at all.

"Terrific, I'll look forward to seeing you then. Say seven? I'll meet you in the lobby."

"Sounds good."

Dane stands up from the table. "I'll walk you out."

No you won't, because I'm missing a shoe. "Actually, I think I'm going to stay a bit longer."

"Alright. Well then, I'll see you on Friday."

"Absolutely."

Dane walks out the door, and once he does, I see Brad coming towards me with his hands behind his back. His crooked smile makes a glowing appearance. "I think you might need this," he says, passing me my shoe from behind like it's a super-covert operation.

I shake my head and roll my eyes at myself. "Thanks."

"Go easy on the heel next time. I don't want anyone losing a head." His voice erupts with laughter as he heads back behind the counter.

Before I head back to post-it land, I pull out my cell phone to text Fran about Dane.

Me: Hey! Guess who I just saw?

Fran: Hmmm...no idea

Me: Dark & Sexy

Fran: You're shitting me

Me: Wouldn't shit you about something like this

Fran: And...

Me: Went to his apartment, then had coffee

Fran: Sounds boring, please tell me there's more

Me: He asked me out Friday night

Fran: Now you're talking

Me: Will need help with wardrobe choice

Fran: Always glad to oblige

Me: See you at home

Fran: Staying at Kyle's

Me: Man you move fast. It's only been eight days! See u in morning. xo

Fran: Hee hee. xo

Chapter Six

I feel a hand pressing on my shoulder. I'm not sure if I'm dreaming, so I roll over, but there it is again. Cracking my eyes open, I vaguely see what look like Fran's ebony strands falling into my face. It's either that or a gigantic spider, and I'm praying it's hair.

"Wake up, sleepyhead!"

My mumbled, sleepy voice comes from underneath the warm blankets and I close my eyes again. "Huhhhh...sleeping here."

"Gabby, get up!"

I slowly sit up and rub my tired blue eyes. "This better be good. I was having a hot dream."

Both her eyebrows raise up. "About Dane?"

A smile creeps across my face. "Maybe. I told you he asked me out tomorrow night, to his *hotel*." I emphasize the last word for effect. "Now it's all I can think about. Oh, and like I said, I need help with clothes."

"Of course you will. We can dig through my closet and find something voluptuous for you!"

"I was afraid of that. Maybe I should get something new."

"Chill, Gab. We'll find something sexy and tasteful and perfect."

After a hot, steamy shower, washing Dane all over me, I pull myself together and Fran and I head out the door for some much needed caffeine. Making our way over to The Brew House, I feel so invigorated. The sun is beaming today. Everyone is all smiles. Or maybe it's just me. The line is ridiculously long, but waiting doesn't bother me today. My patience seems endless, my mind consumed with emerald eyes. When we finally reach the counter, I can't stop smiling.

With a curious smile Brad says, "hey, Gabby. Your usual?"

"Yup, please. And Brad, this is my best friend, Fran. Fran, this is Brad."

"Hey, Fran." Brad's voice is friendly as always. "Welcome to The Brew House."

"Hey." Fran eyes him like a cat on the prowl. When we get to the booth she looks over at me and gestures to Brad, who treats us to a dimpled smile. "He's kinda cute."

"Yeah. He's a nice guy. Cute too. And he always has my drink ready which is a bonus." Not to mention he cleans up my coffee and toilet messes and saves my shoes. Speaking of guys, what's going on with you and Kyle? You've barely known him two weeks, but you've been spending an awful lot of time at his place."

Fran puckers her lips. "He has the ability to rock my world, what can I say?" Then her eyes get a bit dreamy, which is unusual. "I kind of like him, Gabby. He's really sweet, and he's interested in me...I mean, in who I am. He's always asking me questions about me as a kid, California, and...I don't know, he's attentive, I guess."

That makes me happy. "I like him already, then."

Fran's face takes on a look of excitement. She reaches into her purse and then slides something under her palm across the table.

When she lifts her hand, I laugh. "Where on earth did you find watermelon Jolly Ranchers?"

"I have my ways," she grins. "Remember sixth grade in Mr. Flanders' class; I gave you one of these? You didn't waste any time crinkling up the wrapper and popping it in your mouth."

My face brightens. "Of course I remember that. These were my favorite then."

"Mr. Flanders literally stopped class and started sniffing the air like a bloodhound." Fran lifts her nose so her nostrils flare and lowers her voice to imitate his, "Who's eating candy?"

I remember it like it was yesterday. "I can still see chubby, bald, old Mr. Flanders walking in between the two aisles tapping desks and startling kids, the smell of sweet watermelon hovering in the air. Everyone knew it was me. He leaned in close to my face, and then you piped up, 'It's me, Mr. Flanders,' saving me from having to write "I will not eat candy in school" a hundred times on the blackboard during a detention. Why did you do that, Fran?"

She shrugs her shoulders. "You were always saving me, Gabby. Maybe I wanted to save you for a change."

My phone rings, disrupting our nostalgic moment. It's my Mom. Looking down at my watch, I notice it's 8:15, which means it's only 5:15 in California. It's awfully early for a mother-daughter chat. I guess this must be my monthly call. Ugh. I consider not answering it, but for a split second hold out hope she'll be different, so I do. "Hi, Mom," I answer with bland enthusiasm.

"Hi, dear. How are you?"

The sound of her voice causes me to start shredding napkins into tiny pieces and piling them in mounds on the table. "I'm fine, Mom."

"How's work?"

My voice gets smaller and I'm trying to breathe. "It's fine."

"You getting there on time every day?"

What does she think I am, twelve? "Yes, Mom," I reply, crossing my eyes and wiggling my nose obnoxiously at Fran, who's pretending not to eavesdrop.

"Good. Have you thought about applying to any schools for a Master's program?"

I'm silently screaming at her. "No, Mom. Not right now."

"Well, you should. This job you're in will only lead to a dead end. You really need a Master's degree if you're going to get anywhere in this world."

My skin starts to crawl, and inside I'm cringing. Gotta love family pep talks. "Yes, Mom." A change of subject is necessary and I deploy my usual tactic. "So, how are you, Mom?"

And she's off and running. "I'm great, dear. The shop is booming. People always need beautiful clothes to wear, right? So yes, it's wonderful. In fact, I just went to a runway show last week in Paris. It was simply amazing. In between the show I managed to make it to the Eiffel Tower, the Louvre, and the Palace of Versailles. Paris is such a beautiful city. Jim and I are getting on great. It's been seven months now, and he just adores everything about me. He showers me with affection and I can't get enough. I think this one might just be a keeper. We'll see. Anyway, things are going great here. I'm glad you're doing well. We'll talk soon."

"Okay, Mom, bye."

"Goodbye, dear."

I hang up the phone and the tension immediately leaves my body.

Fran reaches over and grabs my hand. "You okay, sweetie?"

"Yeah. I don't know why I ever think things will be different with her. I might as well pre-record my responses." I feel my eyes start to burn and a tear trickles down my cheek.

Fran squeezes my hand tightly.

"Why can't I just have a normal, loving mom, Fran?"

"Gabby, what's normal anyway? I don't think any mom is normal."

"I know," I agree with a sigh of resignation. "I guess I mean an involved mom. One that thinks I'm special no matter what...you know...the kind of mom that wants to hear me gush about my day, my boyfriend, my life. The mom that doesn't care if I'm wearing my Converse sneakers or my hair's in a messy ponytail, or the fact that I haven't taken a shower. The one that wants to take me to the mall and eat giant pretzels while we shop, and help me pick out the right dress for *me*. The one who bumps my shoulder and laughs, who shares her hopes and dreams. The kind of mom that hurts when I'm hurting, and puts her arms around me after I've lost the most important person in my life and I feel like maybe, just maybe, there's a chance that things will be okay..."

Fran gives me a sympathetic smile. "Your mom's doing what she knows, Gabby. It still totally sucks that you got the short end of the stick."

Squeezing the Jolly Rancher out of its wrapper, I pop it into my mouth. It's sweet and perfect, just what I need to distract myself from my crazy mother. She's my mom, and I love her, but I still can't help wishing she could be different.

Chapter Seven

After two excruciatingly long days of waiting since Dane asked me out, Friday is finally here. I truly know the meaning of TGIF. I lean back in my desk chair with my hands behind my head and take a deep breath. I'm meeting him tonight and my body can feel it. Tiny sparks of excitement are shooting off inside me, so much so that it's difficult to focus. I do manage to return fifteen phone calls, get through the oversized pile of paperwork on my desk, and toss a couple of Robby's sticky notes in the garbage after completing the tasks. My stomach is growling as I've completely lost track of time and missed lunch. I grab a yogurt and a juice from the coffee room fridge so I can get through the rest of the day. I'm a bundle of nerves as it gets closer to the time I'm meeting Dane.

When I get home, the first thing I do is rifle through Fran's closet, which is no easy task. The quantity of clothes she has is staggering, and as usual, my decision making skills are letting me down. Just then, the front door slams and in walks Fran. Thank God! I need help.

"Fran, in here," I say, muffled from under a pile of clothes, belts, and shoes.

"Where?"

"Help! I'm drowning in your closet." I hear her loud, melodic cackle. "Come on. You know I'm meeting Dane tonight. What should I wear?"

Fran taps her finger against her temple. "Something revealing. Lots of cleavage."

"I'd like to leave something to the imagination."

"Why bother?"

"Alright, alright. So...?"

Fran eyes all of the choices. "I'm thinking black halter dress."

"Fran! That's way too revealing!"

"Listen, Gabby. Are you going there to have tea, or are you going there to get laid?"

"Okay, okay. Point taken. But you know I'm not very good at this stuff."

"I know, that's where I come in. So let's do your hair. We'll leave it down because that's a lot sexier. Come on. Let me work my magic!"

I take a seat in the bathroom and try to sit still while Fran makes me look extra beautiful. It's taking a while and I'm starting to fidget.

"Stop fidgeting," she barks out, "I'm almost done...There!"

I stand up and glance in the mirror, shocked at my reflection. "Wow." I look beautiful.

Fran was a little pissed that I wanted to go easy on the makeup, but the caked on look just doesn't suit me. "Okay, give me a quick spin around so I can eye my handiwork."

I do my best model walk to the living room and back, without tripping. "You like?"

Fran raises a brow. "Oh, I'm sure someone's gonna like." She gives me a quick hug for encouragement and I head out the door. Just before it closes I hear Fran yell "happy sexing!"

My heels are a bit high, so I walk carefully down the stairs to the lobby, trying not to trip along the way. I'm definitely not taking the subway tonight. I have to keep my hair and my shoes intact. When I walk out to the street, I manage to hail a cab without having to wait too long, which is a miracle in New York. During the cab ride to Dane's hotel, I start biting my nails, something I never do. I also begin thinking maybe this isn't such a good idea. My nerves are definitely getting the best of me. By the time I arrive at the hotel, I'm sweating bullets. I pay the driver and hop out of the cab, nearly catching my heel in a sewer grate when I step out. Taking a deep breath, I talk quietly to myself. "*I can do this. I want to do this. I need this.*"

When I enter the hotel restaurant, Dane's back is to me and he appears to be deep in conversation on his cell phone. Almost as if he senses my presence, he turns around and sees me. A slow, sexy grin spreads like wildfire across his face. He hangs up the phone immediately and saunters toward me like a lion stalking its prey. Holy crap, he looks hot. He's wearing black pants that hug his fine hips and a white button-down shirt with a green tie that, of course, brings out the emeralds of his eyes.

Planting a soft kiss on my cheek, he eyes me appreciatively. "You look fabulous, Gabby."

"Thank you. So do you."

A wicked smile consumes his eyes. I'm on the receiving end of a lascivious look that tells me he wants to sweep me into the nearest broom closet. Sounds good to me. He leads me to the dining room, pulling out my chair like an absolute gentleman. The irony isn't lost on me; he's anything but, and we both know it.

"What's so funny?" he asks.

"Nothing."

"Don't want to share?"

"Not particularly."

We look over the menu. There's a lot to choose from and everything looks scrumptious. "I'm not sure if you like seafood, but the lobster and scallop risotto is really good," Dane suggests.

"I love seafood. That sounds perfect." A bottle of champagne is brought over to the table. "Are we celebrating something?"

"Yes, working with your firm and my new apartment. Not to mention finding the best interior designer's assistant in all of New York."

"Ah, flattery."

"Will it get me anywhere?"

Keep it up and you'll find out. "That remains to be seen."

He leans in over the table. "Well, maybe I have to work a little harder."

Dane's cell phone rings, and after looking at the screen, he motions to me that he needs to take the call. He steps out of earshot to speak while I drink as much champagne as possible to help calm my nerves. In the meantime, I can't help but take in my surroundings. This hotel is absolutely stunning. Contemporary in design, which I happen to favor, with muted brown leather fabrics and burgundies, complemented by candlelight and soft pink roses. Exquisite.

Dane returns wearing a bit of a scowl.

"Everything okay?"

"Yes, just fine."

Guess he doesn't want to talk about it. "So, I'm curious, what do you think of the color scheme in here?"

He looks around the room like any other guy–quickly. "I like it."

"Good, because this is the type of palette Robby was thinking about for your apartment. It's very masculine, and it suits you."

Dane raises an eyebrow. "Masculine?"

"Yes." I blush a little. Masculine, virile, potent. All of the above.

"You know, Gabby, I like that fire in your eyes when you talk about your work. You seem very passionate about it. It's a turn on, actually."

I swallow a gulp of champagne. I didn't expect that. But then again, everything about the way I feel in Dane's presence is unexpected. Excited, nervous, angsty, sexual. My hands are getting clammy. "Yes, I love what I do."

"I'm wondering if that passion extends to other areas of your life?"

I rub my thighs together under the table. "Simply put, I have an appreciation for life. All aspects of life."

Dane must really like his work. He certainly talks a lot about it. I'm reminded of how creative we both are, and it seems to be the one thing we have in common. Other than that, I can't think of anything else. He'd rather be in a suit, while I'd rather wear my red Converse sneakers. He dines on tables with white linens, while I prefer to eat cross-legged on the floor. I doubt he even knows what a Jolly Rancher looks like.

When he speaks, my eyes are riveted to his lush, shapely mouth. And those eyes, well, they're hypnotic. I may not be listening, but I'm most certainly watching.

"Gabby?"

Crap. I've drifted again. What was he saying?

As if he can read my thoughts, he says "Your eyes are stunning."

Your ass is stunning. "Thank you." The waiter arrives to serve our food and saves me. I take a bite and close my eyes. "Dane, you were right. This risotto is absolutely delicious."

"Good. I'm glad you like it."

We eat until we can't eat anymore. Dane clears his throat. "Would you like dessert? I was thinking we could take it up to my room and I could show you the color palette there."

Before I have time to think twice, I reply, "okay."

Dane's cell phone rings again. He lifts a finger, telling me to hold on, which of course I'm more than willing to do. His face grows serious. "What is it, Sarah? I'm the middle of something. Uh huh...okay. That's fine. Tell Clark and James to meet me at my office at eight tomorrow and we can go over the brand strategy."

I freeze. Just hearing his name is enough to pour a bucket of ice water over this entire evening.

Dane ends the call and reaches for my hand. "All set. Shall we go?"

I shift on my heels and stumble a bit. "I just realized I should probably get going. I have a very early morning tomorrow. Can I take a rain check?"

Dane looks back at me in confusion. He seems more than a little disappointed, like I just popped his last balloon, but he shakes it off and walks me to the door. I turn to thank him and realize I forgot my purse. Dane runs back to retrieve it. What is it with me and forgetting things lately? "Thank you."

Dane bends down so close to my ear that I can smell the champagne on his breath. "No, thank *you* for a wonderful evening."

He leans in briefly and touches my lips with his. "Are you sure I can't convince you to come up for a bit?"

"No, I really can't." My hands are shaking and I'm worried he's going to notice that something's up.

He places his hand at the small of my back. "Alright, well, at least let me call you a cab."

"I'm fine, Dane, really. It's only after nine. I'll walk for a bit and then catch a subway."

"Okay, well then, goodnight, Gabby."

"Goodnight, Dane, and thanks again."

His hand moves a bit lower, hovering right over my ass. "The pleasure was all mine. Next time will be even better."

As soon as Dane is out of sight, I sit on the bench in front of the hotel. I bend over and clutch my stomach. My body really wanted this, but my mind, well, it just can't let go. Maybe I just don't want to. It's only sex, though; anyone can have sex, right? Clark and I had sex under the bleachers once. Well, it was more than just sex. It was also a bit cramped, but it didn't bother me in the least, because Clark was wrapped around me. The memory makes me laugh. It was completely dark except for the stadium lights. Clark brought a checkered picnic blanket and spread it out so I wouldn't get dirt in my ass. We were in the heat of the moment and while he was grabbing my breasts I said, "bleacher sex, I'm adding that to my list," and he burst out laughing. We rolled over and I ended up with dirt in my ass anyway. Putting my hand to my head, I forcefully rub my temples. Maybe if I rub hard enough, I can make Clark reappear. If only genies existed. I wouldn't even need three wishes.

I manage to compose myself and start walking. The air will be good to clear my head. There's so much to see here at night, anyway. The walk will be a good distraction. The lights blinking from all the Broadway show marquees, the restaurants filled with people out for the evening, and even a man sitting on the sidewalk with his legs crossed, playing his guitar. People enjoying the music walk by and throw change into a hat. I stop for a second and listen to his strumming. He's really quite good. I pull out a few dollars from my wallet and throw them in. He smiles and continues playing. Clark would have loved it here.

My footsteps continue to lead me forward, and I'm enjoying the fresh air. Hearing a familiar voice call my name, I whirl around. Without realizing it, I walked right past The Brew House. Brad appears to be closing up for the night. When he finally turns and sees me, he stops.

"Wow, Gabby. You look really nice."

"Thanks!"

"You on your way back from a party?"

"No, actually, I met a friend."

"Ah, let me guess. Green eyes, tall…"

I smile. "Ding, ding, ding. You've just won what's behind door number three."

Letting out a small chuckle, Brad replies, "since I'm just closing up, mind if I walk with you? After all, a beautiful woman like you shouldn't be roaming the streets alone."

"Thanks for the offer, but I can take care of myself."

"I'm sure you can. But you never know when my superhero powers might come in handy."

"Superhero powers?"

His dimple returns. "Yup."

"What types of powers are we talking about?"

"I can't tell you that. A superhero never reveals his secrets."

"I see. So I have to trust that should the need arise, these so-called powers will make themselves known."

"Absolutely."

I choke back a laugh. "Okay, in that case, let's walk through the seedy part of the city. I'm anxious to see you in action."

"Never mock a superhero, Gabby. It detracts from our ability to perform." Brad is silent for a moment, and then, "So...how did everything go?"

"It was...nice."

"That's it? Just nice? That doesn't sound too promising."

"Actually, it was *very* promising."

Brad seems like he wants to say something else, but hesitates. He runs his hand through his shaggy brown hair instead. We walk together quietly until we pass Liana's Ice Cream Shop and I look longingly through the window.

"You're looking at that shop like you just found your lost puppy. Want to get some ice cream?"

"I'd love to, but I think I'm a bit overdressed."

"Nah. You look perfect. A bit distracting, but perfect," he says with a wink.

I love Liana's homemade ice cream. Smooth. Creamy. Yum. We had a shop like this back in California and I pretty much got a frequent flyer card there. In my book, the only thing that beats ice cream is warm chocolate lava cake with whipped cream on the side.

Brad grabs a table while I decide on two scoops of my favorite, Double Chocolate Brownie; he orders Monkey Ripple. We take a taste of each other's ice cream. I see him eying mine.

He tilts his head to one side. "I want yours instead. It tastes better."

I move my cup away from him, scraping it across the table. "No way. You had a taste already, and I'm not willing to share any more. Besides, Monkey Ripple suits you."

"What's that supposed to mean? Are you comparing me to a monkey?"

"What's wrong with that? Monkeys are cute."

Brad leans back with his hands behind his head. "So, you think I'm cute."

Time for a subject change. "So...how long have you worked at the coffee shop?"

He moves closer to the table, and to me. "Actually...I own it."

"You do?" I'm not sure why that surprises me, but it does. "Wow. That explains why nobody ever minds when you sit at my table. How long have you owned it?"

"About four years now."

"Wait! I thought it was a new shop?" How did I not know that? I must live under a rock.

"No, we've just had a sudden rise in popularity. A friend of the family, Steve Cooper, owned the shop, and I worked for him part-time during college. He decided he wanted to sell it around the time I graduated, and my brother Matt actually convinced me to buy it and loaned me some money so I could. It's kind of a funny story actually. When we were growing up, I used to always experiment making different drink concoctions...hot chocolate, teas, cappuccinos, whatever struck me. I really enjoyed it, and while it wasn't something I planned, I kind of fell into it."

"Well, you definitely seem happy doing it."

"Yeah, I love it, actually." I see a twinkle in his eyes as they reach up to meet mine. "I get to meet some really cool people."

My face warms, so I eat some more ice cream to cool off.

"Who designed it?" I ask curiously.

"Again, I have Matt to thank for that. He had someone in his firm come out and help. I'm really happy with the way it turned out."

"Yeah, that was the first thing I noticed. It's a little funky, but has a really homey feel. It's very inviting."

Brad rests his elbows on the table. "So...what about you? Where did you go to school?'

"I went to UC Berkeley for interior design."

"So you're exactly where you want to be then?"

I'm not so sure about that. "The job at Landon & Castell is great. It's a really good place to learn and grow and I'm hoping to move up at some point."

"What made you decide to move to New York?" His brown eyes exude interest.

I anxiously twirl my spoon around the cup of ice cream and start making soup. "It was just time, that's all. I was anxious to be on my own. I love California, but New York is fun. It's a lot more fast-paced than northern California." I chuckle. "A lot more people in a hurry here."

Brad swirls some ice cream around in his mouth. "I've been to California several times, but only to visit Matt in Los Angeles. It's really busy there, too. It reminds me of New York a lot, with the exception of the six lane highways, which are insane."

"You planning on drinking that?" he teases, looking longingly at my dish which is now filled with brown liquid.

"Yeah. I'm gonna ask for a straw." I giggle and then push my bowl to him. He seems to want to finish it.

We make our way out of the shop and down a couple of blocks when I realize my high heels are starting to take a toll.

Brad sees me wince a couple of times. "Shall I carry you the rest of the way? We superheroes are incredibly strong."

I laugh out loud. He really is adorable. And funny. "Actually, the subway will be just fine."

Brad walks with me until we get to the entrance stairs, then grabs my arm. "I was wondering if I could have your cell phone number? You know, just to make sure you get home safely."

He wants my phone number. Interesting. I hesitate for a second, but give it to him. I don't think he's a serial killer or anything. At least I hope not. There's really nowhere to hide any body parts in my apartment anyway. He pulls his cell phone out of his pocket and programs my number.

"Thanks for protecting me against any impending villains."

The right side of his mouth turns up. "Don't mention it, Lois."

I shake my head and giggle. He's so kooky.

Walking into the apartment, I'm greeted by a cozy Fran and Kyle on the sofa. She's sitting on his lap straddling him, his hand is up her shirt, and their lips are locked. "Oh...sorry."

Fran looks a bit surprised that I'm not in between 24k gold thread Egyptian cotton sheets right about now. "Hey! Why the hell are you home so early? You're supposed to be in the throes of passion."

Glaring at her so she'll shut her big mouth, she finally gets the message, pulls herself off of Kyle, and walks over to the kitchen counter.

"What happened? Did you chicken out?" she whispers, even though Kyle's out of earshot.

I can't tell her the real reason right now. I don't need her laying into me again. "Kind of."

"Gabrielle Christina Willis. What am I going to do with you?"

"I don't know. I might possibly need a few more of your sex education classes before I'm ready."

"Oh dear Lord. You need a lot more than that at this point."

Kyle interrupts, striding from the living room. "Hey Gabby, do you want to watch a movie with us?" He shows me a DVD case. "We're going to watch Mad Max...and," he dangles the red bag of licorice in the air, "we've got Twizzlers."

I look back over at Fran and quietly mouth, "Mad Max?"

She bobs her shoulders up and down, but smiles.

I rub my eyes. "I think I'm just going to go to bed, but thanks, Kyle."

"You okay?" Fran asks, concerned.

My attention goes back to Fran. "Yeah," I mutter, with the little conviction I feel.

"Goodnight, Kyle."

"Later, Gabby."

Fran stares at me with irritated eyes and shakes her head. I know she wants to say something, but thankfully she doesn't. Instead, she walks over and hugs me tightly. "Goodnight, sweetie. I love you."

"I love you too, Fran."

Throwing on my t-shirt and sweats, I hop into bed. I'm about to get under the blankets when my phone buzzes with an unfamiliar number. Who's calling me this time of night? Quietly, I answer, "hello?"

"You home?"

"Who is this?"

"Gabby, it's Brad."

I smile. Of course it is. "Oh sorry, I didn't recognize the number."

"That's okay. So you're home?"

"Yes."

"Okay, well goodnight, then."

"Goodnight. Hey, Brad? Thanks for checking on me."

"Sure."

"Goodnight."

When I finally close my eyes, I squeeze them shut and concentrate really hard, still trying to imagine Clark's arms around me, needing them around me...I'd give anything, absolutely anything, to feel that again.

Chapter Eight

Mondays suck. Why can't we have three day weekends? It's so hard to get motivated when you've had barely two days to relax. Dane left me a voicemail message that he wants to make good on that rain check. He wants me to come to the W tonight and have dinner with him in his hotel room. This time, I'm not backing down. I can do this. I want to do this.

On the way to The Brew House, my mind wanders to last night and Brad. I find myself laughing out loud, which elicits some stares. I guess Brad isn't the only odd one. There's something about him, though...I can't quite put my finger on it. He's very sweet, and endearing...and funny. He always seems so relaxed and comfortable in his own skin. I have to admit that I look forward to seeing him every morning.

The lines moves blissfully fast at the shop this morning. I reach the register and my lips form a smile.

Brad returns it. "Morning, Gabby. Salted Caramel Mocha?"

"Yes, please." Making my way over to a table, I plop down and pull out my cell phone to call Dane. Just as my fingers begin to dial, I hear giggling and glance over in the direction of the splendid sound. A young couple is in a heated embrace. Dreamy eyes, roaming hands, endless laughter. Clark and I used to be that way; happy. He scooped out pieces of my heart and held them tightly, brought life to them, mixed them up and made me crazy with love...for him.

I remember every detail about Clark. Those cobalt blue eyes that I could gaze into for hours on end, that silky brown hair that I loved to run my fingers through, those sculptured cheekbones, and that sweet mouth that held such hot kisses. Kisses that made me feel so much; until they didn't anymore. "I miss you, Clark." The words fall from my lips before I even realize I've said them. The tears slip from my heart and slide down my cheeks.

Brad stands over me with a box of Kleenex. "Are you okay, Gabby?"

"Yeah, I'm fine. Just having a moment." A Clark moment.

He looks down at the floor, and then meets my eyes. "If you need to talk or anything…"

A quiet sincerity fills his soft brown eyes. They're actually quite lovely.

"Thanks, Brad. Just having one of those days, you know?"

He places his hand over his heart, and I see an understanding glimmer in his eyes. "Yeah, I do know."

I watch as his hand makes a move toward mine, but instantly I retreat, shoving my hand under the table.

♡ ♡ ♡

My nerves manage to get the best of me as I make my way over to the W Hotel. I'm not biting my nails this time, but I'm cracking my knuckles which I'll admit is kind of gross, and straightening my clothes. Silently, I'm giving myself a sexual pep talk; it's not working. My insides are twisting and I'm starting to sweat, but I need this desperately. My brain needs to fall silent.

Passing through to the elevators, I'm met by a couple of stares. That's a good sign. I must be worth staring at. Fran has me wearing a navy blue halter dress and apparently it meets with the approval of random strangers. I make my way up to the twenty-seventh floor, then stand frozen in the hallway as I stare at the door near the end. I recall *The Shining* and half expect blood to pour from the walls. Not a good visual when you're about to have sex. Pausing, I roll my shoulders, hold my head up high, and hope my legs will carry me far enough before giving out.

Dane opens the door and his eyes move up and down the length of my body. "You look spectacular, Gabby. Come on in."

"Thanks," I say, still not understanding why I'm so nervous. I mean, I've had sex before, but there's something about Dane and I just can't put my finger on it.

He gestures with his hand for me to walk in further, and I do. "Would you like a drink?" he asks with his back turned to the bar, ice cubes clinking against a glass.

"Sure," I respond, about to ask for a lemon drop. I think better of it. "I'll have a martini with an olive."

Dane turns around, a look of surprise on his face. "Sure, coming right up."

As he makes the drinks, I'm taking in the room. It's ridiculously large, easily four times the size of my apartment. There's a huge king-size bed covered in very expensive sheets, a sitting area with a plush couch and two matching wingback chairs, and a space where the bar is that has a flat screen television mounted on the wall. As long as there are Swedish Fish on the room service menu, I could totally live here.

Dane brings over our drinks, escorts me to the table, and pulls out my chair.

"Thank you."

I see his eyes move over my cleavage and quickly take a couple big sips of my martini.

He stares at my lips as he speaks. "I hope you don't mind, but I took the liberty of ordering us capellini primavera."

My mouth is starting to feel dry. "Yes, that's fine, thanks."

There's a knock at the door and then a man's voice. "Room service."

Dane gets up to answer it and his fingers graze my bare shoulder, sending shockwaves to my toes. The guy rolls in the cart with our dinner and Dane gives him a sizeable tip. He walks out one happy dude.

As soon as the door shuts, Dane lunges for me, pulling my body tightly against him. He forces my hands behind me as he leans in and pushes his wet tongue into my mouth. The teasing way he strokes it tells me he's done this a million times before. *I'm sure he has.* I push the thought out of my mind as he leaves my lips and moves down to coat my neck with blistering kisses, sucking on my warm, supple skin. His hot breath fans my throat like small gusts of wind as his hands travel greedily down my body, squeezing and kneading my breasts through the fine material of my dress. My nipples harden in response. I draw in a breath when I feel his erection pushing between my thighs.

It's now or never, and my body can't wait a second longer. I shove the dress down my legs, leaving me incredibly vulnerable and open to his wandering eyes; eyes that showcase an undeniable hunger, an emotion reflected in my own.

"You're so fucking beautiful," he breathes as his shirt and pants follow suit and scatter to the floor. His arms sweep under my knees and he carries me to the oversized bed, but not before I reach around and make quick work of the strap on my bra. The thin satin falls from my arms and his fingers play with the tender peaks of my nipples. He draws one into his mouth and the tingling sensation makes me cry out. His lips continues to explore while his hands lower my panties to the floor, baring me completely. When he pushes back up, he whispers, "I want to fuck you so badly, Gabby."

His words inflame my desire and I wrap my arms around his neck, grabbing him hard enough to feel his growing arousal. He pushes me down on the bed and quickly rids himself of his boxer shorts, exposing his rather large erection. "Put your hands on me."

Gripping him firmly, I move my hand lightly up and down his hard length until he gasps, climbing over my body like an animal overtaking its prey. I pull him inside of me and he begins bucking in and out, while blowing rapid, heavy breaths.

Loud moans erupt from my mouth as my body matches his pulsating rhythm. His forehead is beading with sweat and his body dripping with desire as the smell of our lust fills the air. As our breathing becomes more erratic, he holds my hips tightly and continues pounding into me until we both find our release. *Jesus.*

When we're finally sated and our breathing slows, Dane lifts his green emeralds and glares at me wickedly. "That was fucking hot, Gabby. You're incredible."

"Hmmmm" is all I can manage at the moment, because as far as sex goes, yeah, it was pretty amazing.

♡ ♡ ♡

It's just after one a.m. by the time I get home. Fran's leaning against the kitchen counter with her hands on her hips. I smile. Of course she waited up for me. She couldn't help herself.

"Well?!" Geez, she's like a Doberman.

"Can I get in the door first?"

"No. Let's have it."

I string one long sentence together. "We had mind blowing sex and he ravaged me in ways I never thought possible, and he has a seriously hot body and a really big..."

"Oh my God! I just *knew* he had a giant cock!"

"FRAN!" I gasp.

"What?"

"Yes, it was huge, okay, and there's something else, too. He's a bit of a dirty talker."

"Hot damn, Gabby! You've hit the freaking jackpot! Plus, the dirty talk just upped his hotness by a thousand percent. Wait!" she blurts with a raised eyebrow. "Did you really have dinner, or was the whole dinner thing just a front to get you into bed?"

I try to give her one of those wicked looks she always gives me. "Let's just say I'm starving."

She flips her hair back and saunters toward her room. "Good. Now I can go to bed. You've given me some good material to work with."

Chapter Nine

The next few weeks fly by and my routine continues to be, well...routine. The consistency helps me cope, but, at the same time, bores the shit out of me. My job is going well. Dane and I have been seeing, I mean screwing, each other periodically. Brad and I have been hanging out at the coffee shop a lot. I've been getting there earlier in the mornings so we have more time to chat, and we've gone to a movie or two. Fran and I are doing what we always do. Most of the time, though, I just feel like a shell. I'm pretty sure if someone bumped into me, I'd shatter into a million pieces.

Fran has been getting earfuls of sordid sex details and enjoying every minute of it. Apparently, she's enjoying every minute of Kyle too. They seem to be getting on well and it makes me happy. I've been getting to know Kyle since he's been hanging out at our apartment a lot more, and I have to say I completely misjudged him. I made assumptions when we met based on his job, and I was way off. He couldn't be sweeter to Fran, and in fact, every Friday she comes home to a delivery of lilies, her favorite flower. I like the way he wants to take care of her, too. She hasn't had much of that in her life aside from her mom and me, and she needs it. I'm definitely keeping my fingers crossed on this one.

Today has dragged a bit, weekend or not, and I'm ready to go home for a bath and some serious nesting under my goose down comforter. But when I push open the door to the apartment, I find

Fran on the sofa, crying. I run to her and cup her wet cheeks in my hands. "Fran, what's wrong? What happened?"

The tears are sliding furiously down her face and I'm worried. This isn't like Fran. I pull her close to me and just hold her. After a few minutes, she pulls back. "My mom just called. My dad contacted her again, pressing her for my information. He told her he's changed. He's not going to let this go until he finds me, Gabby."

"Fran, listen to me. You're not that little girl anymore. He can't hurt you. I won't let him hurt you, I promise."

She looks at me with lifeless green eyes. She doesn't seem panicked or scared, more resigned. It's shattering to see my strong, independent Fran brought to her knees by the possibility of seeing her father.

"That's just it, Gabby. Whenever I even think about my dad, I am that little girl. I don't want to see him again. I can't see him."

"So you won't," I say with a fierce determination.

I help Fran into her jammies and she climbs into bed with me. I hold her all night long, and watch her as she sleeps. Her ebony hair sprawled across the pillow, her long, dark eyelashes hovering on her face. So beautiful, but so sad. Just a vulnerable little girl who only ever wanted what every little girl wants...a father who will love her and protect her against the horrors of the world, not create them.

Chapter Ten

Saturday morning I awake to a sleeping Fran. There's not a hint of her past lining her face, only peace. That's what I wish for her. As I watch her, I think of the struggle she's had to endure over the years and my issues seem so small in comparison.

I pull on my jeans, a t-shirt, my red Converse, and then grab my iPod. Leaving Fran a quick note on the kitchen counter, I slip in my earbuds and jam to "Candy Girl" by New Edition while I suck on a Twizzler. I've got the perfect plan; subway, fancy coffee, and those special chocolate donuts with sprinkles that Fran loves so much.

The Brew House is packed this morning, but I spot Brad immediately behind the counter. It's hard to miss that dimpled smile. Although, I notice he isn't smiling today. I make my way through the long line, pulling my earbuds from my ears, until finally it's my turn. "Hey, Brad."

"Hey, Gabby," he says with glassy eyes and downturned lips.

"Are you okay?"

He looks over at Erica, his right-hand in the shop. "Can you take over the register for a bit?"

I steer him to a nearby table. His eyes glaze over and all I see is sadness. "What is it, Brad? What's going on?"

He pauses, unsure whether he wants to continue. "It's just that...today is the anniversary of my sister's death. She passed away five years ago, from breast cancer."

"God, Brad, I'm so sorry. I had no idea."

"It's okay. I don't like to talk about it that much."

A lone tear rolls down his cheek, and I have a strong desire to lift my finger and wipe it away, but I don't. Instead, I place my hand over his, ever so briefly. I need him to know that I understand. And I do. I really do.

He looks down at our hands, and I feel the need to say something. "I'd love to hear about her sometime, if you'd like. When you're ready, that is...I'm a really great listener."

We sit quietly for a few minutes, before the shop starts to get more crazy and they need him behind the counter. Brad pats my hand and half-smiles, then goes back to work.

When I get back to our apartment, Fran is awake and watching re-runs of I Love Lucy. As soon as I walk in, she turns the TV off.

I mill around our tiny kitchen, pull a tray and some napkins from a cupboard under the microwave, arrange our breakfast on it, and then go sit next to Fran on the sofa. "Two special chocolate sprinkle donuts, and one caramel latte."

"Thanks, hon. I appreciate it."

"Anything for you. So, how do you feel this morning?"

"Drained. All that therapy I went through so I could heal from that nightmare. My mother dragged me every week for four freaking years. There's no way I can let him back in my life again. I don't know what I'm going to do, but I know that I don't ever want to see that dirtbag again. I don't care how much he told my mom he's changed. He doesn't exist in my life."

"I know, Fran. It's going to be okay. I promise you." I hesitate for a second. "Have you told Kyle about all this?"

She exhales a large breath. "No, not yet."

I cover her hand with mine. "I really think you should, Fran. If your dad is serious, you're going to need all the support you can get."

Chapter Eleven

Sex on a Sunday. That's what I wake up thinking...There's nothing like the tantalizing thought of emerald eyes and wandering hands. Dane continues to blow my mind in the sexual arena and I'm looking forward to another round tonight. He definitely has a gift, that's for sure. If you can consider excelling at giving pleasure a gift. I'll gladly accept it anytime, no twisting of the arm necessary.

I've had sex before, but he's certainly raised the bar. His prowess in this particular area is not unexpected, given that he's an Adonis. Sex appeal drips from every sinew of his sensuous, chiseled body, like warm chocolate pouring seductively from a fountain. Thick, hot, rich.

I need a cold shower.

♡ ♡ ♡

My fashion stylist has chosen my dress for the evening, and apparently it needs to be sexy with a burst of color, like the mint green stretch satin dress with the spaghetti straps that's cut far above the knee. According to Fran, it shows just the right amount of cleavage, while still leaving something to the imagination.

I'm sitting on a chair in our makeshift beauty salon in the bathroom, getting ready for Fran to do my hair. I peek up at her. "So, do you think he'll be turned on by my day of the week undies?"

Fran's mouth hangs open and she nearly drops the hairbrush. "You did not!" she screams out. She's so fun to tease and I can't resist.

I giggle. "Of course not! But don't act so offended, you used to wear them in elementary and middle school, remember?"

A happy noise escapes her throat. "Yeah, I remember. In fact, even then I remember Friday was my favorite day. I seem to remember that you used to wear them too, chickie, even in high school..."

"They made really cute ones! I can't help it! I was addicted." I look around the room covertly and whisper, "truth be told, I still have a pair hidden away in my keepsake box. The ones I was wearing when I lost my virginity to Clark. It was Thursday." I do have a tendency to save things.

Fran looks at me like she's either going to vomit or burst into giggles, and I know she's torn between the thought of dirty underwear in my keepsake box and my sickeningly sweet nostalgia. "Please tell me they've been washed."

"Of course they have! I just couldn't throw them away. They represent something very special to me." I sigh and wipe away a tear.

A hint of laughter tickles her throat before she leans down and kisses my cheek. "That's one of the things I love about you...you're so sentimental." She playfully swats me with the hairbrush. "Okay, enough of this sentimental shit, let's get back to hair."

Fran does my hair in a sexy, casual updo with soft strands dangling on each side of my face. Neck exposure is always good and it encourages nibbling. I like that.

I push back on the makeup, as usual. She wants dramatic and I want simple, so we compromise and go heavier on my pout. Lancome lipstick in *Berry Sensual*. Seems very fitting.

Fran spins me around, then stands back. "You look amazing, Gabby."

"Thanks," I mumble.

"I don't get you, Gabby. Why don't you seem excited? Dane is super hot, he's rich, he wines and dines you..."

I feel like pulling my hair down and ripping off these clothes already. "Fran, the sex is definitely hot, and he totally turns me on, but you know this is just a physical thing...a good distraction."

Her hands immediately go to her hips and her foot starts that tapping thing. "Does Dane know that Gabby? I mean, why don't you open yourself up? Who knows what could happen?"

Staring down at the carpet, I tell her "He's just..."

She cuts me off. "Stop thinking so much, and just enjoy yourself. Leave yourself open to possibility."

The truth is that I don't see possibility. I don't really connect with Dane on anything other than sex. It's hard to admit, even to myself that he's just a "fuck buddy." At the same time though it's kind of nice not to have to worry about an attachment.

Taking one last glance in the mirror, I hardly recognize my reflection. I'm not even sure I like who I see. It doesn't look like me. Oh well.

When I get to Dane's hotel, a tingling excitement comes over me, and I already feel a dampness between my thighs. Eyeing his hotel room door, it feels like I'm about to enter the dragon's lair. I knock once and wait for the dragon to appear. Unfortunately, when he does, he looks less like a mythical beast and more like a dashing knight. He's wearing his trademark black pants and a green button-down shirt that reveals a tiny bit of tanned skin. We match perfectly, almost as if we planned it.

"Gabby, you look absolutely breathtaking." He runs a hand casually from my neck to the hem of my extremely short dress.

My whole body shivers.

He invites me into his suite and I immediately notice the table for two complete with white linen tablecloth, candlelight and a bottle of champagne. Very Dane. Taking my hand, he leads me over to the table and pulls out my chair. Always the gentleman, at least for the time being.

I take in our surroundings. "Wow, Dane, you went all out tonight."

He reaches for my hand and drops a kiss on my palm. "I wanted it to be special for you."

We dine on a luscious meal of brown butter scallops over linguini which is seriously to die for. As we eat, Dane talks a lot about his work...again.

"I just landed this big client that the agency's been trying to snag for the past two years. I was able to put a unique spin on their marketing strategy. We had a meeting the other day and I laid out several concepts. They were extremely impressed and now they're hooked."

Actually, Dane talks about himself a lot. Maybe I've just been ignoring it, but the evidence is glaring tonight. He's pretty self-absorbed. This seems to be a recurring theme in my life; my mom, my dad, my sister. As he continues to talk, I try to appear attentive, though I've completely zoned out. I'm wondering if the hotel has any chocolate cake for dessert.

"Gabby?" he finally asks, bringing me out of my fog.

"Yes."

"Am I boring you?"

Yes, very much. "No, not at all. I enjoy hearing about your work. It's very interesting."

"Would you like some more champagne?"

You don't have to get me drunk, I'm pretty much a sure thing. "That'd be great, thanks."

After pouring more champagne, Dane stands and extends his hand. Before I'm even up on my feet, he descends on me like a wild animal. He's no longer a knight. His hands are fisting in my hair and his tongue engulfs mine with bold, fiery licks. Hot, heavy breaths fall into my mouth as he continues his onslaught. I feel his hands all over my body...stroking, touching, and squeezing while his rock hard chest pushes against the fullness of my breasts. He turns me on and fills me with a desperate lust that I seem to need right now. Panting heavily, I roll my hips against his, begging him with my body to seduce me. He answers by slowly sliding the thin straps of satin down my heated arms, then slipping the soft fabric down past my breasts, past my hips, until it drops to the floor. I'm not wearing a bra. His eyes are immediately riveted to my chest and he licks his lips, pulling me harder against him so I feel every inch of his arousal. Small moans leave my lips and I hear him gasp as he whispers, "your tits are fucking amazing." His words and the burst of air leaving his mouth bounce off my skin, making me hot and wet between my legs.

I unbutton his shirt as he rolls his thumb and forefinger over my nipples, squeezing ever so lightly and causing me to whimper.

"I want to taste those sweet nipples," he says, lowering his head and taking me in his mouth.

I stifle a giggle at his words. There's dirty talk and then there's porno talk. He's walking a fine line.

His breathing quickens and I inhale the soft, spicy scent wafting through the air as my fingertips scrape his chest, glide the linen fabric off, and toss it to the ground. My eyes move lower and I see that his pants have already joined his shirt, his arousal bulging through the seam of his shorts. Pressing his eager body against mine, my thighs are suddenly aching for him.

Dane pushes me against the wall, tearing at my soaked panties, while he exposes the silky hardness waiting for me. "You're so damn wet," he groans.

His head and tongue move lower until I realize where he's headed, and I fist my hands in his hair and bring his mouth back to mine. That level of intimacy isn't something I'm willing to share with him. His lips make their way back down to my nipples, sucking and licking the hardened crest.

"You taste so fucking good."

My head falls back and loud moans pour out of me as he brings me close to the edge. He leans up and enters me with one powerful thrust and I gasp at the intense contact. His large hands palm my breasts as he glides in and out, causing more hungry sounds to leave my berry- stained lips, the smell of champagne flowing out of my mouth.

The smooth, hard wall is pressing against my back, cooling the raw heat we're creating with our scorching bodies.

"I love to fuck you, Gabby!" is accompanied by loud grunting noises.

Puffs of breath blow on my searing skin, making my body tremble uncontrollably. He pushes inside me harder and harder and I long to arch my back, to absorb the intensity of his thrusts into that deep space between my quivering thighs. I feel the pressure building and a sudden need for release, my mouth letting out loud cries of pleasure. Our breathing accelerates and our bodies are wound to the brink.

"God, Gabby, my cock is so hard, I'm gonna come."

We finally climax together and sink to the floor, exhausted and breathless, each of us seeking the calm after our sensual storm.

"That was amazing, Gabby."

Barely having the strength to speak, I just nod my head, my eyes requesting permission to close for a much needed rest. A few minutes go by and I'm finally able to pull myself together long enough to mumble, "I should get going."

"Don't go, Gabby. I'd really like you to stay."

"I'd love to, but I have an early meeting tomorrow morning." Gathering my clothes off the floor, I make my way to the bathroom to dress. Digging around the cabinets, I've opened five before I actually find a washcloth. As my hand is cleaning between my thighs, I'm reminded of when Clark did this for me in his gentle, sweet way. This couldn't be more different. My knees start to give out and I suddenly feel faint, needing to lean against the shower door to try to hold myself up.

After several minutes I hear Dane calling. "Gabby, you okay in there?"

"Yeah. I'll be out in a minute." I latch onto the sink and look in the mirror, staring blankly. Blank is exactly how I feel. Putting myself back into my pre-sex state, I walk out to find Dane waiting for me by the door.

He eyes me like a tiger. "Thanks for tonight, Gabby. I had a really nice time."

Thanks for the wall sex, you mean. "So did I, Dane. Thank you."

Chapter Twelve

Why do Mondays always suck? I feel like I never catch a break. This particular Monday happens to be the morning after my wall sex, and I wake up to a stomach that feels like it's being stabbed with an ice pick. I hold onto it and run to the bathroom. My best guess is the brown butter scallops. Thanks, Dane. Standing over the toilet, heaving and freezing cold is not the way I pictured today. After my stomach is completely emptied and I feel a bit better, I manage to call and let Robby know I won't be coming to work today. Then I slide back under the fabric of my sky blue comforter and drift off.

Hours later, I awaken to the buzz of my phone. In my sleepy haze, I almost knock it off the nightstand. It's Brad.

"Hey, Gabby."

Half-asleep, I try to sit myself up on the bed. My throat is hoarse and extremely sore from all the vomiting. "Hey, Brad."

"You don't sound so good, are you okay?" He seems concerned.

I lie back down. "I'm not feeling well."

"What's wrong?" He sounds a bit anxious actually.

"I've got a stomachache and chills and I've been throwing up all morning."

"How about some chicken noodle soup?"

"What?" The thought of eating anything right now doesn't appeal to me.

He speaks softly. "I'll bring you some soup."

"Really, Brad, you don't have to do that." I know I won't be able to eat it, but I don't want to offend him.

"I want to. Is there anything else you need? Crackers? Ginger ale?"

"No, I'm good, thanks."

"Okay, I'll see you in a flash."

"Let me guess, superhero flight?"

He laughs. "Nah, my cape's at the cleaners. See you soon."

I slowly sit up again and try to breathe. My hair is stuck to my face with a mix of sweat and vomit. I stumble out of bed and head for the bathroom. Looking in the mirror, I'm greeted by a pale face and droopy eyes. How attractive. I take a quick shower to wash all the nastiness off, then dry myself, put some deodorant on, and run a brush through my wet hair. What's the matter with me? It's Brad, for heaven's sake. Yes, it's Brad. Better brush my teeth, too.

I replace my bathrobe with a pair of sweatpants and a t-shirt. And a bra. The least I can do is not look like a granny when he gets here. Forty-five minutes later, the doorbell rings and there he is, adorable sunken dimple and all. His hair is messy and he's breathing heavy. He's holding a brown paper bag and a two liter bottle of ginger ale.

"Hi," I stammer.

"Hey. How are you feeling?" he asks breathlessly.

"A little better, thanks. Did you run a marathon to get here? You look exhausted."

He bends over and places his hands on his knees to try and catch his breath. "I was just concerned about you. You sounded pretty awful on the phone." He sets the bag and ginger ale down on the kitchen counter.

"Thanks. I really appreciate it. I'd ask you to stay, but I don't want to infect you." Oh no. My stomach starts rolling and I hear the toilet calling me like a scrubbing bubbles commercial.

"Gabby, you're pale. Are you okay?" His eyes are full of worry.

"I...feel..." I make it to the bathroom just in time. Brad follows after me and the next thing I know, he's holding my hair back as the remainder of my stomach ends up in the toilet. So much for brushing my teeth. Now I've thrown up in front of him. Way to go, Gabby. I cover my mouth so I don't offend him even more. "This could top the Tom Cruise incident. I'm really sorry, Brad."

He laughs and tucks my hair behind my ear, rubbing small, calming circles around my back. "There's nothing to be sorry for. It's all part of the job description, Lois."

"You know Brad, you've got a serious superhero obsession. Have you thought about getting help for that?"

He smirks. "Tread lightly, Gabby. Remember who's holding your hair back."

When I open my mouth to laugh, the smell is offensive and I close it quickly.

Brad helps me up and over to the sofa, then wraps me in a blanket. Running back to the bathroom, followed by the kitchen, he gets me a cold washcloth for my head and some ginger ale. He sits by my side and presses the cool washcloth to my head. It feels good.

With heavy eyelids, I begin to drift. The last thing I think I remember is a warm kiss being pressed to my forehead.

Chapter Thirteen

It's a beautiful morning in New York City and I'm not nauseous. What a difference a day makes. I forgot to close the curtains last night, and the sun is filtering through them. Wait a minute. How did I get to my bed? The last thing I remember is being on the sofa. Brad must have carried me in here. Oh my God, he's been in my bedroom! I look around, suddenly thankful that I didn't leave any bras on the floor. As I hop out of bed, I'm also extremely grateful for a settled stomach and feeling like myself again. All is right with the world. Fran left a note to meet her at the coffee shop, so I hit the shower. I try to get the image of Brad in my messy bedroom out of my mind, letting my thoughts drift to Dane and those eyes. I can't wait to screw...I mean *see* him again tonight. Well, if nothing else I'll be able to add him to my list. Wow, that sounds bad. Crazy, mind-blowing, no strings sex with a hot guy. Okay, maybe not *that* bad.

On the way to the shop I pass by a couple of corner markets with flowers outside. One in particular catches my eye. They have pink lilies. I pick up a bouquet for Fran and run inside to pay for them. I notice small packages of Swedish Fish at the register, so I get a couple of those, too. For me.

Fran beats me to The Brew House by a few minutes, and when I get there she is chatting up Brad behind the counter. No surprise there. He's cute and she's like a moth to a flame. For some reason the idea of Fran and Brad doesn't sit well with me, regardless of her relationship with Kyle. Brad's eyes meet mine and he flashes those pearly whites. Shake it off, Gabby. There are more important things to think about, like green eyes and a giant...

I hand Fran the flowers and her mouth drops open in surprise. "What's the occasion?"

I smile sweetly. "You're the occasion."

She grabs me and hugs me hard. "Best friend *ever*."

I eye the glass display case for something sweet. A chocolate chip muffin will do the trick. "Brad, can I also have a chocolate chip muffin?" I look over at Fran. "Do you want anything else?"

"No, I'm good."

We grab a booth and plop down. I'm waiting for Fran to say something, which takes all of about three seconds. "Gabby, every time I see him, he gets cuter and cuter, and that dimple is simply luscious. Can you set us up?"

"What about Kyle?" I say with a raised eyebrow.

Fran looks around the shop. "Kyle who?"

"Very funny. I don't even know whether he has a girlfriend or not."

"Girlfriend? I highly doubt that, with the amount of time he spends with you." My face feels a bit tingly at the thought. "Anyway, who cares about that. I just want one night."

With a look of feigned revulsion, I knee her under the table. "Jesus, Fran, keep it in your pants, will you!" I pause for a second with teasing eyes. "So, guess who had her first wall sex ever?"

A loud cackle escapes her mouth; I know it's not as novel to her as it is to me. "So, which do you prefer, wall or bed?" she asks excitedly.

"Well, wall was interesting, but a little too hard for my liking. I choose bed."

Fran snickers. "Oh, I'm sure it was a lot hard."

In mid-laugh, I notice something on her wrist. It's gold and very sparkly. Grabbing her wrist, my curious eyes meet hers. "What's this?"

She touches the bracelet with a shy smile. "Kyle gave it to me."

My mouth drops open. "What? When?"

"Last night," she says, with a blast of color making her cheeks rosy.

I can't seem to close my mouth. "Fran, it's beautiful."

She moves closer to me in the booth. "He's really something, Gabby. He really gets me, you know, and I can be myself with him. When I told him about my dad he was so understanding and supportive. He didn't say a word...he just held me. And for the first time, I'm not embarrassed about my scars. He's always kissing them and telling me that they're a part of me, and he loves all my parts."

I do a double take. "Did you just say love?"

She sighs heavily. "It's just a figure of speech, Gabby. You know what I mean."

Wrapping my arm around her shoulder, I pull her to me. "I'm so happy for you, Fran. That's exactly what you deserve."

We finish our drinks and start to leave when I pause. "Fran, give me a second, okay?" I motion to Brad. He walks over and my eyes meet his. "I just wanted to say thank you for...holding my hair back yesterday."

Brad's sincere eyes caress my face. "Gabby, you don't have to thank me." He smiles. "I enjoyed it, actually, and I'm just glad you're feeling better."

"Well, I am, and I really appreciate you coming over and you know, not being grossed out by my vomiting and all."

He laughs. "I didn't say I wasn't grossed out. Besides, I'm starting to notice we have this bonding thing over toilets."

The corner of my lips turn up. "Gee, thanks for that reminder; I appreciate it. I'll see you later." Brad's expression changes instantly. His eyes look a bit sad and I'm not sure why, I did just thank him and all. "You alright, Brad?"

He slowly turns away, waving the back of his hand at me as he starts for the back of the shop, his voice sounding distant. "Yeah, fine. See ya, Gabby."

Fran and I leave the shop and I can see the wheels spinning. "What was that all about?"

I start twisting the ends of my hair and shifting on my feet. "You knew I was home sick yesterday. When you were at Kyle's last night, Brad came over and took care of me. I just wanted to thank him."

With raised eyebrows, Fran responds, "Reallllly?"

"What?"

"Gabby, you're doing that twirling thing with your hair, and you're fidgeting."

"Yeah, so?" I choke out, a bit frustrated.

"Nothing. Nothing at all."

$$\heartsuit \; \heartsuit \; \heartsuit$$

Robby's in rare form today. He's practically skipping around the office, raving about happy clients and fabulous new furniture. "Good morning, Gabby dahling."

"Good morning, Robby."

"How are you?"

"I'm okay, you?"

He shakes his head back and forth. "When am I going to hear *great* come out of those fabulous lips of yours? I want to hear that you're doing fantastic, splendid, marvelous!" Robby's always so optimistic–he wants everyone to be as happy as he is.

"I'm working on it."

"Well, as long as it's a work in progress, sweetheart, it's all good."

I go back to dealing with the overwhelming sticky note parade marching across my desk. My cell phone rings and quickly transports me from post-it hell.

"Hello, beautiful," a low, husky voice calls from the other end.

"Hey, Dane."

His voice springs up. "I've been thinking about you all day and wondering if I could see you tonight?"

"Sure, that sounds great. What did you have in mind?"

"Why don't we go over to the Sky Bar and have a couple of drinks first, and then come back to my hotel? Sound good? Do you want to meet up at say seven?"

Ooh, we're actually going somewhere other than his hotel! "Great, Dane. See you then."

Immediately, I call Fran. "Hey!"

"Hey, sweetie! What's up?"

"Dane and I are going to the Sky Bar tonight. Do you and Kyle want to come?"

"Kyle's taking me to dinner, but maybe we'll swing by after."

"Cool. Hope to see you later."

♡ ♡ ♡

I'm pacing nervously around my room trying to get dressed for tonight. It's kind of ridiculous since we've already had sex many times, and I should be broken in by now, but I still want to impress the guy with something besides my sexual prowess. Meeting in public is exciting and a little scary. I mean, couples go out for drinks...oh well, I know we'll end up in bed anyway. I try and shake my anxiety when my phone rings. I smile; it's Brad.

"Hey!" He sounds so enthusiastic and I can actually see his dimple.

"Hey!" I respond with the same level of excitement.

He chuckles. "I just said that."

I'm laughing inside. "You've got jokes, I see." Grabbing my heels, I sit on the bed and slide them on, then walk over to my dresser and dig in my jewelry box for my gold earrings. I shoulder the phone to my ear and walk to the bathroom to brush my hair. I've become very good at multi-tasking. Must be all those sticky notes.

"Always. So whatcha doing?"

"I'm getting ready to head out." In ten minutes.

"Where to?"

"I'm going to the Sky Bar. I'm meeting Dane there."

"Oh, okay." His voice deflates and I feel a pang of guilt.

Curiosity gets the better of me. "Why, what's up?"

I hear hesitation, and the line is quiet for a minute. "Nothing. Just thought we could hang out."

"Can we do it another time?" I'm starting to feel bad and try to sound upbeat.

"Sure." He sounds anything but.

"Great. Talk to you later."

"See ya."

When I arrive at the Sky Bar, I'm greeted by the familiar smell of alcohol and body odor. My favorite combination...not. I don't see Dane yet, so I push my way through the crowd of tightly packed bodies to get a drink. It's just seven o'clock anyway. I plant myself on a stool and chat it up with the bartender. Sipping my drink slowly, I eye the door so I can make sure to flag Dane down. It's really crowded in here and I'm not sure he'll see me. When I see the door open, I'm sure it's going to be Dane. But it's not. It's Brad. What on earth is he doing here? Then a tiny thought creeps in my head. You told him you'd be here; you practically invited him!

I watch him walk in. He's wearing tight fitting jeans and a white button down shirt. His brown eyes are dazzling, even from a distance it's hard not to notice them. Walking in further, he appears to be scanning the room. He really is handsome and I'm finding it difficult to look away. Our eyes meet and he smiles, walking toward me with that slow, lazy swagger. I've never really thought of Brad as sexy, but tonight, he looks the part.

When he finally reaches me, he smiles approvingly. "Gabby, you look really pretty."

"Thanks. You do, too. I mean, handsome that is." Gosh, Gabby. Get a grip, you're here to meet another guy. What the heck am I doing? "So, what are you doing here?"

"I don't know. I just felt like a night out." He looks around, obviously searching for my date. "Where's Dane?"

"I'm waiting for him, he's a bit late." My eyes dart to the door again.

"Well, then you have the pleasure of my company while you wait. If that's okay with you."

I look around the room again. No Dane. "Sure, why not?"

We sit and chat for a while. We talk about my life back in California and he tells me some stories about his family. I don't chime in too much, I just let him talk. It's strange, though. I feel so comfortable around Brad. Much more comfortable than Dane. And I'm actually listening to him. I laugh to myself. I guess throwing up in front of someone kind of breaks the ice. I like talking to him, though, so much so that I completely lose track of the time. It's 7:45 and still no Dane. At this point, I kind of don't care whether he shows up or not. My phone buzzes. Speak of the devil.

Dane: Gabby, so sorry, got tied up at work

Me: That's okay

Dane: Can I make it up to you another night?

Me: Sure

Dane: Great

I close my cell phone and throw it in my purse.

Brad looks over at me. "Everything alright?"

"Yes, fine. Dane can't make it, he's stuck at work."

Brad turns away, failing miserably to hide his smile. He seems a little too happy about it. Surprisingly, I'm happy about it, too. I don't mind spending more time with him.

His dimple surfaces. "So, I guess we get to hang out after all."

"Yup, I guess we do." I lean my elbows on the bar and sip my drink with a smile.

He buys me another drink, and then another after that. We talk and laugh, a lot, and I'm genuinely happy that Dane canceled. After my third drink, I narrow my eyes and shake my finger at him. "Are you trying to get me drunk so you can take advantage of me?"

"Who me?" he says with an unassuming smile. "I wouldn't dream of it."

The alcohol is making me brave. "You know, when I first met you, I thought you were kind of odd." I stifle a giggle. "Odd, but cute." And getting cuter by the minute.

He blinks a few times and his face reddens. "You know, when I first met you, I thought you were adorable. Clumsy, but most definitely adorable."

My face flushes, and I almost choke on my drink.

After an hour of a lot more talking and a lot more drinking, I'm feeling extremely giddy. Brad is looking at me with those soft, dreamy brown eyes that, quite frankly, are hard to resist. I take a moment to really look at him. Everything is hazy; well, except for one thing. His lips. Pink, lush, full. There's only one thing on my mind. Kissing them. Scratch that. I want to plunge my tongue into the farthest depths of his succulent mouth. Suddenly, my life's mission is to become an explorer. Holy crap! Where did that come from? It must be the alcohol talking.

The more we talk, the closer he gets. I can almost feel his breath on my face. At some point, his hand moves around my shoulder and his fingers graze my bare skin. I feel tiny goosebumps pop out all over. Holy crap. I hope he didn't notice that.

The music grabs my attention, and I pause for a second. "I love this song."

"'You and Me' by Lifehouse," he says.

"You know them?"

"Yeah, they're one of my favorite bands."

"Seriously?"

"No, I'm lying to you," he says with a teasing smile.

"Ha ha. I can't believe you like them. I don't know anyone else who does. God, Jason Wade's voice...it goes right through me. Plus, he's kinda hot. There's definitely something about a guy who can really sing."

Brad's eyes hold a mischievous sparkle. "I've been known to hum a bar or two."

"Really?" I ask with an arched eyebrow.

"Yup."

I set my hand on my hips. "Okay, well, let's hear it then."

"Here?!" His voice practically squeaks. Apparently he's not drunk enough to sing in public.

"Of course, why not?"

"Well...because I usually reserve it for the shower." He laughs with that deep throaty voice. I bump his shoulder playfully and laugh with him. Brad looks over at me curiously. "So tell me more about what you like to do for fun."

"Well, lots of things, really." Let the rambling begin. "I love the beach, hanging out with friends, reading, parasailing, photography, and then there's my list." That was a mouthful; nice work, Gabby.

Brad puts his fist to his chin, trying to look as interested as possible. "What kind of list?"

"It's sort of like a bucket list. You know, things I want to do before I kick the bucket."

"So, what's on the list?" His eyes light up and I sense he's hoping he can help me cross something off.

"You really want to know?"

"Yeah, I'm interested."

"Okay. Things like traveling. Bora Bora, Italy, Australia, England. Things to do, like skating at Rockefeller Center, a gondola ride in Venice, snowmobiling, visiting the Space Needle in Seattle, helping to build a house for Habitat for Humanity, swimming with dolphins, a carriage ride in Central Park, jet skiing, going on a whale watch...and other stuff."

"You mean there's more?"

"Yeah. There's always more, isn't there? Trying new foods like duck, octopus, maybe bison. Your turn."

"I don't have a list."

"That's okay. We can make one." I grab a napkin from the bar and a pen from my purse. What do you like?"

Brad's brown eyes meet mine. "I like you."

I drop my pen and sip my drink, eyes to the ceiling, trying to look as innocent as possible.

"You know, Gabby, you're super cute when you're embarrassed."

My lips are frozen, so I do the best thing I can think of. I shut up and drink.

Brad opens up a bit more and tells me some pretty funny stories about his old girlfriends. "Yeah, I told Susan my dad wanted to meet her, and she kept telling me how nervous she was and that she wanted to make a good first impression. So, you can imagine how surprised I was when she showed up to my house wearing a ridiculously short skirt and a low cut tank top."

"Oh my God!"

"I know, right? She certainly managed to garner a lot of Matt's attention, but my dad was mortified. That was the exact point when I realized she was a complete whackjob. It turned out she was after Matt all along."

"Oh Brad, that's terrible."

"It's alright. I'm glad I found out when I did."

It's getting late, and the alcohol is really getting to me. "Brad, I think I'm gonna get going."

"Would it be okay if I take you home?"

"Sure." There's nothing I'd like better right now.

There's a chill in the air when we get outside, and I shiver, noticeable goosebumps rising from my skin. Brad picks up on that right away and offers me his jacket, which is warm and smells of him. I let out an audible sigh at how wonderful it feels to be wrapped in his jacket.

The subway and walk to my apartment pass in a comfortable silence. I've had a lot to drink, and at one point, I almost trip over a crack in the pavement. Brad grabs me and stops me from falling. Hmmm. His arms feel good. Strong, supple, and muscular. I can't help wondering what else is supple on his body. The thought makes me snort.

"What's so funny?" he asks.

"Nothing." I say, but then I roar with laughter. I've had way too much to drink.

Brads return laughter echoes in my intoxicated ears. "I need to get you home. The alcohol is making you nutty."

By the time we make it home, my bed is calling me. Brad walks me all the way to the door of my apartment. I'm propped up against it because it's the only thing that's holding me up at this point. Brad leans in so close that I can feel his breath feather my cheek. God, he smells good. He slides his hand behind my neck and pulls me close. Licking my lips and closing my eyes, I wait. And wait. I realize at this moment that I really want him to kiss me. In fact, I'm silently willing him to kiss me. I must be really bad at this, though, because he never does. Instead, he bypasses my lips and leans in to place a delicate kiss to my forehead before pulling away.

Stumbling into my apartment, I sink to the floor, let out a huge breath I didn't realize I'd been holding, and sigh.

Chapter Fourteen

The next morning I'm a bit disoriented, and my head is pounding so loudly I think I hear voices in there. I put my pillow over my head and try to recall last night's events. Oh, that's right. I remember. Of course I remember. Brad. It makes me chuckle. In a weird way, I'm glad Dane didn't show up. I had an amazing time with Brad. My whole face starts to tingle. I wanted to kiss him, badly. I still do.

It's sadly Wednesday, and a workday, so my daydreaming has to end for the moment. I pick out a black pencil skirt and white blouse and pull my black heels from the closet. As I'm dressing, I notice Brad's jacket hanging on the chair. I forgot to give it back to him. Letting out a huge sigh, I walk over and hug it to my chest. It smells like coffee...like Brad.

I'm looking forward to seeing him this morning, and of course I need to return his jacket. I smile to myself. Good excuse, Gabby; like you weren't going to stop there anyway. I walk rather slowly on my way to the shop, holding onto his jacket a little too tightly, my mind on last night and our almost kiss. There's a couple on the street corner in a heated embrace, and for a second, I smile. That is, until I bump headfirst into a woman on her cell phone and her drink ends up all over her white dress. I'm mortified. I look up at her with remorse. "Sorry about that."

"Dammit! Why don't you watch where you're going?"

I want to tell her I'm not sure that would have made a difference, people that spend their time in faraway lands, like me, are destined to crash into others.

The door jingles and Brad flashes me his full-on, no holds barred smile. I don't know why, but it's just what I need, and I smile right back. I make my way through the line of starry-eyed girls who Brad seems oblivious to and finally reach the counter.

"Hey, you," he says.

I bat my lashes like a starry-eyed girl. "Hey."

"You're up early this morning," he teases.

"Yeah, I needed some caffeine."

His lips twitch. "Rough night?"

"Yes, actually. Some drunk guy tried to take advantage of me." I wink conspiratorially. "It was dreadful."

"Really?" He nods as if he's listening intently.

Flipping my hair over my shoulder dramatically, I make my way over to a table. "Yes, it was absolutely terrifying."

Brad makes his way over with my drink and that smile of his. "What a coincidence! The same thing happened to me, except with a cute drunk girl."

I can't help but laugh.

He takes a seat next to me and clinks our coffee cups together. "So, how's that head of yours today?"

I'm liking the table service. "Not bad, actually. Luckily I drank a lot of water last night."

Brad looks over at me with those almond shaped eyes and I melt just a little. "I had a really nice time last night, Gabby."

"Yeah, I did, too." I'm suddenly feeling very self-conscious when I've never felt anything but comfortable with Brad.

"You're pretty funny when you've been drinking. I enjoyed the giggling, it was fairly amusing."

"Well, I'm glad I could entertain you."

"Trust me, you were very entertaining," he says with a wink.

We chat for a few more minutes and I'm almost ready to leave when I remember that I need to give him back his jacket. When I hand it to him, his fingers skim my knuckles and I feel those goosebumps puffing up my skin again. I quickly shake it off. "Thanks for letting me borrow your jacket."

"Anytime," he says, smiling and going back to the counter. "See you soon, Gabby."

I head towards the exit and try to look back without being too obvious; he's staring at me. Turning around quickly, I walk out the door, a smile completely overtaking my face.

Chapter Fifteen

The more I think about Dane standing me up at the Sky Bar, the happier I am that he did. It's been a week since I've heard from him. He's been traveling for business. He finally calls while I'm at work, startling me out of my post-it induced coma.

"Hey, gorgeous! Happy Tuesday! I'm back from my trip. I've been missing you like crazy, I need to see you."

For some reason, I'm not all that excited. Maybe because he didn't even ask how I'm doing.

"Can I see you tonight?"

"Uh...sure."

"Great! How about dinner in my hotel room at eight o'clock?"

"Yeah, okay. I'll see you then," I say with a complete lack of enthusiasm.

"I look forward to seeing you tonight." I can practically hear him leering at me.

"See you then."

$$\heartsuit \heartsuit \heartsuit$$

I make my way down the hallway to Dane's suite. No more horror flick images; no more knights and dragons. That's good, I guess. I knock on his door and he immediately pulls me into the room, sealing his lips over mine with a desperate need. I'm blindsided by his smoldering heat. I feel his tongue wrap around mine, his breath invading my mouth like a foreign predator. Slowly, he starts to unzip my dress, while I eagerly pull his shirt over his head and reach for the zipper of his trousers, setting free his gigantic erection. Our naked bodies are quickly entangled in one another, turned on and dripping with sweat, our breath coming in heavy bursts.

"I want my cock inside you again. It's all I've been thinking about."

I'm momentarily distracted by that comment, but it soon disintegrates as he moves me onto the soft satin sheets of the bed and thrusts his hard length inside me. The feeling is so intense I scream as my body succumbs almost instantly. My insides tighten at his deliberate movements; the rocking sensation of his hips, the sweat dribbling rapidly down my heated skin makes the craving for release overwhelming. After one final, pounding thrust, I let go, and Dane follows my lead as his body quivers and his voice calls out "I'm gonna come so hard, Gabby!"

As our breathing slows, I hear him whisper, "that was incredible."

I don't have a response. I feel numb or sick, I can't figure out which one. Staring up at the ceiling, I suddenly realize what it is. I feel empty. Good. No, not good. Something's different. What is it? It can only be one thing. Shit. After a few minutes I slowly sit up on the bed. "I have to go."

"What do you mean, you have to go? Where are you going? We haven't even eaten yet."

While Dane continues to talk, I'm already out of bed, pulling my panties and bra on, then sliding my dress back up. I grab my shoes and head for the door. I can tell he's flustered but I don't care. I have to get out of here.

"Please, Angel, I want you to stay."

My head whips around. "Don't you ever call me that again," I snap, stomping out the door as quickly as my feet will carry me. Hearing him say that word, one that holds such special meaning for me, makes me sick to my stomach. I start breathing heavily and grab onto the wall as I wait for the elevator. When the doors finally open, I stagger inside and try to catch my breath. I can't help but think that was the biggest blow off in the history of my life; and it wasn't happening to me. I was making it happen.

I'm tired, starving, and feeling the need to lose myself for a little while. Junk food and a movie, that's it. Making my way over to the corner store, I feel the wind on my face and let it carry me away. Away from all the waves of disappointment drowning me. Disappointment in a family I wish could have been different. Disappointment in a guy who gave me exactly what I wanted. But most of all, disappointment in myself for finally wanting to feel something.

$$\heartsuit \heartsuit \heartsuit$$

I awaken in the middle of the night with endless tears streaming down my cheeks and a sick feeling in the pit of my stomach. I throw back my comforter and sneak into Fran's room, crawling into bed beside her. She doesn't wake, but her nearness is enough to calm my tears. Minutes later, she starts to stir and extends her arm to stretch out. She cracks open her eyes when her hand touches my shoulder.

"Hey," I whisper.

"You okay?" The sound of her voice releases more tears and they tumble down my cheeks without ever looking back. I wish I could do the same. Fran pulls me close. "Shhh...it's okay, sweetie...it's okay."

But that's the problem. It isn't okay, and I don't know when it will ever be okay again.

Chapter Sixteen

It's Thursday, day four of this horrific week, and I'm having a hard time concentrating. It's a real problem, since Robby's left me three times as many sticky notes as I'm accustomed to. My mind keeps drifting to Clark.

By the time the day's over, I'm a complete mess. I can't remember the last time I had such a bad day. Well, I can, and that's the problem. I'm walking around aimlessly with no destination in sight, and it suddenly feels like I'm literally on the road to nowhere. Images of Clark's face are flooding my brain and I can't make them stop. My hands are shaking and tears are streaming down my face like raindrops falling from an angry sky. The faster I walk, the quicker they fall. All the tears I've cried for Clark over the years are pounding down on me, overwhelming me. When I finally look up, I'm standing in front of The Brew House. It's almost as if my feet constantly know me better than I know myself.

I take a deep breath, wipe my blotchy face, and walk inside. The door jingles and I see a familiar face. A welcome face. Brad looks up from behind the counter with a smile that quickly subsides once he sees me. He makes his way over and leads me to a booth. As I sit there with tears stinging the back of my eyes, I feel a hand on mine. A warm hand. A feeling hand. And I feel things. Things I'm not supposed to feel. Things I can't allow myself to feel. It's like his fingers are strumming my heartstrings; pulling, plucking, twisting, and I'm helpless. Completely and utterly helpless. I know I need to pull away, but I can't.

"Gabby," he says. There are no questions in his voice, only concern.

After several minutes of silence and using up an entire box of Kleenex, I mutter, "I'm sorry."

He keeps his hand on mine and gives it a reassuring squeeze, then tugs me up by the hand. "Come on."

"What, where are we going?"

"Just come on."

"I can't go anywhere looking like this!"

Brad doesn't let go of my hand. "You look great, now let's go."

We make our way onto the street and I still have no idea where we're going; not that it matters. I look down and notice that Brad's fingers are still intertwined with mine. The moment I notice, he does, too, and quickly pulls his hand back to his side. I didn't mind it, actually. It felt right in some odd way, even though I know, God help me, it shouldn't. Brad doesn't say much to me, so we continue to walk in silence. It's for the best, though; my mind is flooded with too many thoughts I wish I could chase away.

He finally stops and I see that we've reached our destination. Looking up, I see a movie marquee with "Looney Tunes" in giant block letters. My eyes dart over to Brad. "Looney Tunes, seriously?"

He leans back on his heels, and with childlike eyes, shoots back, "Hey, never underestimate the power of Bugs Bunny and Daffy Duck!"

The marathon is hysterical. I don't remember the last time I laughed so hard. A couple times during the movie, Brad caught me brooding and threw some popcorn at me to shake me out of my mood. It worked, for a while anyway.

Walking back to my apartment, we're both quiet. Brad hasn't pressed me once tonight to talk about what's bothering me, and I really appreciate it. I don't know what to say. I feel like a hand is pulling me down a dark hole, and I can't seem to grab the rope to pull myself out.

Brad stops and looks over at me, forcing my eyes to meet his. "I hope you know by now that you can trust me, Gabby. I'm here if you want to talk about it." He hesitates, but then continues. "I can see how pained you are. There's something eating away at you, and I want to help, if you'll let me." There's a softness in Brad's eyes when he looks at me. It's almost as if he's trying to melt away my sadness. His fingers touch the side of my cheek, and for a second, the pain melts away. The disappointment melts away. The world melts away.

Turning to walk inside, I look back and try my best to muster up a smile. "Hey, Brad?"

"Yeah?"

"Thanks for tonight."

"Sure." He walks off into the night.

And just like that, my misery returns.

Returning home to an empty apartment, I shed my skirt, blouse, and rip off my bra and panties as quickly as possible. I make my way to the bathroom and turn the water on until it's just the right temperature. I slide the curtain to the side and hop into the scalding hot shower, attempting to scrub off all the pain, all the disappointment, and all the guilt. But no matter how raw my skin gets, it just won't come off.

Chapter Seventeen

My days are blending together again. I can't even remember what day it is, or whether I have to work today. I'm not sleeping and I'm freaking exhausted. Dragging myself out of bed this morning, I rub my crusty, sleep-filled eyes and knock on Fran's bedroom door. When I don't hear anything, I crack the door, but she isn't there. A note in the kitchen tells me to meet her for coffee.

I putz around the apartment for a while and consider just going back to bed, when Fran's words come back to haunt me. *You have to move on, Gabby. It's time.* Only, how do I do that? Heading back to my room, I walk over to the $90 consignment shop dresser and stand in front of the top left hand drawer, staring at it. I'm not sure what possesses me, because I haven't opened it in a while, but my shaky hand grabs the handle and pulls it open. I gaze at the pile of old pictures and papers, and my fingers itch to flip through them, but something stops me, and I think better of it. Slamming the drawer shut, I run into the bathroom and prepare for the day.

The door does its usual jingle thing when I walk into The Brew House. My feet seem to be in slow motion, or maybe it's my brain, I'm not sure. I take in a couple discussing the benefit of children visiting art museums and notice that, for the first time, my heels aren't sticking to the floor. Maybe Brad's washed it. I see Fran at the counter leaning over it, her cleavage poking through the top button of her green blouse. My feet make their way over to her of their own volition to interrupt whatever it is she's trying to do, and Brad's lips curve into an easy smile.

"Hey," he says quietly.

"Hey."

He looks at me with concern. "You doing better today?"

I twist some strands of my hair. "Yeah, a little bit."

Fran looks annoyed that she's completely out of the loop. I ignore her for a moment and eye the glass case, deciding I need a heavy dose of sugar. "Brad, can I have two double chocolate chip muffins please?"

He stares at me like he wants to say something, until his mouth finally opens. "Two, huh? Serious chocolate craving?"

"Yeah, you could say that. Can I also have extra whipped cream in my mocha?"

"Sure, Gabby."

After ordering our drinks, Fran grabs my elbow and practically drags me over to a booth. "What the hell was that all about?"

"You know, Fran, you'd know about this stuff if you were at the apartment more and not shacking up with Kyle."

She slaps me on the shoulder. "You know you support my relationship with Kyle. Spill."

"Well...Brad took me to a Looney Tunes marathon yesterday night to cheer me up."

"He took you where?"

I can't help the small smile creeping up my face. "I just told you. He took me to see Bugs Bunny."

Fran raises an eyebrow. "And you seem pretty happy about that."

"Well, it was fun. It was just what I needed, actually."

"Gabby, what am I missing here? I thought you were seeing Dane."

"Well, no, I wouldn't say I'm seeing Dane. I would say I'm screwing Dane."

Fran's mouth drops open in disbelief. "Whoa. That sounded seriously bitter."

Taking a deep breath, I try to gather my thoughts before I speak. "Okay, so I saw Dane the other night, and we had sex, just like always. And before you say anything, yes, it was great sex. But, that's all it was..."

Without letting me finish, Fran interrupts. "And the problem is? I thought that's what you wanted, right? Isn't it, Gabby?"

"Yes. No. Yes. I don't know. It's been for the past month or so, but now I'm not so sure." I tap my fingers on the table. "I don't know. I know after we had sex this time I felt empty, and for the first time in a long time, I didn't like it."

"Sweetie, I've known you since fourth grade, and sometimes I actually think I know you better than you know yourself. I've already told you what I think. You've just been too thickheaded to want to hear it. You're running and you've been running for a long time. Dane is a band-aid and that's all he's ever been. It's time to rip off the freaking band-aid; let go of the past, and go after what you really want. Stop messing around, Gabby. This is your life we're talking about."

Fran stops mid-sentence as Brad returns with our drinks. "One Salted Caramel Mocha, extra whipped cream, and one latte." He gives me a quick wink and walks way.

"So, where was I, before we were rudely interrupted by that dimpled cutie?" She smiles. "Oh yes." Her eyes sparkle. "Going after what you want. What do you really want? Because from my perspective, I see things changing for you. Maybe the question isn't what's changed, but who's changing it?" As she says the words, she glances over to the counter and then back to me. "I have a couple of theories."

I pinch her arm hard. "Stop looking over there, Fran. He's going to think we're talking about him."

"Oh yes, things are changing all right." Her whole face smiles. "You may not be ready to admit it, but that's okay. I can tell you this, Gabby Willis; I've seen more genuine smiles from you recently than I've seen in a long time. So, whatever or *whoever* is putting those smiles on your face, I'm rooting for them. She pats my hand and gives me one of her sincere, loving smiles. "Now, getting back to Dane, if you're kicking his hot ass to the curb, can I pick him up and dust him off?"

We burst into laughter so loud, customers turn to stare. "Fran, you're unbelievable!"

Fran and I say our goodbyes and I feel Brad's eyes follow me as we walk out the door. This time I don't look back.

Chapter Eighteen

Fran's words of wisdom seem to be invading my thoughts a lot lately. I laugh out loud; she wants my leftovers. Well, she can have them, and gladly. I'm feeling a bit more confident today and know I have to call Dane. I need to face what happened last week, but I also need to get him Robby's new design plans for his apartment. Above all else, I have a job to do.

On my lunch break, I pull myself up from my chair, which I now seem to be stuck to, and head over to a small conference room. I peek inside and when I don't see anyone, walk in and close the door behind me. I dial Dane's number, feeling pretty confident. He answers after three rings. "Hey Dane, it's Gabby. Listen, I want to apologize for leaving the way I did the other night."

"That's okay. I'm sorry that I upset you. Can I make it up to you, say tonight?"

I'm not giving up my Friday night. "I can't tonight, but how about next week?"

"Sure. I'll call you tomorrow. I can't wait to see you, Gabby."

"Okay, bye Dane."

♡ ♡ ♡

Friday is always takeout and movie night. I rent *Pretty Woman*. Why? Because I'm a hopeless, sappy romantic and I love happy endings...especially one involving Richard Gere. By the time I pick everything up and make it home, I'm completely drained. Ripping off my work clothes in favor of my trademark sweatpants and a tank top, I settle in under a warm, soft blanket with some chicken and broccoli, and Richard Gere.

Just as I get settled, my cell phone rings. I consider not answering it since Fran is with Kyle, but pick it up just in case it's her. It's Brad.

"Hey, you," he says, with that ability to always make me smile even through the freaking phone.

"Hey, yourself."

"Whatcha up to?"

"I'm getting ready to eat takeout and watch a movie. What about you?

"I'm closing up for the night. What movie?"

I'm almost embarrassed to share. "*Pretty Woman*," I answer sheepishly.

"That just happens to be my favorite movie."

Liar. "Yeah right."

"Seriously, I like Julia Roberts."

"I'm sure you do," I say with playful sarcasm.

He laughs. "I don't think I like your tone, little lady."

I think I'd like to see him. "Do you want to come over and see Julia Roberts then?"

"Okay, but only if you have popcorn."

"Why is that?" I don't think we have any popcorn.

"Just in case I need to throw it at you."

I laugh. "See you soon."

"You betcha."

Putting down the phone, I let what I just did sink into my brain. I just invited Brad over to my apartment. What was I thinking? I wasn't thinking. Or maybe I was thinking. I don't know. It's only cute, sweet, adorable Brad. It's not a date or anything. Yeah, okay Gabby, whatever.

I rush into the bathroom to brush my hair and throw a little lip gloss on. Realizing I'm bra-less, I take one out of my drawer and put it on, then fish through my closet and put a different shirt on; one without stains.

The doorbell rings, and inhaling a deep breath, I make my way over to answer it. There stands Brad, smiling with every ounce of himself.

"Come on in, Julia's been waiting for you."

"Oh, I was hoping it was you who was waiting for me."

Gulp. "So, are you hungry? I have a lot of chicken and broccoli left."

"Sure, that'd be great." He hands me a cup with The Brew House logo. "Here. I know it's kind of late for caffeine, so I brought you a peppermint hot chocolate." Brad's eyes roam the kitchen counter and land on the bags of Twizzlers and Swedish Fish. "What's all this?" he asks, obviously excited.

"Ah, you mean my secret addiction. I love candy. I buy it any chance I get and stockpile it. I guess you could call me a candy hoarder."

His amused eyes scan my face. "Well, looks like your secret's out."

"I'm truly relieved," I say, blowing out a breath. "It's been hard hiding that for so long." I stop when I realize what I've said. He has no idea how true that statement is. "So, what do you want to watch?"

"What do you mean? I thought we were watching *Pretty Woman*?"

"Wouldn't you rather watch *Terminator* or something?"

"*Terminator*? You actually have that movie here?"

"Well, no."

Brad looks at me strangely. "Why are you suggesting it then?"

"Because it's more..." I look up at the ceiling, as if an answer is going to fall down in the form of peeling paint. "I don't know...manly."

"Are you suggesting I'm too manly to watch *Pretty Woman*?"

"Well, no...but..."

"Listen, remember me? I'm the one who took you to see Looney Tunes. I think I can handle *Pretty Woman*."

I throw my hands up in the air. "Okay, if you insist."

"I do."

I meander into the kitchen and reach up on my tippy toes, grab a plate and fork for Brad, and load it up with chicken and broccoli, then fill up a glass of ice water for him.

Panic sets in as I make my way over to the sofa. I don't know where to sit. Oh my God, I feel like I'm in freaking high school. Standing there nervously, I start twirling my hair with my fingers and sucking on my lip.

"Earth to Gabby?"

"Um...Yeah?"

"Are you going to sit or do you want to finish eating your lip first?"

"Uh...okay."

I hand Brad the plate and sit down next to him, but not too close. Then I reach around and grab a blanket but when it doesn't quite reach him, he eases over a bit. Our knees are touching and it's making it hard to concentrate on the movie. I put my hands underneath my legs and sit there like a statue. A very tired one.

Somewhere between Julia Roberts watching *I Love Lucy* and Stuckey getting punched in the face, I fall asleep. I awaken to a soft shoulder and tender brown eyes.

"Sorry, I didn't mean to fall asleep like that." I'm completely mortified. I hope there's no drool on my face.

"That's okay. I quite liked it. Except for the part where you were drooling and snoring."

I nudge his shoulder. "I don't drool *or* snore."

"How would you know? *You* were sleeping."

Being this close to Brad gives me a chance to peek at the tattoo around his bicep that I've been eyeing for so long. It looks like two scripted names wrapped around each other, with a small pink rose in the center. Curiosity gets the best of me. "Can I ask you a question?"

"Sure, anything."

"Your tattoo..." I trail off. Brad's expression falls and I immediately regret saying the words. "I'm sorry...I ju..."

"No, it's okay, really. It's...it's in memory of my mom and my sister. The name Clara wraps around the name Sofia. Clara was my sister and Sofia was my mom. My mom passed away when I was twelve, and my sister Clara, who I've mentioned before, passed away five years ago. Both from breast cancer."

I suddenly feel an overwhelming ache in my heart for him. "Brad, I'm so sorry."

"They were the two most important women in my life. I got the tattoo in remembrance, although it would be impossible to forget either one of them. They were both so full of life, and appreciated it in a way I've always admired. You actually remind me of them in some ways."

I don't know what to say. Reaching over, I weave my fingers through his. Brad looks down at our hands and pauses a moment before he continues.

"My mom was so amazing. She was always there for me. When I was a kid, she played with me all the time. Whether I was in the mud, playing basketball, or roughhousing, she was always right there beside me. She was a constant in my life, and I always knew she loved me no matter what I did.

"She sounds like she was very special."

"Yeah," he sighs. "She really was. It was so hard when she got sick, though. I had to watch as the disease took over her body and her mind until I no longer recognized her anymore. After she died, I was lost. I needed her so badly. So I started skipping school and purposely getting into fights. I was so angry, and just didn't know how to handle it."

"I can't imagine what that must have been like for you."

"I just wanted her back, you know. My dad put me in therapy for a while, before he went off the deep end himself. Now he lives in Ohio and is a bit of a recluse. He took her death really hard; not that I blame him. She was the love of his life. After that, he was never the same. He just became...lifeless and bitter."

"So, do you still have contact with him?"

"No, not anymore. He blames the world for my mom's death. I felt that way, too, at first. I had so many questions and I was angry. But over time and with therapy, I realized I'd never know why. And for whatever reason, God felt that it was her time. When my sister passed though, that was the last straw for Dad. It pushed him over the edge. She'd been sick for a while and we had to watch her disappear right in front of our eyes." His eyes have a faraway look and there's a hint of a smile on his lips. "Clara was a real spitfire...larger than life. She had a mind of her own and no one could tell her anything. I remember just before she got diagnosed she was planning on backpacking across Europe. When we found out about the cancer, my dad practically forbade her to go because he was afraid something would happen to her while she was gone." He chuckles. "But did she go? She sure as hell did. She said, "Hey, if I'm dying, I might as well go out with a bang. The living have to keep on living.'" His eyes make their way to mine. "I miss her fire...her spirit."

"What about your brother, Matt?"

"Since he lives in Los Angeles, we don't see each other a lot, but we're really close. We talk on the phone every other day, and make an effort to fly out and see each other at least four times a year."

Brad looks at me now. "How about your family? I've only heard you talk about them briefly."

"Ah...that's a dysfunctional story at best. How much time do you have?" He just stares at me, waiting for me to go on. "My mom and dad are very self-absorbed, so needless to say we're not very close. They never supported my choices unless it was what they wanted for me. I'm kind of a big disappointment to them. My dad lives his own life with his new wife in Atlanta and barely has time for me unless he happens to be in the neighborhood. My mom is so wrapped up with her clothing store in San Francisco and her new boyfriend every six months that the best she can do is call me once a month, if that. I have a sister, but we're not close. They don't get me. They never did."

"I'm really sorry, Gabby." He squeezes my hand.

"It's okay. They just don't know who I am. They don't even know how much I like chocolate. Or that my favorite thing in the whole world is to curl up with a good book and get lost, and when I'm finished reading how sometimes I'm in tears because I'm affected so much. Because I feel so deeply. They tend to do a lot of talking and not much listening. After a while, I just stopped trying to talk to them. I guess I gave up on them ever really knowing me." Tears are starting to surface and I move to cover my face.

Brad leans in and presses a kiss to my cheek. His lips feel so soft. "It's their loss, Gabby. They're missing out on someone very special."

The hour is getting late and Brad and I decide to call it a night. A part of me doesn't want him to leave. I like having him here. He makes me forget.

Grabbing his leather jacket off the chair, I hand it to him, but not before I inhale the faint scent of Brad mixed with coffee.

I look into Brad's eyes with complete sincerity. "Thank you, for showing me who you are tonight."

He leans forward and places a sweet, lingering kiss on my cheek that warms my skin. "Thank you for sharing Julia Roberts with me," he says with a gleam in his eye.

Chapter Nineteen

I didn't sleep well, my mind consumed with thoughts of soft brown eyes and tattoos. In fact, those are the same brown eyes that have been consuming my dreams night after night. Even though Dane and I aren't exclusive, or really dating, feelings of guilt are seeping into my brain but flickers of happiness seem to be melting them away, slowly but surely.

The bright blue sky and warm sunlight awakens me. I must've been drooling last night, because my hair is glued to my face and I'm practically eating it. Gross. I step into the shower and take a little bit too long scrubbing myself as my mind drifts to the soft lips that I'm desperate to kiss.

Fran is still sleeping and I nudge her before I leave so she's not late for work. I don't remember exactly, but there's some big account and she has to go in for a few dreaded hours on a Saturday. Giving her a quick peck on the cheek, I head out the door.

I find myself grinning as I walk the streets of Manhattan today. In fact, I'm grinning so much that I feel as though everyone is staring at me like I have a big secret. Well, maybe I do. On the way to The Brew House, I walk by a store that catches my eye. There are cards and plaques with simple quotes about life in the window, but what I notice most is a wristband with a pink ribbon for breast cancer awareness. I have just enough time to stop. Walking inside the store, I make my way over to the display. Most of the bracelets look pretty feminine, but then I see one that's stainless steel and leather. There are two ropes of black with a tiny pink ribbon imprinted on a stainless steel clasp. Perfect.

Taking a deep breath, I join the line at the coffee shop. When Brad's eyes meet mine, my pulse quickens. There's been a shift of some sort; I can feel it. Something about him pulls at me strongly, like we're having some sort of tug of war and I'm losing. There are no flirty girls today, so I'm able to make my way right up to the counter.

Brad's smile reflects mine. "Morning, cutie."

I melt just like the Wicked Witch. "Morning," I reply, unable to do anything else but smile.

"Did you sleep well last night?"

Yes, because I was dreaming of you, again. "Yeah, really well." I have to look away for a moment to hide the four shades of pink crawling up my cheeks.

"So, what do you want today?" Brad says with his lopsided dimple.

That now-familiar blush seems to have settled in for the long haul. "I'll have an iced vanilla latte, please."

"Absolutely."

I need to give Dane a call. I told him we'd get together this week. He called twice last night and once already this morning. I tried ignoring, but I don't think avoiding him is going to work as a breakup tactic. Given all the calls, he appears to be a bit irritable about it. Perhaps he's sexually frustrated. Although I'm sure there are a million girls out there who could ease his pain. I just don't want to be one of them anymore. I definitely need to make sure we meet in public, so there's no danger of getting caught in his sexual web.

My phone rings and startles me. "Hey, Fran."

"Hey, sweetie! Thanks for waking me up this morning. I would've totally overslept. Kyle and I had a bit of a late night last night."

I chuckle. "I'm sure you did."

"Actually," Fran sings, "Kyle took me to meet some of his family."

"WHAT?" I shout through the phone.

She laughs hysterically. "Gabby, it was amazing. They are the nicest people. Do you know he's got three brothers and three sisters? I met four of them last night, and his mom and dad. We had dinner and then we played Scrabble. It was so fun!"

I'm shocked. "*You* played Scrabble? You don't even like games! Wow, Kyle's really doing a number on you."

Her tone gets serious. "Yeah, he is Gabby." Now I hear her smiling brightly through the phone. "You know, he didn't let go of my hand the entire night and I really felt like I was a part of his family. It was...amazing."

"Well, I want to hear more about this later. I want details!"

"Cool. So listen. Kyle and I are going to the Sky Bar Tonight. Do you feel like coming out with us?"

This sounds like the perfect neutral place to have a conversation with Dane. "That sounds great. I'm going to ask Dane, too."

"You mean the Dane you don't give a shit about?"

"FRAN!!!" I bark.

"Well, let's be real. He's nothing more than a good screw. *Your* words."

I laugh. "Well, I have to talk to him tonight, and I don't want to do it alone."

"Ah...afraid you'll get caught up in his web of sex?"

"Something like that."

We agree to meet at the Sky Bar at seven o'clock. I call Dane after and leave a voicemail.

Brad brings me my drink and slides into the booth next to me. I'm still loving the table service. When he hands it to me, his fingers deliberately skim mine and I feel that familiar shiver. He hesitates, and for a moment I think he feels it, too.

I play nervously with the smooth ends of my hair. "I have something for you."

His eyes light up. "For me?"

I take out the bracelet, which is artfully wrapped in tissue paper, and hand it to him. He slowly opens the crumpled pink tissue and runs his fingers over the leather and the clasp. I wish I knew what he was thinking.

He looks up with a hint of tears lacing his eyes and shakes his head as if in disbelief. "Thank you, Gabby. No one's ever done anything like this for me before. I can't tell you how much it means to me."

I see his eyes dart over to my wrist. I bought myself something, too. A pink wristband that says *celebrate courage*. He runs his fingers over the writing and looks up at me.

I shrug my shoulders. "I wanted to wear one, too."

His fingers wrap around my wrist, his thumb resting on the bracelet. My insides quiver. While his mouth is moving, it's his eyes that are speaking to me. "Really, Gabby. Thank you." His thumb continues to rub my wrist gently and we just sit there, staring at one another. I know I need to get up, but every cell in my body is so relaxed and happy that I can't move.

Finally, Brad is the one who gets up. "I need to get back behind the counter."

I look up shyly. "Yeah, I really need to get to work."

Brad helps me up from the booth, grabs my portfolio, and hands it to me.

"I guess I'll see you later."

His dimple smiles at me. "You can bank on that."

With my portfolio and latte in hand, I finally make my way out the door. This time, I take a prolonged look over my shoulder. As the door closes, Brad's eyes meet mine, and the corners of his lips rise sweetly. Adorable. Absolutely adorable.

Chapter Twenty

It's Saturday night, and the Sky Bar is packed like sardines in a can, and it almost smells the same. The music is blaring. People are practically having sex on the dance floor. *Get a room.* I get on my tippy toes and try to spot Fran and Kyle, but it's hard to see over all the giant heads. I hear a voice calling me and follow the direction of the sound. I think I see Fran and Kyle at a table near the bar, holding hands casually and scanning the room for me. Bumping into some guy on the way over to the table, he spills his drink, and I hear him mutter a curse at me.

"Watch where you're going." Like I can even see where I'm going.

I finally make it over to the table and Fran grabs me and plants a big kiss on my cheek, then I hug Kyle. "Let's sit closer to the door, otherwise Dane won't be able to find us." That's assuming he doesn't stand me up again.

Fran, of course, eyes him the moment he walks in the door, and elbows me-hard. Watching Dane's eyes scan the room is like watching a wild animal searching for its next meal. His eyes finally settle on me and he gives me that panty-dropping smile. Unfortunately for him, I don't want to drop my panties anymore. He reaches me quickly, and when he does, pulls me into a kiss. A long, deep kiss. The kind of kiss that other people shouldn't be seeing; the kind that I'm trying to avoid. I make to pull away from him quickly and notice Fran appears to be gasping for air, while

Kyle looks turned on. They'll be rushing home for hot sex in a minute, I just know it.

"Dane, you already know Fran. This is Fran's boyfriend, Kyle."

He greets Kyle in his all-business demeanor. "It's a pleasure to meet you."

Kyle eyes Dane up and down, protectively, taking in his finely-tailored suit and tie and his outrageously expensive Berluti leather shoes. "Likewise."

Dane goes to the bar to get a round of drinks for all of us. Kyle looks over to me with a huge grin. "Gabby, have you seen this girl play Scrabble? She beat the pants off of us again last night."

Interesting choice of words. "I heard something about that, Kyle, and you must have some sort of magic up your sleeve, because I've never been able to get her to play Scrabble in the entire fifteen years we've been friends."

Kyle and Fran make googly eyes at each other and kiss. I'm a bit jealous.

Dane returns with our drinks: martinis for Fran and me, and gin and tonics for the guys. The conversation is flowing freely and everyone's getting along. I know Dane and I need to talk, but I'm not ready to do it just yet. I need to get a buzz on to calm my nerves; I might even need to get trashed. Kyle and Dane seem to be hitting it off, which is great because Fran and I have a chance to talk. At some point during our conversation, Fran motions over her shoulder and I wonder what she's staring at. I follow her gaze and see Brad standing at the bar with a woman. What's he doing here, and who the hell is that?

"Gabby, Brad's here. He's been here for a while."

"I know, I see him." My stomach flips. I eye the girl. She looks vaguely familiar, with long auburn hair, blue eyes, a tight-fitting dress and a figure to die for.

"Who's that chick he's with? She's pretty hot."

"How the hell should I know?" My tone is biting and I immediately regret it. Fran can pick up the jealousy scent a mile away.

"Whoa, Gabby. Get a grip. You're not dating or anything."

A knot forms in my stomach and I need to find the bathroom, fast. I might just throw up again. This is becoming a habit around Brad. It's so freaking crowded in here and I have to push through a maze of intoxication, sweat, and ass grabbing to get there. Thankfully my legs are moving quickly and I've almost reached my destination when I feel a hand catch my elbow. I spin around like a top and practically knock someone over.

"Gabby. Hey."

Just that simple touch makes me tremble. "Hey, Brad. I'm in a hurry, what do you want?" I feel my whole body tense up at my harsh words.

Brad looks slightly offended and I suddenly feel bad. "I just wanted to say hi. I had the night off tonight so I came out for some drinks."

Even though I already know the answer, I ask the question. "You here by yourself?"

"No, I'm here with Erica from work." He waves a hand at her standing at the other side of the bar, and then eyes me curiously. A bead of sweat forms at the corner of his brow and he reaches up to swipe it away. The touch of his fingers causes his hair to sway. And there it is, a crinkle. Right smack in the middle of his damn forehead.

I don't know how I never noticed it before. My breathing picks up, and suddenly the walls are closing in. I'm pushing against them with all my might, but they won't move, so I need to. "Let me go, Brad."

"Gabby, what is it? What's wrong?"

"Nothing. Just let me go."

I'm feeling the need to stomp my feet, cry, or hit something. I crash into several people on the way to the bathroom, but I don't care. Pushing open the door, I scan the room and am relieved to find it empty. I pace the length of the pee-stained tile floor; back and forth, back and forth. He has a freaking crinkle on his forehead! What the hell?! I suppose he also enjoys picking up super absorbent tampons in his spare time, too. I kick my heel firmly into the back of the stall door. Dammit!

I have to get out of here now; I can hardly breathe and I need air desperately. I finally find a path back to the table and lean over to Fran. "Hey, I'm leaving."

"Are you okay?" Fran whispers, making to stand.

"Yeah, I'm fine." I know I sound less than convincing.

I hear her mutter under her breath and she pulls me away from the table; away from Kyle and Dane, who didn't even notice I was gone. "The hell you are. Talk to me, Gabby. Is this about Brad?"

"I just want to go, Fran." I'm edgy, bordering on whiny.

"Gabby, listen to me. Brad's been staring at you all night. He hasn't taken his eyes off of you. He may be here with someone else, but he's barely noticed her. You may not want to hear this, but I think he's into you. I saw the way he was looking at you at his shop. It couldn't be more obvious."

"What are you talking about?"

"Come on, Gabby. This is me you're talking to, and you can't pull this shit with me. I see the way he looks at you, and that's not how you look at a friend. It's not just that, either. You've been different, too." She sighs and puts her hands on either side of my face, forcing me to look in her eyes. "It's okay, you know. It's okay to let yourself be happy."

I shake her hands away and then, slowly and *very* casually, look over my shoulder. Our eyes meet. Brad's been watching me. Immediately, I look away and resume my conversation with Fran. Somewhere, deep down, I know she's right. I've been trying to ignore it, but it's becoming impossible.

I can't stay here. "Fran, I want to go."

"Kyle and I will come with you if you want, and I mean that."

"No, you guys stay. I'll be fine. I'll see you later." I give Fran and Kyle each a hug, and walk over to Dane. He's been practically ignoring me anyway, first talking to Kyle and now to his female colleague from the ad agency, who's apparently joined our table.

I place one hand on my hip. "Dane, I'm leaving."

"What? We just got here." He's caught completely off guard.

I breathe deeply. "I just want to go."

"Okay, then I'm coming with you."

Really? Why bother? My panties are off limits. "Fine."

Dane says his goodbyes to his colleagues and follows me out of the bar. I feel him trying to keep up with me as my feet hit the pavement with long, quick strides. When I look over at him, confusion covers his face. The same confusion that I feel.

He stops suddenly, grabs my shoulders, and turns me around. "What's going on, Gabby? What's wrong? I don't understand. The nights we've spent together over the last several months have been...well, amazing. But the past couple of weeks, you seem distant and distracted. You ignored my calls all weekend, and tonight we've barely spoken at all."

Unsure of what to say, I just lift my shoulder and stare at him blankly. I know it's not good enough. It's also not fair to Dane. "I'm just tired, and I want to go home."

Hesitantly, Dane reaches for my hand. "Can I come with you?"

I really don't want to hurt his feelings, but that's the last thing I want. I need to be alone. "Can we talk tomorrow, Dane? Right now I want to go home. I just want some time to myself."

Dane nods with understanding, and at that moment, I see a flicker of something I can appreciate about him. "Let me at least hail you a cab."

I'm in no mood to fight with him. He gives me a chaste kiss on the lips and helps me into the taxi.

My mind is racing and so is my heart. If I was in a cartoon, steam would be leaving my head right now. Picking at the dirty leather on the seat of the taxi, I just keep shaking my head. It's all I can do. It feels like someone's playing a cruel joke on me, only the problem is, it doesn't feel so cruel. It kind of feels like fate.

My phone buzzes, and it startles me. I don't want to answer it, but when I see it's Brad, I can't help but smile. Why the hell am I smiling? I'm mad at him!

"Gabby? It's Brad."

"I know who it is," I reply with a bit more anger than I'd intended.

"Are you okay?"

He sounds genuinely concerned, which only increases my guilt. "Yes, I'm fine, why?"

"You seemed upset with me earlier. Did I do something? You left without even saying goodbye, and before..." His voice trails off, and he sounds hesitant, as if weighing something over in his mind.

"Before what?"

"Before I could ask you to dance."

Did he say dance? "What?"

"I wanted to dance with you."

"With me? What about your *date*?" I can't help the sarcastic drip in my voice.

"Erica wasn't my date. She's my friend. She works with me at the shop."

"She's pretty," I say reluctantly, because it's true.

"Yes, she is, very. But she's just a friend."

A temporary feeling of relief floods my body.

"Where are you?" he asks, his voice anxious and demanding at the same time. A side of him I haven't seen.

"I told you, I'm in a cab on my way home."

"Yeah, but where?"

I peek out the window. "We're on Broadway, about to pass Bloomingdale's."

"Okay, can you get out at Bloomingdale's? I'm on my way there."

"What? Wait!" Too late; he already hung up. "Stop the cab!" I've always wanted to say that.

I fumble with my fingers. What am I doing? I'm standing in front of Bloomingdale's waiting for Brad, that's what I'm doing. Just when I change my mind and decide to leave, I see him jogging towards me. He's breathing heavily, his cheeks flushed and muscles flexing underneath his shirt, his wavy brown hair blowing in the breeze. I'm not going anywhere.

When he finally reaches me, he's completely breathless. "Thanks for waiting for me."

"Brad, what on earth are you doing here?"

He grabs my hand, his touch making me tremble. "I told you. I want to dance with you."

"Here?" I gesture to the crowded New York sidewalk.

"Why not?"

It's confirmed, he's absolutely insane. "Okay, now I know you're certifiable."

His dimple flashes like a neon sign as he places one hand at the small of my back and laces his fingers through my other hand, bringing it to lay upon his chest. I can feel his heart beating rapidly. He leans in and presses his forehead to mine, so close I feel the warmth of his breath tickle my nose, sending a shiver up my spine. The wisps of his shaggy hair massage my face, and the smell of java mixed with his own scent whisks me away. All the anger has suddenly left my body. I can no longer hear the taxis honking, feel the muggy temperature in the air, or notice the constant rush of people bumping into us and staring. The world has completely fallen away.

Our bodies sway from side to side and all goes silent except for the soft humming that fills my ears. The hum is oddly familiar, then completely recognizable. Brad's voice begins its caress, the sweet melody of 'Lover You Should've Come Over' sweeping over me.

"Jeff Buckley," I whisper. "He's one of my favorites." I feel him smile against my cheek. When the humming stops, I instinctively pull away and gaze into his sweet brown eyes. Suddenly, I feel vulnerable, like he can see inside my heart, and I'm not sure I'm ready for him to see that much of me. I lean my forehead back against his and enjoy the rest of our very first dance together, silently hoping that it won't be our last.

$$\heartsuit \; \heartsuit \; \heartsuit$$

When we finally reach the subway platform, disappointment looms. Brad pauses for a moment and rubs the back of his neck with his hand. I'm not sure if he's nervous or deep in thought; I can't put my finger on it.

"Can I ask you a question?" He doesn't wait for me to answer. "Are you and Dane exclusive?"

I have to resist the urge to roll on the ground, grab my stomach, and laugh hysterically. I'm not sure what we are, but we're definitely *not* exclusive. "No, we're not."

The curve of a smile touches his lips before he speaks. "Good. So...I was wondering if you'd like to go out tomorrow night?"

"Go out? You mean like on a *date*?" I emphasize the last word with a grin.

Brad shifts his feet. "Yup, a date." His smile is endearing and I want to accept immediately.

The problem is, I don't do dates. Mindless screwing, yeah, that's what I do. But I can't tell him that, he'll think I'm crazy. The thing is, as much as I keep telling myself that, the thought of going on a date with Brad does something to me. "Well, I really don't do dates."

Brad looks at me with a strange expression and I suddenly want to eat my words. "What do you mean you don't do dates? Aren't you doing dates with Dane?"

No actually, I'm just doing Dane. "Not exactly." Now I'm really embarrassed. I can't imagine what he thinks of me.

"Okay. So then we'll do what we always do. Two friends just hanging out together. I mean, we are good friends, aren't we?"

It's not what I usually do, but that works. "Yes. We are. And yes, I'd like to hang out."

The full-on dimpled smile I get after I say yes nearly makes me combust on the sidewalk. "Great! So until tomorrow then?"

"Yes. Until tomorrow." He lifts my hands to his face and places a single kiss on the inside of each of my palms.

As the subway doors close, I'm squealing inside. The earth has suddenly shifted on its axis.

Chapter Twenty-One

I'm in the middle of an amazing dream, full of giant dimples attacking my mouth, when my phone rings the next morning and wakes me up, which stinks because it's Sunday and I could've slept in. When I see who it is, I debate hitting ignore and going back to my fantasy because it's much better than the reality. The one with my mom. I suck in a breath and pick up the phone. "Hi, Mom," I exhale.

Her voice sounds as chipper as ever. "Hi, dear."

"What's up, Mom?" I try to sound somewhat interested.

"Well, as luck would have it, I'm coming to New York City two weeks from this Saturday for Fashion Week."

Who's luck would that be? I'd rather win the lottery. My nonexistent excitement is blaring. "Great."

"I thought we could have lunch together."

"Okay. Well, you know I'd ask you to stay here but..."

"Oh no, I certainly can't stay in that tiny space you call an apartment. I'm staying at the Waldorf. It's going to be a busy weekend, but I'm hoping we can manage to squeeze in lunch."

She always knows how to win me over with her kind words. "Sure, Mom."

"I'll call you when I get in."

"Okay, Mom." As soon as I hang up, I get a sick feeling in my stomach. I'm rummaging through the medicine cabinet for anything resembling Tums, or even Valium at this point, when I hear the front door latch click. "I'm in the bathroom, Fran!"

"What are you doing, Gabby? I have to get ready for my date with Kyle," she whines. "He's taking me to the Botanical Gardens."

"I'm looking for some Tums," I say, diving into the box of crap under the sink. Nothing's there either.

"Let me guess. Patricia Willis is coming to visit."

"Ding, ding, ding. You've won! You're going on an all-expense paid solo date with my mom."

Fran cackles, then moves past me to turn on the shower. "So when is crazy coming?"

"Two weeks, so I have time to mentally prepare. Not to see me, of course. It's for Fashion Week; I'm just a detour."

"Well, you can handle that, can't you? At least it'll be a quick visit."

Fran strips down, reminding me that she wants to shower.

"Yeah, I guess," I agree, then sigh, because I'm not so sure everything will be fine.

She turns the water on and hops in the shower. "So tell me what the hell happened last night."

My phone buzzes and I see it's a text from Brad. I can't help but smile.

Brad: Good morning friend

Me: I see your sense of humor is in full swing this morning

Brad: :) It's tomorrow, you know

Me: Yeah?

Brad: We have a date...cough, cough. I mean, we're hanging out tonight

Me: Yup, hanging out

Brad: See you tonight. I'll pick you up at 6

Me: See you then

Brad: See you tonight friend

Fran sticks her head out from behind the shower curtain and eyes me curiously. "What was that about?"

I let out a long, contented sigh. A night with Brad will make me forget everything else, including my Mom's visit. "I'm hanging out with Brad tonight."

"Oh, you mean you have a *date* with Brad?" she coos, then goes back to washing her hair.

"NO! I say adamantly. I didn't say that."

Fran pokes her face out again, her sudsy hair dripping on the floor. "You didn't have to, your eyes gave you away. Gabby's got a date, Gabby's got a date," she sings playfully. "So, back to telling me about last night."

A swoony sigh escapes. "The night ended up to be pretty spectacular."

She makes a seductive voice. "You spent the night with *Dane*?"

A silly grin spreads over my face like melted butter. Picking up my lip gloss off the counter, I apply two coats then check my pucker in the mirror. "I actually spent the rest of the night with Brad."

"What the?" Her head weaves its way around the shower curtain and I hear her mutter, "Shit!" and then, "grab me a towel, I've got soap in my eyes."

I throw her a towel and pucker my lips a few more times. "Yup, the night was spectacular."

"I'm waiting here, Gabby..."

"Get your mind out of the gutter, Fran, I don't mean I had *sex* with him!"

I can hear her disappointment. "Oh, my condolences then."

I playfully punch her arm and push her back into the shower. "We danced together...right outside of Bloomingdale's."

"You did what?!"

"I just told you. We danced outside Bloomingdale's. It was one of the coolest things I've ever done, really."

Fran makes a gagging sound. "I can't believe I'm about to say this, but it sounds pretty romantic."

"Fran, you have no idea." My body starts swaying back and forth on the wet floor as I hear Jeff Buckley in my head and remember the feel of Brad's arms around me.

"I love seeing that smile on your face," she says.

It feels good to me, too.

My body is tingling with excitement and my brain is crackling with nervousness. I can hardly contain myself and realize I haven't been this excited since...well, in a long time. Which reminds me that I need to call Dane. Instead of doing the grown-up thing and calling him, I chicken out and send him a text instead, to let him know I won't see him tonight, but will make a point of it tomorrow. He seemed less than thrilled, but honestly right now I only care about one thing. That one thing will be here in twenty-five minutes, so I need to get my ass in gear.

I decide on my snug skinny jeans and a blue sleeveless silk blouse that Fran once said brings out my eyes. Yup, that'll do. I curl my hair so it falls in soft waves down over my shoulders, and keep my makeup light, as always. A little shimmery blush, soft eyeliner, and another touch of gloss to my already ruby lips. I pull on a pair of strappy black sandals and I'm ready to go. Now all I need is my hot date. I mean *my friend.*

Only ten minutes to go and I can't sit still. Fran's been out with Kyle for hours, so I have nobody to talk to. My head is swimming with thoughts I can't control, my heart is thumping loudly, and it feels like tiny fireflies are lighting up my heart. I can't wait to see Brad. I don't know what it is, but being around him always makes me smile. I'm starting to sweat just thinking about him, so I open a window, but quickly close it when a blast of muggy August air forces its way in. Not a good thing if I want to have perfect date hair. I organize the magazines on the coffee table, straighten the pictures on the wall, then sit down on the couch and wait.

The doorbell rings and startles me from my wandering mind. I open the door and the moment I see him I relax. A huge, bashful smile spreads across his face. He's so damn handsome. His silky hair is still wet from a shower and he looks great in dark jeans and a cream long-sleeved shirt.

From the way he's gazing at me, I can tell he likes the view. "You look beautiful," he says with genuine appreciation, chocolate brown eyes smiling at me.

I fiddle with my belt loops. "You look pretty stunning yourself."

He blushes and brings his hand down gently to lace his fingers through mine. "I couldn't wait to see you tonight."

My pale skin turns pink and I smile. "So where are we going?"

He grins mischievously. "You'll have to wait and see."

When we get down to street level, I see a car sitting at the curb. Who owns a freaking car in the city? Well, I guess Brad does. It's a grey Audi S4, with the license plate "WE BREW" on the back. Cute. I figure whatever it is we're doing, we're most likely leaving the city to do it. I'm kind of excited, I haven't left the city that much since we moved here.

An air of confidence proceeds him as he opens my door. "I can see the wheels spinning up there, Gabby, but trust me you won't figure it out."

"Don't be so sure. I have special powers as well."

"Really?" he says with raised eyebrows.

I wish it was x-ray vision. "Remember? I'm indecisive. I'm also pretty persistent. If I wanted, I could coax that secret right out of you."

When we're buckled in, Brad turns to me. "So what kind of music do you want to listen to?"

Keep surprising me. "I like all kinds of music. Alternative rock, jazz, blues, r&b. Oooh, do you have any Lifehouse?"

Brad grins, clicks the CD and I hear the croon of a guitar and then John Mayer's voice. Another one of my favorites. Looking out the window, watching all the buildings go by in flecks of light, my face forms a hopeful smile. Brad reaches across the seat and places his hand in mine. His skin is warm and soft; it feels good. I notice he's wearing the bracelet I gave him and it makes me smile. My bracelet's also hugging my wrist, and I roll my fingers over the words *celebrate courage.* Maybe I need to *find* mine.

We sit quietly until Brad breaks the silence. "Do you want to play I Spy?"

Nearly breaking out into a fit of laughter, I shoot back, "I Spy? I haven't played that since I was a kid."

"You scared?" He tries to look intimidating, but it's a lost cause. He's too darn cute.

"Nope, I'm not afraid of anything. " At least not right now.

Brad starts "I spy with my little eye something that is white and bright."

"That's easy," I respond. "The moon."

"You're good at this," he chuckles.

"My turn," I call out excitedly. "I spy with my little eye something that is tall and pointed with bright lights."

Deep in thought, he thrums his index finger against his mouth, and guesses, "The Toys 'R' Us store?"

I make a loud beeping noise. "Sorry, but thanks for playing."

"I give up," he says, sounding a bit defeated.

"You give up? You only guessed once!"

He lets out that loud throaty laugh. "What can I say? I have a low tolerance for games. Back to me!"

He's staring straight ahead, but I feel his eyes on me. I like the way it feels.

"I spy with my little eye, something that is so beautiful, it leaves me breathless."

Swallowing hard, I take a deep breath and answer, "the Manhattan skyline?" When I turn my head to look at him, I see serious brown eyes staring back at me.

"Nope...you."

His words melt my heart. Pulling my hand to his lips, he softly kisses the inside of my palm, and I feel those familiar goosebumps multiply. I don't know what to do with myself, so I start biting the inside of my lip and fiddling with the door handle.

When I look around, it appears that we're fairly close to Central Park. I still have absolutely no idea what we're doing. Brad finds a parking space, grabs my hand, and leads me toward the park.

"Okay, so what are we doing?"

With a relaxed smile, he says, "patience, grasshopper."

I can't help but laugh and hold up two fingers. "I've got two words for you. Corn and ball."

"That's three." His dimple comes out to say hello.

I playfully flick his arm with my finger, and he loops his pinky through mine. We make our way through a clearing in the park and a sign comes into view. *The Loeb Boathouse.* "What is this place?"

He chuckles. "The word 'boathouse' doesn't give it away?"

I squeeze his arm and he yelps.

"Just come on," he says, tugging on my arm, pings of excitement radiating off his fingers.

The early evening sun is bouncing off the water, sparkling brilliantly. Wow. As I scan our surroundings, I notice what appears to be a gondola in a far corner of the water. I look over at Brad and a squeal of excitement jumps from my mouth and lands on the ground.

Quietly, and with a look of pride clinging to his face, he says, "I know it's not Venice, but it's the next best thing."

Without thinking, I throw my arms around his neck and hug him. Then I quickly retreat.

Brad's eyes fill with...something. "We can come here every day, if you like." He grins and I let out a happy giggle.

Reaching the gondola, we're greeted by a tall gentleman with sandy blond hair and blue eyes. "Welcome to the Loeb Boathouse. My name is Andre, and I'll be your guide this evening."

Andre helps me into the gondola, and Brad follows behind me. We take a seat next to one another; very close. Brad laces his fingers through mine and a tingle runs through me. I gaze at his lips, for no special reason other than I want to kiss them.

As the gondola begins to move through the water, a peace settles over me and I find myself opening up. "I've always loved the water, ever since I was a child. My family had a small cottage at the beach and we'd stay for weeks at a time throughout the summer. It was so much fun. We'd make giant sandcastles and walk the beach for hours collecting shells." I can still feel the sting of the sunburn on my shoulders.

"I can just picture you, those bright blue eyes dancing with excitement, running through the waves at the beach. You must've been a real cutie."

"Let me put it this way. When I was cast in *The Wizard of Oz* in fourth grade, I was chosen to play a munchkin. So that should give you some indication. Thankfully, I'm five foot seven now so I'd qualify for another role."

Brad squeezes my hand. "Well, munchkins are quite cute."

"Yeah, okay. You just keep telling yourself that," I joke with a wide-eyed smile.

Brad looks out over the water and seems thoughtful. "My mom and dad had a boat. It was nothing to write home about, but it didn't matter. The five of us used to go out on the water a lot. I remember spending all day on the ocean. My mom would bring peanut butter and jelly sandwiches with potato chips for us, and Matt, Clara and I would crush the potato chips on our sandwiches. My dad used to say how gross it was, but the three of us would just laugh and throw potato chips at him." I see a tiny tear slide down Brad's cheek and I reach up with my thumb and catch it. He turns around and smiles, and it's like a hotline straight to my heart. The very thing I'm trying to protect, and at this moment, I feel weary.

After a gondola ride around the lake, we make our way inside the restaurant, hand in hand. We're escorted to a table, and from every angle there's an incredibly romantic view of the lake. While waiting for our food, I delve a bit more into Brad. He's my favorite subject these days. "So, what was it like growing up in Westchester? Pleasantville, right?"

His expression shifts before he speaks. "Yeah. It was okay; hard at times because I didn't have many friends and I got picked on a lot."

"Why?"

"I was a gawky kid, a bit of an oddball actually, and unfortunately, that didn't make me much of a friend magnet. Plus, once my mom passed away, everyone saw how angry and damaged I was, and they didn't want anything to do with me."

I lay my hand over his and give it an empathetic squeeze. "I know what it's like to be damaged."

Brad raises his eyes to mine. "I don't know, Gabby. We're all damaged, right? It's what we make of the wreckage that matters. Anyway, once my dad mentally checked out, I was lucky that I had Clara and Matt, and my therapist, of course. Otherwise I probably would've ended up in juvie. What about you? What was your childhood like?"

"Actually, it was great. I had a lot of friends and tons of fun. Although I always felt that I was a bit of an oddball too, in the sense of my family." I pause and take a breath. "Or, now that I think about it, maybe they just made me *feel* like an oddball. Nothing I ever did was good enough, and if my mom and dad couldn't understand something about me, they'd chalk it up to me being strange. I remember one time, I must have been about fourteen, and Fran and I had gone to the mall with Fran's mom to buy some new clothes for school. Fran helped me pick out a new blouse that was bright and colorful with tiny butterflies. I loved it the minute I saw it. There's something about butterflies, you know," I say as I stare out at the lake, "they're free. Anyway, the next morning when I came down for breakfast, my mother took one look at the shirt and told me I had to change. She said, 'you're fourteen years-old, Gabby, and you're wearing the shirt of a seven year-old. Go and change. You don't want people thinking you're weird, do you?' I sat on my bed and cried, then reluctantly put on another shirt and went to school."

Brad's eyes meet mine and I feel a hand reaching out to touch my heart. "Do you still have the shirt?"

"Yup. I put my butterfly shirt in a big keepsake box I kept hidden in my closet. No one was going to take my butterflies away from me."

Throughout dinner, Brad never lets go of my hand. When we finish, I look over at him and his eyes are alight with excitement. It's most certainly contagious. There's no way I'm ready for this date to end. He helps me from the table and we make our way through the restaurant until we're outside again.

Looking over at him with a broad smile, I quietly ask, "so, what now?"

Brads face beams. "We're going to Top of the Rock."

"Top of the Rock? What's that?"

His brown eyes grow large. "You live in New York City and you don't know what Top of the Rock is?" He pulls me along. "It's an Art Deco skyscraper forming the center of Rockefeller Center, and it's very cool. I think it's like 800 feet above street level. The view is amazing."

Apparently, it's about two miles from the park, but instead of driving, we take a gypsy cab, where you can negotiate a price and it's a steal at four dollars. When we get there, we step onto the elevator and the first thing I notice is a transparent ceiling leading to the wide open sky. As we rise, different colored lights are popping all around us. Once we finally reach the platform, I realize that Brad's description couldn't have been more accurate. I'm rendered utterly speechless. Colored lights twinkle from various buildings and there's a clear view of stars that sprinkle the night sky. There's the Brooklyn Bridge, the Empire State Building, Central Park, and the Hudson and East Rivers. You can see it all. I look over at Brad, who's waiting on my reaction. "Wow. It's just exquisite."

Brad takes a deep breath. "It is, isn't it?"

I lean against him, my back to his chest, and he rests his chin on my head. I feel a strange sense of calm. He laces his fingers through mine and we walk around the platform a bit, enjoying the view, until something catches his eye. When I look over to see what it is, I notice there's a plaque attached to a long piece of rock that reads *This is a good kiss spot.*

Catching me by surprise, Brad grabs me and pulls me close. He threads his arms around the curve of my shoulders, causing my heart to pitter-patter wildly and my breath to come in giant gusts. His breath is blowing on my lips like a soft breeze as he whispers, "I've been wondering something all night." My eyes go wide. "Have you ever been kissed by a superhero before?" My mouth won't move, so I simply shake my head back and forth. His eyes are burning up my lips as he breathes, "because you've never been truly kissed until you've been kissed by a superhero."

With a small gasp and a hoarse voice, I strangle out a reply. "Will it be life-changing?"

He dangles his lips over mine. "Oh yes, life as you know it will never be the same."

My heart slams against my chest as his mouth claims mine. His lips are warm and soft, his tongue gliding across my bottom lip, caressing and teasing before sliding inside. The taste of him awakens my senses. I feel his breath whisper to me as he continues to explore my mouth, the wetness of our tongues soaking each other and twirling about like vines dancing in the wind. I reach up and slide my hands behind his neck, the strands of his soft, silky hair tickling the space between my fingers as his arms encircle my waist to deepen the kiss. When we finally pull apart, breathless, he leans his forehead against mine.

"I've been waiting my whole life for your kiss."

My pulse skyrockets at his words and I'm not sure what possesses me, but I pull his mouth to mine again. Sucking his bottom lip softly, my tongue traces the outline of his lips before realizing we're in public and pulling away. With Brad's hand in mine, we make our way over to view the lights of the Empire State Building. He stands behind me again and wraps his arms around my waist; I lean my head back against his shoulder and he dips down to place a soft kiss to my temple. I could get used to this.

It's getting late. The stars in the night sky and the darkness tell us that it's time to head home, though I can smell the hesitancy in the air. After what seems like hours of enjoying the view, the silence, and the feeling of his arms around me, Brad puts his arm around my shoulder and leads us down.

We're both quiet as we make our way back to the car. I'm so happy I feel like tiny bright stars are surrounding my heart. But it's not the stars, it's Brad. My mind is soaking him in. He's incredibly endearing and I feel so lucky when I think about the hordes of women who flow in and out of his shop every day that would kneel at his feet. For some reason, he chose me. The thought makes me smile.

Brad opens the door and helps me in. Just before he starts the car, he leans in, lifts my chin, and gently brushes his lips against mine. His mouth lingers, leaving me wanting more. A lot more. Then, flashing that dimpled smile I've grown to love, he starts the engine and we head back.

James Taylor's voice croons softly, singing about smiling faces, fire & rain, and being the only one. With my head back on the seat and my hand in Brad's, I feel a wonderful sense of peace, like this is where I'm meant to be. We ride in comfortable silence back to my apartment. Brad puts the car in park and comes around to open my door, ever the gentleman. I find myself fumbling with my fingers and staring nervously at my toes.

He gently places his hands on either side of my cheeks and lifts my eyes to his. "I had a wonderful time tonight, Gabby. Thank you." His gaze is so intense it makes me want to look away, but I can't.

I look deep into his eyes. "I did, too."

He stares down at my mouth and then slowly presses his lips to mine. My lips part, and our tongues tangle ever so briefly before he pulls away. "Goodnight, sweet Gabby."

"Goodnight."

I run into the apartment, anxious to tell Fran all about my night. I drop my purse to the ground and sprint down our tiny hallway, pushing through her door. I use her bed as a trampoline until she bolts upright and I realize she's not alone. Rubbing her eyes furiously, she points to the spot next to her.

I see Kyle's honey blonde hair poking out from the blanket. "Gosh, Fran, I'm so sorry!"

"Shhhh...it's okay," she whispers. "Let's go in the other room."

"Sorry, Kyle," I hiss, scampering into the kitchen.

She pours a glass of water, then sits down, pawing at her eyes furiously to try and wake up. "So, spill it, sister, how was the date?"

"It was amazing Fran. I feel like I'm walking on clouds." I'm pretty sure I have a ridiculous grin plastered to my face and I'm giddily rocking back and forth on my heels. If Kyle wasn't sleeping, I'd be squealing like a teenager right now.

Fran looks at me with raised eyebrows and a cunning smile. "So, did you kiss?"

My face comes alive. "Yup."

"And..."

"Hmmm..." I stare dreamily into space, recalling the strength of his arms and the softness of his lips.

"You're holding back on me! What was it like? I want details!"

"It was hot."

"Yeah?" She smiles eagerly and gives me a tiny swat on the arm. "Come on, tell me!"

I sigh. "But it was also sweet, and sexy, and tender." Another sigh escapes. "And...romantic."

"Whoa...seriously?"

"I don't know, Fran. I was so nervous. I wasn't sure what to expect because Brad's so unassuming. But the way he kissed me was anything but unassuming."

Fran smiles confidently. "I knew there was a tiger behind that dimple."

I twirl my hair around my finger. "Well, I'm going to bed now."

"Gee, thanks a lot. Now that you woke me up and made me all flustered."

"So go wake up Kyle. I'm sure he can help you out with that." I giggle and practically float down the hall to my room.

"Goodnight, Fran."

"Goodnight, sweetie."

I pull on my sweatpants and a soft cotton tank and climb into bed feeling hyper. So much so that I just can't get to sleep. I keep replaying the kiss over and over in my head. The kiss that made my heart dance. My phone buzzes and snaps me from my train of thought. It's Brad. Sigh.

Brad: You still awake?

Me: Yeah

Brad: I can't sleep

Me: Me neither

Brad: I wish I hadn't left

Me: Me too

Brad: Your kiss made my heart flutter

Did he seriously just say that? I feel a squeal coming on.

Me: Mine is still fluttering

Brad: Goodnight Gabby

Me: Goodnight

With that, I fall into a peaceful sleep.

Chapter Twenty-Two

It's Monday, and it doesn't suck anymore. I wake up to the sound of heavy raindrops pounding on my windows. I love the rain. I love the sound of it, the feel of it as it falls lazily onto my skin, the...my alarm goes off, but I smack it silent, allowing myself to drift back to last night...to Brad. Just thinking about him makes my insides melt. He completely dazzled me and I feel as though I've fallen under his spell. My phone buzzes and I grab it quickly, thinking it might be him. As soon as I see Dane's name appear on the screen, my smile disappears. Dragging this out is only going to make things worse, so I reluctantly accept the call.

"Hello," I say with the lack of enthusiasm I feel.

"Hey, Gabby, it's Dane." His voice sounds a bit apprehensive and I'm wondering if he can read my thoughts. "I thought I was going to hear from you yesterday?"

"Yeah, sorry about that. Fran and I just hung out and relaxed."

"I was wondering if I could see you tonight?" His tone sounds a bit more desperate now that I think about it, and it puts me on edge. It's a familiar feeling with Dane.

"Yeah, we really need to talk," I reply with determination, dragging myself off the bed and rifling through my closet.

"Can you meet me in my room at seven o'clock?"

There's no way that's happening. "Let's meet in the lobby restaurant," I say casually.

"Oh, okay. I'll see you then."

"See you later, Dane."

Ugh. I dread tonight. I don't want to hurt Dane, but I just don't feel anything for him, which sounds weird, even for me. I actually *want* to feel something. I mean, the sex is incredible, yes, but it's just not enough anymore. Shaking off my nerves, I quickly hop in the shower so I have time for my caffeine fix...and my Brad fix.

Everything looks so much brighter today. The rain has cleared and the sky is a magnificent cobalt blue, the clouds look like puffy white marshmallows, and I'm happy. Not the fake, suck-it-up-and-put-a-smile-on-your-face-happy. Really happy. For the first time in a long time.

The only thing that makes me happier is when I hear my favorite door jingle and see Brad. The moment his eyes meet mine, I see the sunshine in his smile and it lights me up inside. He leaves the counter and comes right over, his lips landing softly on mine. "Good morning, beautiful."

"Good morning, yourself," I reply, my entire face beaming.

"Do you do realize this is a first for us?"

"A first?" I answer with a confused grin.

"Our first kiss in my shop."

"Oh, that, yes." I chuckle softly. "Well, I'll cross that off my list."

"I was on your list?" There's a smile in his voice.

"Well, yes, but I didn't know it."

Grabbing my elbow, he escorts me to a table and goes to make my drink. He's back in a flash, taking a seat beside me and handing me my Salted Caramel Mocha, extra whipped cream. "So, I was thinking maybe we could catch a movie tonight?"

I pick at my fingernails and look down. "I can't tonight, actually. I have something I have to do. Listen, I want to be honest with you. I'm seeing Dane tonight." A frown spreads across his face and my heart sinks. Feeling the need to immediately make it right, I continue. "It's not a date. Really, it's not. I'm only meeting him tonight to tell him that I can't see him anymore."

Brad's mouth shows a hint of a smile. "Really?"

"Yes." Reaching around my drink, I place my hand in his, and he lets out a huge sigh of relief.

$$\heartsuit \heartsuit \heartsuit$$

My anxiety kicks in as I make my way to Dane's hotel. I don't like confrontation and I don't want to hurt him, but the need to be honest outweighs it. The irony of this whole situation makes me laugh. When I first saw Dane that day on the street, all I could think about was how his hot body would feel underneath me. If I'm honest, it was freaking amazing. At least that's what my body said; my head just couldn't catch up. I've tried to keep living on the edge; I've tried to be the one with no emotion. But when I think of Brad, that's the only thing I want. I want emotion. I want to feel. Everything about him draws me in, and I find myself wanting more. Definitely more kissing, at least.

My body starts to heat just thinking about Brad's soft lips and his strong, muscular arms. Shaking off the feeling, I head in to face Dane. When I see him in the lobby, my heart stops for a moment, for no other reason than the fact that he's drop dead gorgeous. It's hard not to notice him. The moment his emerald eyes meet mine, guilt consumes me. When I reach him, he comes closer to kiss my lips, and I offer him my cheek instead. His forehead wrinkles in confusion, which intensifies my need to get to the point.

"Gabby, I've missed you. I thought we had such a good time together and then suddenly you pulled back. Did I do something wrong?"

"Why do you keep asking me that?" I ask, completely irritated.

He crosses his arms over his muscular chest. "I don't know, Gabby. Maybe because you keep disappearing."

I pull my thoughts together and take a deep breath. "Dane, you're a great guy. I've really enjoyed our time together, and the sex was great." He furrows his brow, but I continue. "But, whatever this is we're doing, I just don't see it going anywhere."

Before I can say anything else, Dane chimes in. "I think you're lying to yourself, Gabby. Your body gave you away. I know you have feelings for me. Maybe you're scared, but whatever we have here is worth exploring, don't you think?"

My eyes meet his. "No, Dane, I don't. We had sex, nothing more."

Without hesitation, he says, "I don't believe you."

My feet are tiptoeing backwards when they need to be running full speed ahead. "Dane, I'm interested in someone else. *Very* interested in someone else."

He's just about to say something when he glances over my shoulder. His eyes grow wide and his face turns pale. When I look over my shoulder, I see a leggy blonde with blue eyes and a body to die for, heading towards Dane. Everything that happens next is almost as if I'm watching a movie play out in front of me. She runs up to Dane, throws her arms around his neck, and kisses him passionately. When she finally takes a breath, I hear her whisper, "hey, sexy, I missed you." What the hell?

Feeling the need to pick up my mouth off the floor and control the anger that is bubbling inside, I take a calming breath. "Aren't you going to introduce me to your *friend*, Dane?"

Without hesitation, the woman whips her head around and extends her hand to me. "I'm Susan, Dane's fiancée."

I passed my hearing test with flying colors, so I'm pretty sure there's no mistaking what she said. My anger bubble pops. "His *fiancée*?!" I practically shout, pure contempt drenching my voice. With a look of absolute horror, Dane starts to speak but I cut him off. "Well, I certainly wish you two the very best of everything." The desire to spit on him almost overtakes me but I don't want to ruin my new shoes. Instead, I turn on my heel and head towards the door.

I rush down the street to the subway, wanting to kick every brick wall I can find. It all makes sense to me now; the brief periods of not hearing from him, the mysterious phone calls. Even though I didn't want anything more from Dane, the simple fact that he could screw me while he was engaged to someone else is pathetic...and mess around on his fiancée, the bastard. Not to mention, he told me he wanted more. The word "asshole" keeps playing over and over in my mind. He's lucky I don't go back and kick his ass. I just keep shaking my head. Unbelievable; he had sex with me while he was engaged to be married. If that doesn't shout jerkoff, I don't know what does.

When I finally arrive back at the apartment, it's empty. Fran's at Kyle's again tonight. I just want to see Brad. His phone rings several times before he picks up.

"Hey!" I say, my voice rising at the thought of him.

"Hey yourself. I was just thinking about you." He sounds so sincere, so real.

"You were?" That gets me curious.

"Well, I'm always thinking about you. How did it go with Dane?"

"Let's just say it was interesting."

"What do you mean? What happened?" He sounds edgy now, almost a little angry.

"I discovered something about Dane tonight. Kind of an important tidbit he left out."

"What's that?"

"He's engaged," I drawl, "to be married."

"What? Wow, what a jerk." Brad sounds appalled but relieved.

"Yup, my sentiments exactly." Talking to Brad helps lessen the sting.

"Want me to kick his ass? Because as a superhero, it'll be fairly easy."

I snort. "I considered doing it myself, but he's not worth it. I did almost spit on him though."

He chuckles. "Now that's something I'd pay money to see."

"I'd really like to see you. Do you want to come over?" I close my eyes and cross my fingers. The desire to see him is overwhelming.

"Hmmm...I'll have to think about it."

"Take too long and I'll rescind my offer," I warn.

He snickers. "I'll be right over. I can't wait to see you."

I push all thoughts of the world's greatest asshole away and let all thoughts of Brad in. He's on his way over! I run to the bathroom and brush my hair and my teeth, twice. I'm so excited to see him; I feel like a school girl with a big crush. I find myself pacing the living room when I frantically start cleaning anything that looks remotely dirty. By the time I've finished, the kitchen counter is sparkling, the brown carpet actually looks relatively clean, and there aren't any crumbs under the sofa cushions. I run in the bathroom and slather on a bit more deodorant, then brush my hair again and dab some perfume behind my ears. Oh no! I realize I have my butterfly undies on, so I bolt into my room and pull a pair of purple lace ones out of my drawer, then slide them on...just in case.

After about half an hour, I hear the doorbell ring and let out my new signature Brad squeal. Thankfully, it's one he can't hear. When I see him, it's like an instant charge. He has a wide grin on his face and mine lights up from the sheer sight of him. In fact, I'm smiling so big, it hurts, in a good way. Brad comes in and drops a brown bag on the counter.

"Hey," he says as he walks up to me.

"Hey," I greet him with a shy smile.

"I already said that."

"Yeah, I have this weird tendency to repeat what you say. Must be because you're so cool."

He tucks a strand of hair behind my ear. "I've been thinking about you all day."

"Yeah?" I stand on my tippy toes so I can look into his eyes.

His eyes meet mine as his fingers graze the curve of my cheekbone. "I've been thinking a lot about the color blue for some reason, about a cute little nose, and lips that I hope I get a chance to kiss again."

I look up into the many hues of brown I see in his eyes. "Well, if you play your cards right, you might just get another chance."

"Lucky for me then, I'm an ace at cards."

"Oh *yeah*?"

He inches closer. "Yeah." He brushes his lips against mine, teasing me with his tongue. I open willingly and he slips inside for a taste then pulls back with a knowing smile. "Mmm...you brushed your teeth for me?"

I'm mortified he knows. "It was really for the first guy who showed up here, you just happened to be the lucky one."

A mischievous sparkle alights his eyes. "You're right, I'm damn lucky."

I look over at the brown paper bag resting on the kitchen counter. "What's that?"

Brad opens the bag and hands me a large glass jar covered with a red bow, containing hundreds of Swedish Fish. "For you," he says with a sweet smile. "I wanted to feed your addiction."

He's so freaking adorable. I lick my lips and eye his. "I can think of other ways you can feed it."

He lets out a small chuckle and closes the gap between us. Settling his long fingers around the nape of my neck, he brings me in close and sweeps his lips over mine.

"Thank you," I whisper quietly against his mouth.

He threads his fingers through mine and walks me to the couch. We sit, thigh to thigh; I rest my head on his shoulder while he quietly strums his fingers through my hair. After a moment, he looks down at me. "Do you want to talk about what happened?"

"Well, let's see. There's not really much to tell. I met Dane's leggy fiancée and discovered he was a complete asshole. But, not before I told him I didn't want to see him anymore because I didn't feel anything for him. He kept pushing the issue, so I told him the truth..." My voice trails off and I squeeze his hand, "I told him that I was *very* interested in someone else."

I feel him smile against my temple. "Really? And who might that be?"

"Oh, I think you know," I flirt, a wide smile encompassing my face.

"No, I think you might have to spell it out for me," he responds playfully.

Tilting my head back so I can look into his eyes, I grab handfuls of his hair, pull him close, and give him a chaste kiss on the lips.

He just shakes his head. "I think I need a bit more convincing."

Slowly, I rise up and place my knees over his legs so I'm straddling him. My hands cup his sweet face while my lips tease the corner of his mouth then duck inside to capture his tongue and stroke it against mine.

Eventually, we come up for air, both of us short of breath. He pushes a few long strands of hair away from my face and looks into my eyes. "Do you have any idea how beautiful you are?"

I smile shyly and shake my head from side to side.

"Well, you are. You're the most beautiful girl I've ever laid eyes on." He gently presses his lips to mine and I melt against his mouth.

We end up watching *Bridesmaids* and laughing until our stomachs ache, eating popcorn, all the while snuggling together on the couch. It feels good. When the movie's over, I don't want him to go. I look down at my hands and make my move.

"What would you like to do now?"

He bites his lip, something I've never seen him do before. "Gabby, I'm not...I just..." Taking a deep breath, he says, "Can I just stay and hold you?"

I have no idea what that means. Does he want to hold me naked or with clothes on? Shit. My voice grows quiet. "Okay." I have no idea what I just agreed to.

We shut off the television and the lights and make our way to my bedroom. I'm shuffling my feet and I think I might throw up. Not a good idea, even though he's already seen me do that. The nearness of him is making me crazy. Why am I so nervous? I head to the bathroom and change into a tank top and sweatpants. When I return, Brad has his t-shirt and jeans still on, but no socks. Is he going to take them off? I hope not, or I hope so; I don't know which one. He pulls back the covers and motions for me to join him. Nestling my head on his chest, I inhale his intoxicating scent, and he rests his chin against my head. Being this close to him is harder than I thought. I want to wiggle nearer to him, but I don't. Instead, I lie very still, afraid he can hear my heart pounding into my chest, afraid he can read my thoughts. He has no idea what I'm hiding, what I'm thinking, what I'm feeling. If he only knew how much I want to let him into my heart, into my life, in between my legs. I can almost feel him tracing my curves with his slender fingers. It's driving me crazy. A frustrated rush of air leaves my mouth and lands on his muscular chest.

I see the light of the moon peeking through the pale blue curtains, casting a shadow on Brad's face. I'm not sure what suddenly comes over me, but I lift my leg and hook it over Brad's waist, resting my crotch right on top of his apparent erection. He stirs and I grab courage from somewhere and climb on top of him, straddling his groin and feeling his hard-on between my thighs. I lick my lips, then lean forward and press them against his mouth.

He makes a strange noise in his throat. "Gabby, what are you doing?"

I press myself harder against him. "I think that's pretty obvious," I breathe against his lips.

He props himself up on his elbows. "I can't, Gabby. I can't do this." His words sting and I push myself off of him, stunned.

"You don't want me that way?" I ask with a voice full of hurt.

He runs his hands through his shaggy hair, as he so often does. "My God, you have no idea how much I want to be with you, or how long I've wanted you. I'm so hard for you right now it's driving me insane. I want nothing more than to bury myself inside you and sit in between your thighs all night long. But I want all of you. I want your body and your heart, and I won't accept anything less. I want the whole of you, Gabby." His hand finds my face in the darkness, and he holds me in place. The moonlight is shining in his eyes. "You're not ready for me yet, as much as I wish like hell you were. But I'm patient. I'd wait forever to be the one who gets to hold your heart." He kisses me like I haven't been kissed in a long time, feeling his every word with his every breath. Breaking away, I go back to resting my head on his chest, and he kisses my hair and whispers, "goodnight."

I lay in Clark's bed, naked, awaiting his return. I stare at the beautiful diamond on my finger. I'm going to be Mrs. Clark Thompson. A huge grin spreads across my face. This is the moment I've dreamed about for seven years. I can't wait to tell the world. My parents won't be happy about it, but I don't care. I'm happy. Happier than I've ever been.

I must've dozed off, because in my sleepy state, I think I hear my cell phone ringing. I crack open my eyes and glance over at the clock, noticing two hours have gone by and Clark isn't beside me. Where is he? I wish he'd hurry up. My cell phone continues to ring. I reach over to grab it from the table beside the bed. It's probably Clark. "Hello?"

A hysterical voice is on the other end. "Gabby... this is... Mmmrs. Tttthompson."

I bolt upright in bed. "What's wrong?"

"Gabby, whhhere are you?"

"I'm at your house waiting for Clark. What's wrong? You're scaring me!"

"Mr. Tthhompson is going to come over there right now... There's been an accident... Gabby...sweetheart... it's our Clark..."

My whole body freezes. "What about Clark?"

"Sweetheart, I'm so sorry...there was a head-on... collision... he didn't... make it."

I drop the cell phone to the ground and all I hear are my own screams.

I'm moaning loudly and feel shaky. Sweat is gushing from my skin and tears are spiraling off my checks. Brad sits up quickly and flips on the light. "My God, Gabby, what's wrong? Are you alright?"

I can't speak and uncontrollable sobs are the only thing that make their way out of my body. Brad holds me in the safety of his arms for what seems like seconds, minutes, hours. I lose track. When I finally stop shivering, he sits back and lifts my chin to meet his gaze.

"Gabby, talk to me. Please. What is it that's got you so upset?"

I take a couple of deep breaths, and with a shaky voice it all pours out from the overflowing river of my mind; I tell Brad about Clark. "Clark was...he was everything to me. My first...love. Back in those days, the person I thought would be my life. We dated all through...high school...and college. He asked me...asked me to..."

"Shhh, baby, it's okay."

But I have to do this, I can't stop now. "He asked me to marry him...that night. He left me...and then he never came back...an accident...he died..." Pausing, I swipe the tears with my arm. "After that, everything went...black for me. I became numb. It's been...well...over three years now and it's been stuck inside of me. I haven't been able to let it go."

Brad cloaks me with his arms. "I'm so sorry, Gabby. I'm sorry you lost Clark, and that you've lived with this pain buried inside for so long." He holds me close and gently strokes my hair with his fingers. "It's okay, baby. There's no time limit on grief. Breathe it, feel it, let it seep into you. When you're ready, and only when you're ready, you'll be able to let it go. And even then, it will stay with you, somewhere in a part of your soul. The part where you don't want to ever forget, because there's no forgetting love, especially a love like that." He wipes a stray tear with his thumb before he continues. "I understand what you're feeling, though. Grief can be overwhelming. I felt like that when my mom and sister died. There's a part of me that didn't want to go on living, not without them. I kept seeing their faces everywhere, feeling them, breathing them. I wanted them back so desperately. It took me a long time to come to terms with it." Brad lays me back down and wraps his arms around me, letting my tears soak into his chest and fall onto his heart.

Chapter Twenty-Three

My puffy eyes are disturbed by the bright sunlight trying to break in. I rub the sleep away and try to crack them open. When they come into focus, I see that Brad is gone. There's a handwritten note on the table.

Hi Baby,

I had to open the shop early but didn't want to wake you. Hope you managed to get some sleep. I slept well knowing you were in my arms. I'll remember how beautiful you looked all day.

Brad

I'm exhausted, but for the first time in a long time, I feel like I can breathe again. Brad's support and understanding lifted me. He made me feel safe, like the world couldn't hurt me anymore.

I sit up in bed, feeling the full weight of my emotional exhaustion. My head and body hurt and my eyes are sore from crying. It feels like I've got whiplash. All I want to do is go back to bed. It's a work day, so no such luck. I drag myself out of bed to shower. As soon as I open my bedroom door, I see Fran standing in the hallway, smiling wickedly and tapping her fingernails against my doorframe, fresh from her shower. "So...I bumped into someone this morning when I woke up...a cute someone with a dimpled grin."

My lips turn up into a ginormous smile. "Oh, him?"

"Don't 'oh him' me, Gabby! Did you have sex?"

"NO...we didn't!"

"So what were you guys doing in there then?"

"Uh...sleeping. I called him after I found out about Dane's fiancée." I walk to the bathroom and Fran follows behind me. Grabbing a towel off the shelf, I pull my sweatpants off and slide my t-shirt over my head.

"His WHAT?"

Reaching through the shower curtain, I turn the water on then look back at Fran. "Yeah, he's freaking engaged to be married, Fran."

"What a fucking asshole," she growls, seriously annoyed.

Hopping in the shower, I close the curtain and let the warm water wash over me. "I couldn't have said it better myself."

"So what happened?"

"Nothing. After I met her, I stormed out of the hotel. I actually feel sorry for her. She's in for a future full of heartache and God knows what else."

"Honey, I'm so sorry."

I smile as I massage shampoo through my hair. "I'm not. I told Brad about Clark last night."

"How did he react?" She's concerned and has every right to be. I've never told anyone about Clark.

"He was compassionate and understanding. God, Fran, he was so amazing. He held me all night while I sobbed."

"I'm glad you finally told him, Gabby. You've been holding on to that for way too long. You needed to let it out so you can be rid of it once and for all, you know."

I sigh deeply. "I know."

Stepping out of the shower, I cover my body with a towel. Fran walks over and wraps her arms around me, my hair dripping on her shoulder. "Thank goodness. Now maybe you can start letting yourself be happy. Clark would want you to be happy. You know I love you so freaking much."

"I love you, too."

She pulls back and scans my face. "So getting back to this no sex thing...you really didn't do it?"

"No. He was a perfect gentleman."

"I'm sorry to hear that."

I stick my tongue out at her. "It's different with him, Fran. It's hard to explain, it's just different. In a good way."

"I know, chickie. It's all good, and I'm happy for you. But, when it does happen, I want a full report."

"You'll be the first one to know," I respond. "Promise."

When Fran leaves the bathroom and I see myself in the mirror, I'm mortified. A blotchy face accompanied by dark circles and puffy eyes jump out at me. I reach in the drawer for my makeup bag and attempt unsuccessfully to cover it all up.

I'm almost finished dressing when my phone rings, and I immediately regret answering it when I hear Dane's voice. "Gabby, I want to explain everything. I need to see you. Please tell me you'll meet me."

I'm tired of this crap. "Dane, there's no need to explain," I snap. "I have absolutely nothing to say to you. Besides, whatever we had is over. I told you that I'm interested in someone else. Go back to your fiancée and leave me alone!" I hang up abruptly. That was annoying, but I refuse to let him get under my skin. I have somewhere important I need to be.

That familiar jingle alerts Brad to my presence. His eyes immediately meet mine and I see that smile; the one that opens the door to my heart. Brad skips over and locks his lips with mine. It's a good thing there are other people around, because I have an intense desire to pull him close and deepen the kiss.

He leans in and studies my face with concern. "How are you?"

I exhale a large breath. "I'm better now." I am better now. I feel different. Lighter. Freer.

He takes my hand and leads me to a booth. "I'm gonna make you a latte. I'll be right back." When he comes back, he moves in and sits close to me, taking my hand in his. "You look so tired, baby. Did you manage to get any sleep?"

"Yeah, a little bit. I'm more emotionally exhausted than anything else."

He brings my hand to his mouth. "Thank you."

Why is he thanking me? "For what?"

"For opening up to me. I knew there was something deep troubling you, but had no idea what it was. I can't imagine what the past three years have been like for you."

I move in closer and rest my head on his shoulder. "Thank *you*."

"For what?"

Picking my head up, I look in his eyes. "For being here, and being you."

Chapter Twenty-Four

This week has flown by, and it's been the best week I've had in a long time. It's Friday, and I know that for two reasons. One, I'm seeing Brad this evening, and two, I saw the pink lilies courtesy of Kyle's Friday delivery sitting on the coffee table this morning.

First though, I have to get through the day. My annoying red light is blinking, but I only have thirty-two voicemail messages, and nobody needs anything yesterday. Robby has completed a couple of penthouse redesigns and has two very satisfied clients. Needless to say, he's in a very good mood, which is precisely why I choose this time to talk with him about Dane.

I walk nervously over to his office door and then hesitate, biting on my lip. "Hey Robby, can I talk to you?"

"Sure, dahling, come on in. Have a seat, sweetheart." Robby says absentmindedly. He's concentrating heavily, typing away at his computer while he eyes design plans on his desk.

I sit down, cross my legs, and begin playing with the fabric on the chair. "Well, I'm not sure how to say this, but..."

He continues to type without looking up. "Gabby, if you're handing me your resignation, you can forget it. I won't accept. You're my most valuable asset here, dahling."

Pausing, I'm even hesitant to say his name. "No, it's nothing like that. It's actually about Dane Rhodes."

Now he stops and meets my gaze. "Yes, what about Dane?"

"Well, I'm wondering if there's any way Valerie can take over his project? We had a..."

He lets out a knowing smile. "Dahling. Say no more. You think I don't know what happens with these hot, rich types. I can't tell you how many times I've heard it. If I had a dollar...well, anyway...I'll put Valerie on the account. I'm sure she'd *love* to get on board with that." He leans back in his chair and lets out a rich laugh.

"Really?" I ask with both surprise and relief.

"Listen, sweetheart. If that's the most difficult issue I'll come across today, I'm in heaven. You're now officially off the hook."

Wow, that was easy. I love Robby.

♡ ♡ ♡

The day is flying by and my mind is wandering to thoughts of tonight. I can barely contain the excitement bubbling up inside. Brad told me he'd pick me up at seven and to make sure I'd eaten beforehand. His wish is my command.

I'm sitting in the last of our client meetings with John Roche, picking at my fingernails and staring at the clock. It's 5:45 and I need to get home. Paying attention should be my first priority, and John's lips are moving, but I don't hear anything. The only thing I do hear are the freaking seconds ticking by loudly in my ears. Come on, people. After fifteen more minutes and practically wearing the point down on my pencil, thankfully the meeting ends. I run back to my desk, grab my purse, slam my drawer closed, and head out the door. Running for the elevator, I hear my phone buzz and smile. It must be Brad. My face falls instantly; it's a text from Dane.

Dane: I have to see you. We need to talk

Me: We've been through this. I don't have anything to say to you

Dane: Please give me a chance to explain

Me: No. I told you. We're done Dane

I turn my phone off. He's the last person I want to be thinking about right now.

I'm tearing through my closet, pulling clothes off hangers. I don't like anything I see. Before I know it, my bed is covered in a heap of fabrics and I'm still standing there in my matching blue lace bra and panties. I let out a burst of air, and throw myself on top of my bed. Now I know what the princess felt like in *The Princess and the Pea*. I'm on top of sixteen outfits and I swear, there's an earring digging into my ass. After five more minutes of sheer frustration, I finally decide on black jeans and a green silk blouse. I put on a little pink blush to make my cheeks look rosy, a drop more lip gloss, and a bit of mascara. I dab perfume behind my ears, on the back of my neck, and in between my breasts. Heading to the bathroom, I brush my hair for the fourth time, and my teeth for the second, then go out to the living room and sit on the couch. Crap! I forgot to floss. Running back in the bathroom, I pull the floss from the cabinet and have at it as particles of food fly around the bathroom. Good thing I remembered. When I come back out, I notice a *People* magazine on the coffee table, so I sit down to read it, but it doesn't hold my attention. I turn the television on and flip the channels, but can't focus on that either. The pillow cushions look like they need fluffing, so I snag one...and hear a knock.

Finally! I feel like I've been waiting forever. I glance at my watch. Forty minutes is an eternity when you're anxious. Taking a deep breath, I straighten my blouse, fluff my hair, and open the door. The minute the door opens, I do what I've been wanting to do all day. I grab Brad, tangle my hands in his hair, and pull his mouth to mine. Parting his lips with my tongue, I slip inside and am welcomed by his sweet warmth. I explore him, softly at first, then with more intensity. Pulling back with a breathy voice, I whisper, "I missed you like crazy today."

"Me too, baby," he says breathlessly, trailing wet kisses from the corner of my lips to the nape of my neck.

My skin tingles all over. We may not make it out of my apartment. But we have to, so I pull away. "So, where are going?" I ask with a smile larger than life.

"I can't tell you that." He shakes his head and taps his finger against his temple.

I put my hand on my hip, my hair bouncing off my shoulders. "I have ways of finding these things out, you know."

"Tell me more," he encourages, winking. "I might be persuaded."

Brad has a habit of keeping me in the dark, and I kind of like it. I've loved surprises since I was a kid. But surprises with Brad far surpass any of those childhood memories.

We take the subway to our destination. Typically, I'm grossed out being on here. Dirt-filled seats, the smell of urine and booze wafting through the air, and endless stares from strangers when all you want to do is look away. Tonight though, nothing bothers me. Brad pulls me close beside him, and I lay my head in the crook of his neck, relishing his warmth and breathing in his scent.

We make it to street level, strolling hand in hand. Brad swings my arm as we walk and I feel very much like a teenager on a first date; excited and just a little terrified. We don't go far before I see a gleam in his eye, and realize we must be getting closer. I feel the excitement rippling off of him in waves and rolling straight on to me. Our fingers toy with each other's and Brad gives me little squeezes periodically. I marvel at the soft, gentle quality of his hands. I love when he touches me.

The horse-drawn carriage sitting near the path to Central Park comes into view. I immediately let out a squeal and jump into his arms. "This is on my list, too!" I shout.

"I remember," he says as he kisses my earlobe, sending little shocks to my toes. There's a glow in his eyes. "Do you have any idea how adorable you are when you're excited?"

I can barely contain myself. "I can't believe we're doing this!"

Brad raises my chin to meet his gaze. "I love seeing you happy."

All I can do is sigh. He's so freaking thoughtful and sweet, and funny.

He helps me up into the carriage, climbs in, and snuggles close. The driver takes off almost as soon as he's seated. The clip-clop of the horses' hooves, mixed with the night's quiet bathes us in a sweet tranquility. I lean against Brad's shoulder and he softly kisses my hair. Bringing my hand to his chest, I feel the rapid beat of his heart.

He inches closer and whispers, "Do you feel that? That's what you do to me." His hand moves to the back of my neck before he brings my lips to meet his. He gently strokes my tongue with his and we taste each other's sweetness with each tender flick. His breath heats my skin while his scent hovers in the night air, intoxicating me.

This moment with Brad in this carriage, surrounded by the stars dancing in the sky and the brilliance of the moon, is just perfect. I'm discovering that every moment I spend with him is nothing less than perfect. It's almost too good to be true. I just hope it's not.

We talk quietly amidst the steady clip-clop. "So, how's your brother doing?"

"He's great. I spoke with him the other day and he's coming in for a visit in a couple of months. I want you to meet him."

I'm excited to meet Matt. I know he's the only family Brad has, aside from his dad, of course, who doesn't speak to him. That tears at my heart, but he never seems sad; maybe he hides it well.

He's grinning widely. "I've mentioned you to Matt a couple of times."

I stick my bottom lip out in a pout. "Just a couple of times?"

"Yup," he says.

My excessive curiosity gets the best of me. "So what kind of honorable mentions did I get?"

"Who said they were honorable?"

I bump him with my hip and give him my most intimidating glare.

"Hmmm...let's see. Well, I told him how witty you are, and adorable, and I couldn't leave out feisty."

I smack him on his shoulder.

"See, I told you...feisty."

"Oh, I'll show you feisty." I grab him and kiss him furiously, something he didn't see coming. I have a few surprises up my sleeve, too. I pull away. "How's that for feisty?" I whisper.

He smiles and holds his hands out in front of him, palms up. "I'd like more of that, please."

And then I punch him again.

He continues the conversation, unruffled. "Oh, by the way, I passed by Parsons The New School of Design today and it made me think of you. I'm not sure if you've ever considered it, but they have a really great Master of Fine Arts program. Matt got his Master's there in architecture and it's a really good school."

"I've heard about the school, but never thought about it before."

He kisses me on the nose. "Well, it might be worth checking out. I know you're hoping to stay in interior design."

I lay my head back onto his shoulder and smile at our linked fingers. It's quiet again, except for the clip-clop of the horses. I lean up and his lips meet mine. This carriage ride with Brad doesn't begin to compare to my dreams. It's a million times better.

When we hop off the carriage, I take his hand and kiss it softly. "Thank you for adding something magical to my list."

Brad's shy smile is back again, the one which makes my insides melt. I just sigh; it's all I can do.

We walk for a while until Brad stops short. "Are you hungry? I'm kind of in the mood for some Double Chocolate Brownie ice cream."

"Oh no," I say incredulously. "You're more of a Monkey Ripple kind of a guy."

"I've decided I like *your* flavor better," he declares with a cocky grin.

We walk for a while until we hit Liana's Ice Cream Shop and make our way inside. There aren't too many people tonight, so we don't have to wait. We both order Double Chocolate Brownie except I get whipped cream and he orders hot fudge. I'm in heaven, because besides coffee and candy, chocolate is my other secret addition. I crave it and can't go a day without it. Hmmm...there's something else I'm starting to crave daily.

Brad sees me smirk. "What's going on inside that pretty little head of yours?"

My eyelashes flutter. "Wouldn't you like to know?"

He leans over and licks some chocolate from the corner of my mouth. "You know, I wanted to do that when we came here last time."

"Do what?" I ask innocently.

"Lick chocolate off of those pouty lips of yours," he replies with a sexy smile, and I want to freaking jump his bones right here.

That dimple is driving me crazy. I divert my attention elsewhere. "So I was thinking maybe next weekend we could spend some time with Fran and Kyle. Fran wants to get to know you better."

"She does, does she?"

"Yeah. I gave you a couple of honorable mentions too."

"Well, if she's important to you, then I definitely want to get to know her," he says sweetly.

As we're finishing our ice cream, I stifle a yawn and Brad notices. "You're tired; do you want me to take you home?"

"I don't think so."

"Then what do you want to do now?" he asks.

"I don't know. What would you like to do?" I ask coyly.

Brad seems to be deep in thought before he decides to speak. "Well…we would go back to my apartment? I could give you the grand tour and you could give me your unbiased professional opinion on the overall design scheme."

With a little too much eagerness, I agree. "I'm interested to see how a superhero lives."

We're both carrying around these ridiculous smiles as we head back to Brad's apartment. I can't deny I'm a bit nervous. I'm not sure what to expect, but I know my heart is finally open.

Brad lives in a one bedroom apartment in Central Park North. It's a nice location. Certainly a bit different from mine, as his place lacks the delightful view of the back alley. He ushers me through the door and I'm instantly taken aback by what I see. It's not the typical bachelor pad I expected. It's incredibly neat and he has real furniture. Tasteful artwork fills the walls accompanied by framed landscape photographs.

"I'm impressed," I blurt out.

"Really...why is that? Were you expecting empty beer cans and clothes all over the floor?"

"Maybe." I grin. "This really is a great place. In fact, I don't think there's much I could do here to improve it."

"You just being here improves it." He throws his keys on the kitchen counter and gently reaches up to cup my face, his gaze moving intently from my eyes to my lips. Pulling me in, he wraps his hands around the base of my neck, my smooth skin settling underneath his fingers and causing tiny shivers to run through me.

I grab handfuls of his hair, drawing him in so close that his warm mouth layers mine. His soft breath teases the sensitive space between my lips, causing me to open and take in the wetness of his tongue. It feels like heaven inside and stirs my need for his touch, my desire to touch him.

I slowly let my hands roam from his waist to the thin cotton of his shirt and ease my palms underneath to feel his smooth, supple skin. Bursts of air float from his lips and land on the nape of my neck, making me feel lightheaded. My toes curl, and my knees weaken.

I stop and look up at him. "Brad?" I whisper.

"What, baby?" he says as he continues nibbling on my neck.

"It's yours..." I say breathlessly.

He pauses and looks up. "What is?"

I gaze into his brown hazy eyes. "My heart."

He immediately lifts me up and carries me until I feel the texture of the plush green sofa beneath us. Brad's lips find mine again as he slowly unbuttons my blouse and I willingly help him slide it down my heated skin. He pulls me close and dips his tongue into my mouth, licking every space he can find. He leaves me and rains hot kisses down the curve of my neck, easing lower. My breathing accelerates, and my arms prickle with goosebumps. He pinches the front snap of my blue lace bra and it pops open. His tongue brushes the curve of my breast as his wet lips surround my nipple and a tiny whimper slips from my mouth. Brad drags his hands over every inch of my body, setting off fireworks, my body crackling and popping in response. I feel his hands reach the edge of my jeans and he waits, for my approval, I think, before he eagerly pulls them off, then propels them into the air without a care as to where they land.

"Touch me," I whisper.

He exhales loudly. His fingers scrape the lacy edge of my panties and a soft mewl escapes my lips. When I feel the fabric tickling my legs, I arch my head back in anticipation as his hand slides between my thighs, the warmth of his fingers meeting with the damp folds of my skin. More moans fall aimlessly from my lips as his touch sends me to another place; one I can't wait to go to. My body trembles when his fingers begin massaging that moist spot within me. I latch onto him with a quiet desperation, blending our bodies together, clawing at him so I can climb into his heart like he's climbed inside mine. My breathing grows heavy as I dig my nails into his muscular shoulders. My body is climbing and my mind is lost. His sweet scent, mixed with the feel of his skin against mine, intensifies my need to release the rapture building inside of me.

He pauses as if to speak. His eyes look deeply into mine and I try to slow my breathing as I wait for his words. "Gabby, I need you to know something. You make me feel things inside, things I've never felt…"

I quiet him with my mouth. His words are my undoing and my insides quiver with the feel of his fingers sliding in and out of my wetness and the sound of his heavy breaths. I let go, moaning against his lips, vaguely aware of his hoarse voice.

"God, baby, you're so beautiful."

As I float back down and my breathing slows, I become intensely aware of Brad's aching hardness through his jeans, pressing against my inner thigh. I unzip them and tug, hoping for a little help. He slides them down and I glide my hands across the muscles of his chest as my fingertips graze the trail of hair that leads to the elastic of his boxer shorts. Pausing until his eyes meet mine, I place my hand over my heart. "I want to touch you, the way that you touch me."

He lets out a gasp of air at my words and I reach in and grab hold of him. I'm amazed at the softness of his skin as I stroke his hard length and moans of pleasure pour from his lips. I caress him tenderly at first, then more fervently, his hot breath blowing on my neck as his pants become more intense. The sweat beads off his brow and I watch his beautiful face contort with the oncoming contentment of his release. He lets go, calling out my name, then pulls me close and tenderly strokes my mouth with his tongue.

As we calm, my fingers wander aimlessly across Brad's muscular back, lazily drawing invisible doodles over his smooth skin.

He lifts his head to mine with utter sincerity in his eyes. "Are you okay, baby?"

"Never better," I respond happily. "You?"

"I think you know the answer to that."

"Yeah, I do."

He reaches behind the sofa and grabs a soft flannel blanket, tucking us in under the warmth that we've already created. We didn't make love tonight, but it doesn't matter. Brad has officially climbed into another corner of my heart, curled up into a ball, and settled there.

When I wake up in the morning, I feel disoriented until my blue eyes open to a handsome face, a sunken dimple, and lips that call to me. I lift my fingers to Brad's cheek. His skin is soft and flawless. He really is beautiful.

His eyelids flutter and when he opens them, they're filled with wonder. "Hi, beautiful," he says in that deep throaty voice that makes my insides churn.

"Hi, yourself."

"Some host I am, I didn't even offer you my bed." He rubs the back of his neck and drops a kiss on my nose.

Smiling contentedly, I move some stray hairs away from his face and kiss his pink lips. "That's okay. I like what you offered."

Brad watches my mouth and then his lips land on mine. Even with morning breath, he tastes divine.

My face goes flat. "Ugh, I forgot to tell you that my mom's coming next weekend."

"You don't look that happy about it. Are you looking forward to seeing her at all?"

A small groan forces its way out. "Not really. She's not even coming to see me, she's coming in for Fashion Week." Brad lifts his fingers to my cheek and I let out a resigned sigh. "It's okay. It is what it is."

Chapter Twenty-Five

Today, my grin and good mood are because Brad and I are going to the beach, my absolute most favorite place in the whole world.

We're headed out of the city to Fire Island. It's a place Brad suggested, and while I've never been there, I've heard it's quite beautiful. Excitement bubbles up inside of me. I can already smell the salty water, feel the yellow sunshine warming my back and the wind blowing through my silky hair, and hear the rhythmic sound of the waves lulling my soul into peace.

One day, I want to live in a house by the ocean. I can't imagine anything better than starting and ending my day with the splendor of the sea. Breathing in the ocean air, feeling alive and exhilarated, yet relaxed and at peace; it's the best. It takes all of your troubles and whisks them away, sweeping them out with the tide, never to be heard from again. Come to think of it, that's what Brad has done for me.

I'm dancing around my room singing "Kiss Me" by Sixpence None The Richer as I gather things up for our trip. I dig into the back of my closet to find my blue and white flowery bikini, the one I haven't worn in years. I'm hoping it still fits me. Thankfully, I pull it on and it does! The blue shorts and white tank top still fit, too. I pull my hair into a messy ponytail and strap on my white sandals. I need to let out one more squeal of excitement, so I do. Brad plus the beach! I'm not sure what could be better.

Brad picks me up early and we head out. It's a glorious day. The temperature is about eighty degrees, the sun is beaming brightly, and there isn't a cloud in the clear blue sky. The sunroof is down, the windows are open, and the voice of Van Morrison is cradling us in the moment. Brad takes my hand in his and tells me he wants to learn everything about me during our drive. He's too darn cute to refuse.

"So, favorite color?"

"Purple."

"Favorite food? Wait, never mind...chocolate."

"Yup."

"Favorite band I already know...Lifehouse."

"Ahhh..."

"Alright, alright...I know how you feel about Jason Wade."

"Jealous?"

"Maybe a bit. If only I could sing." He grins. "I do have other talents, though."

I play with his fingers. "Well, that remains to be seen."

"Is that a challenge?"

"Why, do you think you can *rise* to it?" I manage to ask with a straight face.

"Baby, they don't call me a superhero for nothing."

Then I burst out laughing. This is going to be a great trip.

When we finally arrive at Fire Island, I'm completely mesmerized. The water is crystal blue and the sand is smooth with hints of seashells buried throughout. There's a smattering of boats in the distance, drifting on the water, floating free in the greatness of the ocean.

We unload the car and plant ourselves fairly close to the water. Brad is all smiles and he looks radiant. Especially when he takes his shirt off and I get a good look at those golden brown abs. Dear Lord. He looks over at me as I admire the view. It's becoming my favorite one.

"Am I the only one taking anything off, or are you planning on swimming with your clothes on?"

I think I'll have a little fun. "Actually, I swim in the nude."

Brad's eyes grow wide. "Baby, I hope you're kidding. I really don't feel like sharing you with anyone else."

"Of course I'm kidding."

His eyes grow even larger as I remove my shorts and tank top and reveal my relatively skimpy blue and white flowery string bikini. In fact, I didn't realize how skimpy it was until just now. I've been feeling more and more comfortable in my body lately; but I haven't worn a bikini in years. Perhaps I should've chosen something a little less revealing. Although, since Brad looks like he wants to devour me, I think I made the right choice after all.

The sun feels amazing, but I need to make sure I don't burn. California girl or not, my fair skin burns easily. "Brad, can you rub some sunscreen on my back?" I'd like him to do my front too, but unfortunately, I can reach there.

"It's a tough job, but someone's got to do it," he says wickedly. The blistering sun and the feel of his fingers gliding over my shoulders in circular motions are causing tiny little prickles all over my skin.

Brad leans into my ear and I feel his hot breath. "Turn over so I can do your stomach." I nearly fall to pieces at his words. His eyes never leave mine as he rubs lotion all over my belly. His touch is driving me crazy, and definitely not the asylum kind. In a minute, I'm going to pull him on top of me without a care for anyone else on the beach. He leans over me, running his long fingers down the side of my face, and then moves his lips over mine, slowly and deliberately. The sensation of his wet mouth, the salty air, and the sound of the waves fills me with desire. When he lifts his lips from mine, he blows out a breath that cools my searing skin. He tilts his head and gives me a devious grin. "I think we need to go in the water to cool off...like, now."

My lips turn down in a pout. "I'm not ready to go in just yet."

He smiles again, but this time says nothing. Instead, he lifts me up over his muscular shoulder and I squirm as he carries me into the cold sea. My hands slap his back while my feet hang in mid-air.

"Ahhhh...put me down! Brad! Put me down!"

He just holds on tighter until we get further into the water and he throws me wildly against the waves.

"You're going to pay for that!" I warn with a lighthearted tone that burns with playful revenge.

There's that magnetic smile. "Oh, I hope so, baby, I hope so."

We splash each other until there are no splashes left, only hysterical laughter and abundant smiles. Brad pulls me close and grasps handfuls of my soaking wet hair and I let my tongue venture into the depths of his mouth, both of us pulled in by the ocean's seductive charms.

I can't resist Brad, but mix Brad with the fresh scent of the ocean, the summer breeze, and the sand between my toes and I'm powerless. Our hands wander up and down each other's bodies and I feel him grab my ass and bring me in so close I can feel his erection through the thin cotton of his swim trunks. I want him so badly, but as much as making love on the beach is a fantasy of mine, I don't feel like fulfilling everyone else's fantasy today. With that, I pull back abruptly and push him down in the water. He needs to cool off.

♡ ♡ ♡

It was a perfect day, and as exhaustion settles over me, I can only think of one thing right now that would make this day more perfect. Climbing into bed with Brad.

We're on the stairs up to my apartment, Brad and I are giggling hysterically like twelve-year-olds, until we get closer to the door. All laughter is halted by the sound of Fran's screaming voice.

"Get your hands off of me, and get the fuck out of here! I told you I never wanted to see you again!"

Jesus. My hands fumble for the keys, but Brad doesn't wait. He uses every bit of force he has to kick the door open, finding Fran in the clutches of an older man. A tall, graying, fierce man. It can only be one person. Fran's dad.

Brad pipes up immediately. "Didn't you hear what she said? She *said* take your hands off of her!"

"Who the fuck are you?" Fran's dad bites out.

When Brad sees Fran crying, he springs into action. Just like a freaking superhero. My superhero. He grabs Fran's dad by the arm to pull him away and gets knocked against the wall, hard. I panic. Brad's hurt, Fran's shaking, and there's a psychotic asshole in our apartment. I vaguely hear Brad mumble "call the police," and I start digging furiously for my cell phone.

When Fran's dad hears the word "police," his posture suddenly changes. He bolts for the door, but not before he eyes

Fran one last time. "I'm your father, Franny. I deserve to be in your life, and this isn't over, not by a long shot."

As her father disappears out the door, I'm left with the pain of the two people I care about most. My instincts tell me to go to Fran first, but the need to see if Brad's okay pulls me in his direction. I run over to him. "Are you okay, babe?"

"I'm fine, baby. Go take care of Fran."

I walk over to Fran. She's shaking violently and tears are staining her cheeks.

"Jesus Fran, come here." I wrap my arms around her and hold her tightly, wishing I could take this one thing away for her. The one thing that almost destroyed her life. I walk her into her bedroom and tuck her under the false security of her blanket, press my lips to her forehead, and send her off to a troubled sleep. "I'm here if you need me." I pick up the cell phone off her nightstand and leave Kyle a message to come over as soon as he can.

When I come out of the bedroom, Brad is still leaning against the wall. His head is back and his eyes are closed. I grab an icepack from the fridge, sprint over, and gently hold his face in my hands. "Are you sure you're okay?"

"I'm fine," he repeats, reaching for my hand.

"You're absolutely insane, you know that?" I say, letting out a huge sigh and pressing the ice pack to his jaw. "You know, I already believed you were a superhero, you didn't have to go out of your way to freaking prove it to me." Brad tries to smile, but winces. "Seriously, I'm so sorry you got caught up in all this. Her dad is crazy, and you could've been seriously hurt."

Chapter Twenty-Six

After the nightmare with Fran's dad, we somehow managed to get through the week, although Fran has been in a funk since last weekend. She definitely needs a fun night out. I also need a fun night out to prepare for my mom's arrival tomorrow. Instead of our usual Friday night bar escapades, we decide to play pool. It was actually Kyle's idea and Brad is pumped for a little competition. Little do they know, Fran and I know our way around a pool table. Back in college, Fran, Clark, and I used to hang out and play pool...a lot. Clark and a couple of his friends taught us to play, and while we're no sharks, we're more versed than the average girl. We know how to break and we certainly know how to sink balls; not to mention, we're masters of distraction! This should be interesting. Very interesting.

When we arrive at the pool hall, Fran and Kyle already have a table. As we walk over to the table, I whisper to Brad, "I can hold my own with a cue, so be forewarned."

Brad's eyebrows lift and he grins. "I was hoping." Then he pinches my ass. Oh, this is definitely going to be fun.

We're playing girls vs. guys and I watch their surprise as Fran nails the break, sinking two balls right off the bat. We call stripes and continue to sink balls, another two before Fran miscues. When it goes back to them, I'm eyeing Brad as he leans over the table. He looks so hot, and him bending over the table is giving me a *lot* of ideas. He raises his head and catches me in mid-stare, puckers his lips, and grins.

When he comes back around the table, he leans in and nibbles at my earlobe and I melt. "Baby, I hope you like what you see."

I definitely like flirty Brad. Two can play this game. I slink past him and chalk my cue ever so slowly, fully aware that Brad's watching my every move. I lean *way* over to take the shot, making sure he gets an eyeful of cleavage. I hear a sudden choking sound and know I've succeeded.

Fran and I are about to win when Kyle looks over at Brad. "I don't know about you, man, but I think we're being hustled. These beautiful ladies have definitely played pool before." Just then, Fran leans over to take a shot, her breasts poke out from her yellow blouse and Kyle beams. "Actually, I like being hustled. Let's play another game. Double or nothing."

Fran playfully shoulder bumps him. "Why not?"

We play one more game, this time couples, and Brad and I end up losing and buying dinner. We grab a booth and order something to eat. Kyle snaps his fingers suddenly and his brown eyes shine. "So, did Fran tell you she kicked our butts again in Scrabble last night. You should've seen her. I'm kind of thinking she needs to enter some sort of competition. She's becoming quite the wordsmith."

Fran turns to Kyle, glowing. "Uh...wordsmith? I don't think so."

Kyle leans over and gives Fran a kiss then takes her hand in his. She smiles contentedly. She looks so happy tonight and this seems to be just what she needed. I'm so glad. Not to mention, Fran and Brad seem to really like one another and that puts me over the moon. They're both so important to me. Just when I feel like all is right with the world, Fran opens her mouth.

"So, Brad, what are your intentions?"

Kyle gives her a piercing glare.

I kick her under the table and she screeches. I give her my most evil death stare; I can't believe she just said that.

Brad doesn't seem the least bit ruffled, or if he is, as usual, he doesn't show it. "My intentions..." He pauses. "My intentions are to make Gabby deliriously happy."

You already do.

Fran has a humongous grin on her face as she winks at me. And me, well, if I'm not as red as a hot juicy tomato right now, I'd be shocked.

Brad leans in close to my ear. "I have other intentions, too...for your ears only." He nips my earlobe and I nearly choke on my drink. He has a habit of making me do that.

Fran stares at me with a twinkle in her eye. She moves in so close only I can hear her words. "I like seeing you like this. I haven't seen you this happy in a long time."

She's right. I haven't been.

Chapter Twenty-Seven

My mom is coming into town today, so waking up with a hangover is a given. After I take two Tylenol to calm my pounding head, Fran and I spend the morning cleaning up the apartment so I don't have to hear Mom complain.

"Gabby, you need to relax. Everything's going to be fine. She's not even gonna be here that long." Thank goodness for Fran, she's always the voice of reason.

"Well, you wouldn't know it, the way we're scavenging the apartment looking for rodent cadavers. You haven't seen any cockroaches recently, have you?"

"Very funny. So, are you going to introduce her to Brad?"

I sigh. I've been debating introducing Brad to Mom. It could go great, but I doubt it. "I was thinking about it. But I'm not sure she can control herself."

"Gabby, he's absolutely adorable, she'll love him."

I put my hands on my hips. "Yeah, well, I don't care if she loves him or not."

Fran crosses her arms over her chest. "Whoa. Rein it in there, chickie. I'm on *your* side, remember?"

I stare at her as I make swirls in the carpet with my feet. "I know, Fran. I'm sorry. It's just... You know how I get whenever I'm around my mom. I become a completely different person and I'm so uptight."

Right on cue, as if she knows we're talking about her, my cell phone rings. I cringe when I see her name pop up. I might as well get it over with. "Hi, Mom."

"Hi, dear! Guess where I am? New York City! Right smack in the middle of fashion central. It's fabulous! I'm so glad I decided to come. The couture lines are amazing. I've got lots of great ideas for my shop." Take a breath, Mom. "I've had a chance to meet some of the designers *and* the models. It's so exciting!"

"That's great, Mom." I roll my eyes even though she can't see me.

"So, I'm going to finish up at around four o'clock, and thought I could come by the apartment so we could grab a bite to eat. It's really going to be the only chance I'll have to see you. Tomorrow is a full day and then I head back home."

"That sounds fine, Mom."

"Great, so I'll see you later."

"I will. Bye."

Fran looks over at me. "So what time is she coming?"

"Around four. Where do you think we should go to eat? If it's up to her, she'll want to go somewhere ritzy and I'm not up for that." I look down at my Converse. Definitely not up for ritzy.

Fran taps her finger against her cheek. "What about Carmine's on the Upper West Side?"

"Perfect. I'll call Brad to see if he wants to come along. Do you want to call Kyle?"

"He has to work tonight, so he'll have to miss out on the fun." She chuckles. "I'm sure he's all torn up about it."

I dial Brad and wait to hear the sound of his throaty voice.

"Hey, Baby."

My heart skips a beat just hearing it. "Hey!"

"What's up?"

"So do you want to meet my crazy Mom? She's here and we're going out to dinner."

"Absolutely. What's the plan?" Wow, he actually sounds excited. I hope he feels the same way after he meets her. Ugh.

"I think we're going to head to Carmine's. Do you want to meet us there after work?"

"Sure. That sounds good."

"I'll text you on the way, okay?"

"Okay. I can't wait to see you."

"Me too."

♡ ♡ ♡

At four o'clock sharp, there's a knock at the door. I throw a couple more Tums in the air and they land in my mouth. Now I'm ready. I fling open the door. There she is; impeccably dressed as always. She's wearing a navy blue pencil skirt and a white silk blouse. Subtle gold jewelry adds to her look, and I notice she still wears those ridiculously expensive Borgezie shoes. Her makeup is perfect, right down to the waterproof mascara, and her hair is pinned up in her trademark bun with a rhinestone clip.

"Hi, dear." She hugs me gently and pats my back awkwardly, as an afterthought. Whoever invented this uncomfortable hug, I'll never know.

"Hi, Mom."

"Let me look at you. Have you been eating? You look a little thin, dear."

My eyes go to the heavens. "Yes, Mom, I'm eating."

"Well, I certainly hope it's not only that dreadful candy you can't seem to stay away from," she says with disgust.

Let's not talk about me. "So, we thought we'd go to Carmine's. They've got great food and it's relatively casual." Thankfully, here comes Fran.

"Hey, Mrs. W." Fran walks over and gives her a big hug. My mom doesn't know what to do with herself. She's not used to this kind of affection; giving it or receiving it.

"Franny, wow, you look terrific!" Nice. She looks terrific and I look emaciated.

"Thanks, Mrs. W. It's good to see you. How's the fashion business?"

Ready. Set. Go.

"Oh, Franny, it's fantastic. I'm living the dream, what can I say? I'm loving the energy of New York; I'm meeting so many amazing people."

"That's great!" Fran sounds genuinely excited. I wish I could have that same level of enthusiasm around my mom.

"So, let's head out," I chime in. And get this over with.

On the way to Carmine's, I text Brad. I hate to expose him to my mom, but I'm looking forward to seeing him. Fingers crossed that she can behave herself and not offend him with any of her snobbish remarks.

When we arrive at the restaurant, Brad's already there. He flashes me his dimple the moment we walk in the door, and I want to do a lot more than just smile back. I fold my arms around his waist and give him a gentle kiss on the lips. I hear my mother clear her throat. "Dear, who might this be?"

"This would be Brad, Mom, my boyfriend. Brad, this is my mom."

"You haven't mentioned him before." She sounds affronted *and* she just insulted Brad.

"Yes, and that would be because I rarely hear from you."

She shoots me a dirty look. I look over at Brad with an apologetic smile. He grabs my hand and squeezes. All is right with the world.

From the moment we sit down, my mother starts in on him. "So, what do you do, Brad?"

"I own a coffee shop in Midtown."

My mom gives me a disapproving glance. I'd expect nothing less. She hesitates before she speaks. "That sounds...nice. What did you get your degree in?"

"Business Management."

"Yes, and where did you go to school? Do you have your MBA?"

I chime in. "Oh my God, Mom, enough of the third degree."

She never disappoints. Perfectly poised, but impossible to hide the shards of ice that surround her.

Fran knees me under the table and gives me a sympathetic glance.

"I'm just trying to get to know your boyfriend, dear."

Brad continues. "I went to Pace University, and no, I don't have my MBA."

"I see," my mother says, disapproval dripping from that nasty little tongue of hers. "It must be somewhat interesting, meeting people from all walks of life."

Someone shoot me now. Brad doesn't skip a beat, though. My superhero. "Yes, it is Mrs. Willis. I get to meet all sorts of people, some pretty wonderful ones actually. That's where I met your daughter." Score.

"Still addicted to coffee, Gabby?" My mom shakes her head and turns down her nose at me. "It's a terrible habit and so unhealthy."

She says it like I'm addicted to crack. Get a grip, Mom. I raise my eyes to meet Brad's and grab his knee under the table. "Yes, especially now." God, I just want to plant my lips on his and kiss him senseless. I'm sure my mom would appreciate that.

"So are you enjoying being in New York, Mrs. Willis?" Leave it to Brad to save the day and change the subject. This should get her going for a good fifteen minutes.

"It's fantastic. There's so much to see, it's hard to take it all in. Plus, I'm so just busy with getting new fashion ideas for the store, that I don't have time for much else. It's a nice change from California, though. Things definitely move at much faster pace here." She turns to me, planning her next move. I can see it on her face. "So, Gabby. Have you managed to get a promotion yet? It's been almost three years, after all."

"Not yet, Mom."

"Well, maybe you need to start working harder. If you're going to have a chance of moving up in the company..."

Thankfully our food comes and there's so much of it that it takes the pressure off the conversation for a little while. That is, until my mother opens her mouth...again. "So Brad, tell me what you like about my daughter."

Fran chokes on her salad. I'm turning blue and silently being rolled away by Oompa Loompas. Gah! I never should've invited Brad. This is so humiliating!

"Well, I'm not sure where to start. It's a pretty long list." A man after my own heart. Oh, that's right, he already has it. "She has a knack for clogging toilets."

I burst out laughing and the spaghetti flies out of my mouth and lands on my mother's shirt. Brilliant.

"Gabby! This is a new blouse, for heaven's sake." Oh well, not anymore.

"Actually Mrs. Willis, your daughter is incredibly special. I first noticed her sense of humor, and then everything else followed. Her thoughtfulness, the way she cares about other people, the way she appreciates life. Her overall sweetness. She has a beautiful spirit."

Sadly, all of the things Brad listed my mother knows nothing about. My mother sighs and looks bored and completely unimpressed. Completely unfazed by the man singing her daughter's praises.

Brad captures my chin between his fingers. Brown eyes to blue, we're lost. He leans close to my ear and whispers. "I want to kiss you like crazy right now." I have an incredible urge to take him in the bathroom and let him do just that. Eh, What the hell.

I look over at my mom. "Can you excuse us for a minute?"

Fran winks and Brad looks confused, but stands anyway. Grabbing his hand, I lead him towards the ladies' room. Now I'm the one who's completely insane.

"Gabby, what's wrong? Are you okay?" He always shows such concern for me; little does he realize I tuned my mother out in seventh grade.

When we get to the hallway, I turn my head from left to right, and then duck inside the ladies' room, pulling Brad with me. It's a single bathroom, hooray; but locking the door is essential. I push Brad up against it and crash my lips to his, plunging my tongue into his mouth as he grabs my hips and pulls me close.

He breaks the kiss, stunned and panting. "Gabby, what was that for? Not that I'm complaining, but *whoa*."

"You talking about toilets turned me on."

He runs his hand through his shaggy hair and laughs, then takes my hand and kisses my fingers one by one.

I look up at him with apologetic eyes. "I'm sorry about my mom."

"There's nothing to be sorry about. She's nice...in a nasty sort of way."

I give him another quick kiss. He sure knows the way to my heart.

"I'm actually having a hard time believing you're really her daughter. You're nothing like her."

I lift up on my tippy toes to find his mouth. "You get another kiss for that."

We walk back out hand in hand, and I suddenly feel so much better. When we arrive at the table, Fran's smirking and my mother looks confused.

"Everything okay, dear?"

"Yes, Mom, everything's fine." More than fine.

My mother looks at her watch and then at me. "I hate to cut the evening short, but I have to get back to review some details for tomorrow's events."

"No problem, Mom." No problem at all.

One by one, Mom gives us all her conventional awkward hug. "It was great seeing you, dear. I'll chat with you soon. Brad, it was a pleasure meeting you. Franny, great to see you as always."

We say our goodbyes and I can finally breathe again.

Chapter Twenty-Eight

Brad's traveling out of town for two days to meet with some people about possibly opening up another shop. It's the first time we've been apart since we started dating a couple of months ago. I'm going to miss him, a lot.

I've been thinking about what Brad said to me that night in Central Park, about going back to school, which is why I'm on my way to Parsons The New School for Design on Fifth Avenue to get some brochures and meet with the program director. I did some research online and apparently they do have a terrific Master of Fine Arts program.

When I arrive, I'm met at the front desk by a very professional looking girl wearing a brown pencil skirt, cream silk blouse, and what appear to be black Jimmy Choo heels. Her blonde hair is pulled up in a perfect ponytail and her diamond studs are a fabulous complement. Seems appropriate, after all, this is a design school. I'm feeling seriously underdressed in my blue blouse, skinny jeans, and blue Converse sneakers. At least I'm color-coordinated. I take a seat and pick up a magazine called *Spaces* until my name is called.

All of about two minutes later; "Gabrielle Willis."

"Yes, that's me."

"Hello, Gabrielle. I'm Edith Hanley. Come on in."

Making my way to her office, I trip on the hardwood floor and hear a girlish laugh from the reception desk. There's absolutely nothing on the ground; I tripped over my own sneaker. What a lovely first impression.

I take a seat in one of two velvet wingback chairs that face a large glass window overlooking Fifth Avenue.

Edith takes a seat in a chair opposite me, crossing her legs and propping her notebook on her lap. Her features are sharp; she has short, cropped red hair and big blue eyes surrounded by a pair of black designer glasses. She's wearing a black tailored suit with a crisp white shirt. Her outfit screams serious, but her smile is welcoming. "So, what brings you here, Gabrielle?"

"Well, I'm interested in learning more about the Master of Fine Arts program. I currently work at Landon & Castell as an assistant and I have my Bachelor's in Interior Design from UC Berkeley."

"That's fabulous! Then you have a bit of a head start. We have a very comprehensive program with both seminar and studio classes, as well as the opportunity for work outside of the classroom."

"That sounds great." I'm pretty excited. It feels good to be here, and I finally feel like it's the right time for me to do this. I can probably complete the program on a part-time basis in two years.

"I'd like to give you some brochures and additional paperwork for you to review. Also, we're having a program information night next Wednesday at six if you're interested."

"Thank you, Edith, I appreciate it."

She gives me a big smile with those huge blue eyes and pats my hand. "Here's my business card. Just give me a call and let me know if you have any additional questions."

"Terrific. It was great meeting you." I shake her hand. "Thanks again." I make my way out of the building, taking my two clumsy feet with me. Once I'm outside, I lean against the glass, look up at the sky, and smile.

$$\heartsuit \heartsuit \heartsuit$$

Fran and I are having a girls' night tonight. With Brad out of town, Fran's taking a break from Kyle and spending some time with me. I stop at the corner store on the way home to pick up a giant bag of Swedish Fish and a box of those Devil Dogs Fran loves so much. I'm excited to spend some quality time with Fran. She's been with Kyle so much lately, and now with Brad and me spending all this time together, we're like ships passing in the night.

I browse through the narrow aisles to see if they have any Twizzlers and pick up some orange juice.

"Clark, put that back, we need to get going."

Immediately, I twist my body to the voice. A frazzled woman is speaking to a little boy with dark hair and wide blue eyes, his little fingers clutching a Hershey's Bar. Closing my eyes, I draw in a deep breath. Our little boy might have looked just like him. I could really use that Hershey's Bar right about now.

I walk back to our apartment, devouring the entire Hershey's Bar along the way. By the time I get to our door, I've got a wicked stomachache. I open the door, excited to share my goodies, but am completely unprepared for what I see. Fran is sitting on the sofa, her mascara-smeared eyes riveted to what appears to be a spot on the carpet. I call her name, but she doesn't respond.

"Fran, what's going on? What happened?" She still doesn't look at me. If I didn't know better, I'd think she was in a catatonic state. I shake her shoulders until she looks over at me, fresh tears forming in the green of her eyes.

With a shaky voice, she exhales. "My-my mom called me. She...told...tol-told me that my dad committed suicide yesterday."

Dear God. I pull her to me and hug her tightly. Holding on to her, I feel the overwhelming grief over the loss of a father she never even knew, who had no interest in knowing her, only hurting her. The problem is, your father is still your father.

After several minutes, I force her green eyes to meet mine. "I'm so sorry, Fran. But listen to me. This *isn't* your fault. You didn't push him to this. He had severe issues and..."

Fran stops me mid-sentence. "I'm not crying because I blame myself, Gabby. I'm crying because I'm relieved that he can never hurt me again. I'm fucking relieved because he's dead. My own father. Isn't that sick?"

The tears start, and they don't stop. I'm crying, too: for her, for her mom, even for her dad, who made his own decision. We sit together for what feels like hours, until Fran's tears subside. I lift her chin and look into those beautiful green eyes. "Fran, your father hurt you in horrible, unthinkable ways. He was never a real father to you. We're brought into this world helpless and innocent, with nothing but love and trust for our parents. Your father took that away from you, and took advantage of that love. He didn't deserve your love. So, no, you're not sick."

She lets out a long, cleansing sigh. "I love you, Gabby."

"I love you, too, Fran."

Fran and I didn't watch movies tonight or eat junk food. But we did have our girls' night. Two girls who care about each other more than life, shut out the world and cocooned themselves with the strength and love of one another.

When Fran's finally asleep in my bed, I slip out to get a drink. My heart feels so weighted. She didn't deserve to have such a shitty father.

I take a seat on the sofa, curl up under a blanket and grab my book, feeling the need to get lost, even for just a little while. Concentrating on the book isn't even an option. I can't stop thinking about Fran's dad, about Clark, and about the source of disappointment I am to *my* parents. That's when the tears start to fall. It's then that I hear my phone buzz. It's Brad.

"Hi, baby." The sound of his voice soothes me.

My shoulders slump down. "I'm so glad you called."

"What's wrong? You sound like you're crying?" He's immediately concerned. He really cares about me.

"It's Fran."

"What about Fran?" His sincerity warms my heart.

I pull the blanket high up to my chest, as if it can shield me from the nightmares of the world. "She found out today that her dad committed suicide." It feels so good to let it out and tell Brad.

"God, Gabby. How is she?"

"She's sleeping now, but it's been a rough night."

"Do you want me to come home?"

I want to say yes, but I know he'll be home tomorrow. "No, it's okay."

"Will you tell Fran that I'm thinking about her?"

"Of course."

"You okay, baby?"

I'll be much better when you come home. "Yeah. I just feel so bad for Fran, you know? She didn't deserve any of this."

"I know."

"How are your meetings going?" I ask, desperate for a change of subject.

"Good, except I miss you."

"I miss you, too. Oh, I have some good news, though. I went to Parsons The New School for Design today to talk about their Master's program."

"That's great! How did it go?" His enthusiasm gives me so much self-confidence.

"Really well. It's given me a lot to think about. They actually have an information night next Wednesday, and I might go."

"Well, if you want some company, I'd love to come along. Remember how much you love my apartment? I do have a knack for design, after all." I hear the smile in his voice and it makes me smile, too.

"I'd like that."

"So I'll see you tomorrow, okay?"

"Okay. Hey, Brad?"

"Yeah?"

"I've been feeling really bad about some of the things my mom said to you at dinner the other day."

"Don't feel bad. You're not responsible for your mom. You're completely separate from her. In fact, I think she's actually from another planet."

His dig makes me giggle, but does nothing to ease my guilt. "She was just so freaking condescending."

"Baby, I've heard a lot worse. Anyway, it's just life, right?"

Clark bumped my shoulder and shrugged his. "It's just life, right?"

All the blood drains from my body and I go silent.

"Gabby?"

Nothing.

"Gabby? You still there?"

"Yeah?"

"Dream of me, okay."

"Okay. Goodnight."

My face feels wet and my nose is dripping. Running to the bathroom, I splash cold water over my face. My heart is beating fiercely and I can't control my breathing. Bending over the sink, I lean down on my knees. It feels like I'm choking. There's a lump in my throat and I'm struggling for air. Breathe, Gabby, breathe. I exhale a harsh breath. Jesus. It's been well over three years, but I still see his face, feel his presence, and yearn for him like it was yesterday. Brad's words. Clark's words. This has to be a sign. I was supposed to be with Clark. He was my happily ever after. But dammit, he's dead and I'm very much alive. I'm supposed to feel dead inside, but I'm starting to feel life. I just can't.

I'm getting too close. I can't do this. I'll end up losing him, just like I've lost everyone else. I look down at my courage bracelet and watch a single teardrop fall.

Chapter Twenty-Nine

The sun wakes me up the next morning, and for the first time in a while I'm not smiling. My eyes are puffy and my body feels stiff. I can barely drag myself out of bed. There's nothing to look forward to today. My insides are twisting at the thought of what I need to do. I just hope I'm strong enough to do it.

I'm on my way to Brad's apartment, pushing through the millions of bodies in the subway. I see no faces. Everything is blank. Just how I feel.

When he opens the door and I see his face, I almost lose it. He pulls me close and for a second I tell myself everything will be okay. But I know that's a lie.

Brad kisses me tenderly. "I missed you, baby."

I pull back and stare into those penetrating brown eyes, my brain running wild, my heart beating crazily against my chest. Sweat drips from my brow and I'm afraid I can't do this. I have to do this. How did I even let this happen? Everything was perfect in my controlled little world, even though somewhere deep inside I was imploding, my organs stretching until I couldn't breathe. I didn't even realize how numb I was until Brad came along. He brought it all to the surface and I just want to stuff it back down. It's easier not to feel; feeling leaves you vulnerable to so much pain.

He strokes my hair gently. Lovingly. "You look like you've been crying. What's wrong, baby? Talk to me. Is Fran okay?"

"She's okay," I mumble. "Kyle's with her."

"That's good," he says, sighing into my hair.

I squeeze my eyes shut. I have to do this. I couldn't bear it if he ever left me. I have to walk away before he does. Taking Brad's hand, I lead him over to the couch.

All the color drains from his face.

The tears are threatening now and my breath is coming fast. "Brad, I think we need some space." His eyes go wide, but I continue. "You're...well, you're amazing and wonderful and witty. You're kind and sweet. You make me smile."

He interrupts me, holding his hand up. "Stop. Don't do this."

"Let me talk, Brad." I rush the words out as fast as I can. "I've never felt so much before. For a long time, I shut off my feelings because it hurt too much. Somehow, you found your way into my heart. But..."

"Gabby. I don't want space. You don't know what you're saying. I want *you*. I...I care about you so much."

I look down at my hands, the pain filling his eyes too much to bear.

Brad lifts my chin to his, not letting me break eye contact. His hands cradle my face. "How can you think this will be better for me, Gabby? Better for us? You're the best thing that's ever happened to me. I know what you're doing. You're not giving me space, you're walking away! Dammit, Gabby, I'm not going to let you walk out of my life. You don't freaking get it! I was dead inside before I met you. You awakened something in me, and if you think I'm letting you walk out of my life, you're more insane than I am. If you want space, I'll give you that, but I'm gonna fight like hell for you. With every breath that I have, I'll fight for you."

I push him away and stand up, trying to put some distance between us. "Brad. Just stop. You have to listen to me."

"No, I don't. You listen to me now," he demands, moving towards me. He rakes his hands through his hair and begins pacing the blue shag with heavy feet. "I get it. I really do. I know you've pushed away feeling for so long. You want to stay numb; it's easier that way. That's how I was, too. First after my mom, and then Clara, I shut down and wouldn't let anybody in. Then, one day, I woke up and realized that they wouldn't want me to die inside. They'd want me to be happy. They'd want me to live. So I honor their memories by living, by being happy.

"It's not that..." But he's right, it is.

He stops pacing and grabs my hands in his. "I know you miss Clark. But he wouldn't want you to shut down, Gabby. He'd want you to live your life, to find happiness again."

I choke back my anger and twist my body away from him. I don't want him to see me. "No, Brad, I don't know what he wants, because he's *dead*!"

A shocked look overtakes Brad's face. I might as well have slapped him.

Teardrops continue to crash to the floor and break apart, just like my heart. I want to run. I want to hide. Mostly, I want to scream. I want to scream at all the people who've ever hurt me. I want to yell at my parents, who always expected me to be something I'm not; for not loving me, unconditionally, no matter my choices. I want to yell at my sister for not being there for me, not loving me enough. But mostly, I want to scream at Clark for leaving me that night, for not taking me with him.

Brad grabs my arm and spins me around, tears rolling silently down his cheeks. "Gabby, please don't do this. I can't bear the thought of being without you. You're too important to me. I need you so much."

"Let me go, Brad. You have to let me go!"

There's only one other person I've felt this way about in my entire life. Now, the thought of not being with Brad makes me want to curl up in a little ball in a corner and just stay there. With one touch, with one word, with one breath, he can unravel me. I've worked so hard up to this point not to let anyone get too close to me. Tears are falling down my shirt and soaking the carpet. I hold on to Brad so I can imprint him in my memory, then I pull away. The door is inches from me now. All I have to do is walk through it. I can do this. The carpet moves beneath my feet and the door creaks open.

"Dammit, Gabby. Don't fucking do this! You can't do this!"

I take one enormous breath, and without so much as a look back, walk over the threshold. The door closes, and just like that my heart slams against my chest and I know I'll never be the same. I hear a loud crashing sound and the echo of shattered glass; it mimics my heart.

I stumble with shaky legs down the hallway and out to the street, a burst of cool air smacking me in the face. I need Fran. Frantically, I dig through the clutter in my purse and pull out my phone. It's ringing, and I'm silently praying she's there.

Thankfully, she picks up, her usual, perky self. "Hey, sweetie!"

A sob betrays me. "Fran, are you at home? I really need you."

"Gabby, what is it? Why are you crying? What happened, honey?"

The tears come, but the words don't.

With a fierce resolve, Fran says, "I'm here, honey. Kyle just left. I'm not going anywhere."

My trembling legs barely carry me to the subway. I feel eyes all over me as tears crawl down my mascara-smeared cheeks, and I'm silently telling them all to fuck off. Squeezing my eyes shut, I suck into myself and pray that no one touches me. Tonight, I won't be responsible for my actions.

When Fran opens the door to and sees my face, she says nothing, just pulls me forward and holds me while I sob in her arms. We stand there for several minutes until the tears subside. She takes my hand and leads me to her bedroom, then sits me down and removes my shoes. After fluffing up her pillow, she pulls the duvet over me. Kneeling on the bed next to me, she takes my hand in hers. "Talk to me, Gabby. Tell me what happened."

"I broke Brad's heart, that's what happened. I told him I needed space. But I'm really letting him go."

With concern in her voice, she sighs, "Oh, Gabby." She strokes my hair. "Why would you do that, honey? I know how much you care about him, and you'd have to be blind to not see how much he cares about you. You've finally opened up, Gabby. I haven't seen you like this since Clark. Is that what this is about? Because he's not Clark, Gabby. He's not going anywhere."

"I know he cares about me. Right now, anyway. But ultimately, I'll end up disappointing him like I do everyone else in my life. I don't deserve to be happy, Fran, not while Clark's laying in the ground."

Fran takes a deep breath. "Gabby, listen to me. I know you've been hurt. I know the people you loved the most in your life let you down. I know, deep down, you feel that if they loved you enough, they wouldn't have walked away from you. I know your family has made you feel that you're not worthy of love. But let me fucking tell you something, Gabrielle Willis. If there's anyone on this earth who deserves to be loved, and loved hard, it's you. You're my best friend, and one of the most amazing people I've ever met. The way you live your life, the way you appreciate everything, is admirable. You're such a giving person and you appreciate it all, the good and the bad. You know it has value in your life. Life's lessons, you always tell me. You take those lessons and turn them into something positive. I love that about you. I'm not the only one, Gabby. It's impossible not to love you."

I bury my face in the comforter, smearing my tears all over it. "I just can't do this, Fran. I don't have the strength."

Fran's voice becomes stern. "Now you listen to me. Brad's not your family, Gabby. He's not. I know you're scared. I know you think he'll end up being just like them, or that you'll lose him. Clark loved you, Gabby, and he would've wanted you to go on with your life, to be happy."

"I was supposed to be happy with him, Fran. I thought we were meant to be."

"I know, sweetie. But none of us know what life has in store for us, or how much time we have. Life is a risk, and you have to take risks if you're ever going to have a chance at happiness. I want you to be happy. I've seen the way you are with Brad; he makes you happy. Take a chance. What's the worst thing that can happen? I know you're worried about getting hurt. But isn't there also a chance that you'll end up experiencing the happiness you've been searching for, for so long? Regardless of what happens, Gabby, I'll be here for you. I'll always be here for you."

Fran's words swirl around in my head. "I just don't know if I can, Fran. I just don't know if I can get past the fear."

We sit in silence as Fran wipes the last of the tears from my face. In the comfort of her bed, I fall into a restless sleep, haunted by soft brown eyes, pain, and overwhelming disappointment.

Chapter Thirty

The days drag on but, before I know it, another week is over. It's been seven whole days and I haven't heard from Brad at all. Why would I? I told him I needed space. He's just doing what I asked. I force myself to go back to Starbucks so I don't have to see him. I can't even share with him that I went to the information meeting and actually applied to Parsons for next year. Concentrating is so much harder than I thought. Everything in my being craves him. I miss his smell. I miss his smile. I miss his dimple. I miss that adorable wink he always gave me when I walked into his shop. I miss his touch. The way he made my skin shiver and my heart skip a beat. I miss *him*. I recognize this longing. It's all too familiar. It hurts. It physically hurts.

When I get home, Fran is waiting for me with compassion in her eyes. "Hey sweetie, how are you?"

I walk over to the sofa and fall backwards with a thump. "I'm okay, Fran."

She comes over and takes a seat next to me, resting her hand on my thigh. "I saw Brad at the coffee shop today."

The sound of his name makes me lose my breath. Is he okay? Does he miss me? The question looming in my head makes its way out. "How is he?" I ask in a hoarse whisper.

"He asked about you. And Gabby? He looks miserable."

Fran doesn't leave my side all weekend except to buy me some of my favorite things. She holds up an overstuffed grocery bag and a handful of DVDs. "I've got Twizzlers, Swedish Fish, Hershey's Kisses, and a couple of chick flicks."

No matter how many Twizzlers or Swedish Fish I eat, I can't stop thinking about Brad.

"Oh, and I almost forgot, I picked up your favorite ice cream."

When she pulls out Liana's Double Chocolate Brownie, I practically lose it.

Chapter Thirty-One

It's day ten without Brad. The pain isn't going away. If anything, it's getting worse. I have so much freaking work to do and don't feel like doing anything. I'm deleting messages without even listening to them and I'm making sticky note puzzles on my desk.

Robby finally calls me into his office and I panic. I'm afraid he's on to me and I'm going to get fired. When I walk in, he's got his hands behind his head and his feet up on his desk, looking the opposite of what I expected. "Gabby, sit down, dahling, you look like you need a chair." Then he pauses. "What's going on with you? You haven't been yourself lately. Is there anything I can do, sweetheart?"

"No, thanks, Robby. I've just got a lot going on right now."

He nods sympathetically. "Yes, by a lot going on you mean a guy, don't you?"

"Kind of."

"Gabby, honey. There's either a yes or a no, there's no kind of."

"Yes."

"Well, let me know if you there's anything I can do. In the meantime, shake it off and get that cute little head wrapped around my sticky notes."

When I get back to my desk, I grab my coffee, hoping it will revitalize me, and go to the lunch room to heat it up, though hot or cold, it still tastes like shit. I plunk back down in my chair and manage to make it through a good chunk of Robby's to-do list. I type reports all morning, which is pretty mindless, so it gives me a much-needed break. At lunchtime, though, thoughts of Brad are unavoidable. The receptionist arrives at my cubicle with a dozen lavender tiger lilies that were delivered for me, with a card attached.

Gabby,

I told you I'd give you space, but I never said I wouldn't fill your space with flowers.

Brad

My heart swells. He's thinking about me. He hasn't given up on me.

It's hard not to stare at the flowers throughout the day. They're so damn happy. Just like Brad. They're also my favorite color. He remembered. The smell pervades my office and makes it difficult to concentrate. What the hell? I couldn't concentrate anyway. Who am I fooling?

Chapter Thirty-Two

The days march forward, and the flower deliveries keep coming. On day two, yellow sunflowers. On day three, pink chrysanthemums. On day four, red gerbera daisies. Every day there's a new note and I have to do everything in my power not to break down and call Brad.

By the end of the week, it looks like a botanical garden in here, and I can't help but smile. At this point, I'm nervously twiddling my fingers in anticipation of today's flower delivery, but it never comes. Instead, after lunch, a kid in a baseball cap wearing a red cape stands beside my cubicle, holding a cup with The Brew House logo on the side and a bag of Twizzlers. I smile. Of course I smile. I wonder how much Brad had to pay him to wear the cape.

By now, I'm prepared with tip money. He hands me the cup and Twizzlers and waves goodbye. The cup holds a piping hot Salted Caramel Mocha and the Twizzlers have an envelope taped to the side.

Dear Gabby,

It's been fifteen days of no special coffee for you. I was afraid you might be going through withdrawal. Although it can't be nearly as bad as the withdrawal I'm going through without you. I miss you, baby.

Brad

My heart hurts. I miss him so much I can hardly stand it. There's a part of me that wants to reach out to him, but I'm so scared. I notice a longer note folded inside the card; my hands shake a little as I open it.

Dear Gabby,

There are some things I need to say to you. I didn't want to put this in a letter, but you're leaving me no choice.

I know you're scared. I'm scared, too. I know you feel like everyone in your life has let you down. People walk away from you just because, or they're pulled from your life unexpectedly. That's not me, Gabby. I'm not walking away from you. Ever. There's no way that will happen. Do you want to know why, Gabby? I've never felt this way before about anyone. The moment I think about you, I smile. When you're near me, I feel calm. I can relax. I can be myself. I feel acceptance. You let me be me. I know I'm crazy sometimes, but with you it's okay. God, Gabby, it's so hard to put all this into words, because sometimes there are no words. You've shined a light on me, exposed me, left me bare. I'm not embarrassed, though, because I feel free.

People have left me too, Gabby. Important people. My mom, my sister, even my dad. The people in my life that I trusted, that I thought would be there for me always. Family isn't supposed to do that, right? So, I get it. I know what you're feeling. I want to prove to you that I'm different, if you'll let me. I'm not like everyone else in your life. I accept you, Gabby. I'll never judge you and I don't expect you to be anything you're not. Just be you. That's all I want. That's all I'll ever want.

I want you to be happy, truly happy. I thought being with me made you happy. I know you make me happy. A sense of contentment washes over me when I'm when you. You arouse all of my senses. You make things real for me. You see me in a way no one else has, or has ever wanted to. It's almost like you opened up a window that I've been banging against for so long...screaming and clawing and trying to get out. Yet, that day you walked into my shop, you simply opened the latch and I poured out. Every bit of my heart and soul was exposed. I wasn't scared. I'm not scared with you.

I know I'm asking you to take a chance and trust me, but I promise you, it'll be worth it. We're worth it. The possibilities are endless when we're together, Gabby. I feel it, and I know you do, too. Please don't let your fear and your guilt overwhelm how you feel when we're together. Give me the chance to show you I'm not like everyone else. I care about you so much.

Even though I feel like I'm breaking apart inside right now, I'll continue to give you space. I'm not giving up on you, though. I won't give up when I've found the one person who truly makes me feel like a superhero. You make me feel like I can leap tall buildings, like I can take on anything that life throws my way. I feel invincible as long as you're by my side.

Please don't give up on us. Think about me. Because I'll be thinking about you.

Love,

Brad

♡ ♡ ♡

Fran comes into my room later that night with anxious eyes. "More flowers today?"

"No. Coffee, Twizzlers, and a letter."

"What did it say?" She holds her hand out for the letter and I rifle through my purse to find it. As she reads it, she shakes her head.

"What, Fran?" I don't know why I'm asking, I already know what she's going to say.

"What do you mean, what?! He's fucking crazy about you, Gabby. For the love of God, get your head out of your ass and tell him you feel the same way."

"It's not that simple, Fran."

"Bullshit, Gabby. It is." She tosses the letter at me and gives me an encouraging pat on the back. "It's simple if you just let go."

After Fran leaves, I lay in bed, exhausted and craving sleep. My brain is wide awake, though, filled with jumbled thoughts. I feel my insides crumbling and my walls along with them. It's getting harder to keep them up. Brad's making it very difficult for me. He just won't give up. There's a part of me, deep down, that doesn't want him to. So many other people in my life have given up, and I realize now that it scares me most to think that he might, too. All my life, I've wanted someone to accept me and when I finally find another someone who does, I push him away. Yet, he keeps coming back. How can I not try to trust him, the way he's trusted me? I want to, I really do, but the fear is overwhelming. I close my eyes to find relief and am drawn into sleep.

I see him. Clark. He's surrounded by the glow of a beautiful white light. The brightness of it blinds my eyes. I keep walking until I reach the edge of the light. I can go no further, something stops me from crossing into the light. He stops me. He doesn't say anything, though. He just looks down at the ground. This is my chance to tell him. I need to tell him. The tears are welling up in my eyes, but I can't let that stop me. I take a deep breath.

"I miss you so much, Clark. It's so hard to believe you're not here anymore. Everywhere I go, I hear your voice, I smell you, I feel your touch. I long to see you, to talk with you, to hold you again. I miss the way you held my hand when we walked on the beach. The way you laughed when you got really nervous. The way you kissed me and held onto me like I was the air you needed to breathe. The way the world fell away when you looked at me. The way you could heal me with a simple touch, a glance, a smile. I loved you, Clark. I'll always love you, and I promise I'll never forget you. You'll always hold a special place in my heart."

He finally lifts his eyes to me, and I see the tears rolling down his cheeks, falling away into the surrounding light. "I loved you, Gabby, so much. You were the light that brightened my life, my heart, my soul. Your spirit wrapped around me and warmed me. I thought we'd be together forever, but God had other plans for me. I'm just grateful that you weren't in the car with me that night. You're alive. Go live your life. Let yourself feel. Be happy. Let yourself love. Find someone who will hold your heart.

You're with me, Gabby, in my heart. Your love surrounds me always. And someday, when you've seen an endless array of those sunsets that you love so much, I'll see you again."

He blows me a kiss, turns to the luminous white light, and is swept away.

A knock awakens me. Fran cracks the door open and sees the tears streaming down my cheeks. She sits next to me on the bed, holding my hand lovingly and then pressing it to her cheek.

With a shaky voice, I say, "I saw Clark. He seemed so real. I told him how much I loved him, and I said goodbye. I loved him so much, Fran."

"I know you did, sweetie, and he loved you." She kisses my hand and smoothes my hair.

"But I miss Brad. I miss him so much it hurts. I...I love him, Fran. I love Brad."

"I know."

Chapter Thirty-Three

My eyes open to a new day. Life. The life where there are no guarantees. The life where every moment counts, because you never know when there will be no more moments. My only hope is that I haven't destroyed my chances with Brad. I think about him every minute. All the times he made me smile. All the times he made me laugh. All the times he held my hand. All the times he held my heart. I haven't been the same since I walked out on him sixteen days ago. Sixteen days, yet it feels like a lifetime. I can't get him out of my mind or my heart.

I grab my phone and dial Brad's number. It's ringing and my hands are shaking.

"Gabby?" Brad answers, surprised. The sound of his voice nearly makes me crumble.

"Hi," I say in a small voice. "Thank you for the beautiful flowers, and the coffee, and the letter."

I hear him breathe deeply. "Do you have any fucking idea how much I miss you? I can't see straight. Please tell me you've changed your mind."

My voice raises an octave. "I've changed my mind."

"Seriously?" I hear the nervous excitement in his voice.

"Seriously. The cape clinched it," I say, with a huge smile he can't see. "Can you meet me somewhere tonight?"

The excitement in Brad's voice is palpable. "Anywhere, baby."

"Top of the Rock, say seven o'clock?"

He doesn't hesitate. "I'll be there. And Gabby?"

"Yeah?"

"I'm so glad you called."

I hear his happiness, and I can feel it too. "Me, too."

I hang up the phone and walk over to my dresser. Standing in front of the drawer, I pause and take a deep breath. I reach out and pull the handle with trembling hands. Lifting up the pictures, my fingers dig further until I feel it. I pull out the burgundy velvet box and just stare at it before my fingers shakily open the lid. It still shines just as brilliantly as when Clark first put it on my finger. Holding it close to my heart, I go to my closet and stand on my tippy toes to pull my keepsake box off the top shelf. I place it on the bed and sit down, open the shiny gold latch, and run my fingers over my butterfly shirt, my day of the week undies, but most especially the pictures of Clark and me. My favorite picture of us is here, the one at the beach during sunset. I hug it close to my chest for several minutes, right against my heart, then let out a sigh before I put it back in its special place. The velvet of the ring box makes its way to my cheek, and I hold it there as tears fill my eyes. "I love you, Clark. I always will," I whisper. I place it inside the keepsake box, tuck it away in my closet, and walk away, smiling.

♡ ♡ ♡

I may as well have called in sick today. Thank goodness it's Friday and Robby has left an alarmingly small number of sticky notes. But I can't think of anything except Brad all day. I'm going to tell him that I love him and we can finally be together. I can't wait to see him and wrap my arms around him. I'm never letting him go, ever.

Most of my day is spent flicking a pencil against my desk and watching the clock tick slowly by. I manage to answer twelve of twenty five voicemails and make a couple of baskets with Robby's completed sticky notes, which helps pass the time, too. My heart is vibrating loudly and my stomach is doing belly flops. I love Brad and I can't wait to tell him. I smile at the fragrant garden my cubicle has become. This is it.

At 6:30, I clean up my desk, gather up my jacket, grab my purse and the single red rose I bought for Brad, and make my way over to Rockefeller Center. Even the supreme nastiness of the subway doesn't bother me tonight, nor the fact that my foot has been stepped on twice, nor that I just sat on a piece of gum.

Clark's words suddenly come back to me...*let yourself feel, let yourself love, be happy.*

I will, Clark; I promise.

I don't see Brad when I get there, so I take a minute to try and compose myself. The delicate petals of the rose are shaking, but steadying my hands is an impossible task. My heart is racing. I can't wait to see Brad. Taking a deep breath of the night air to settle my nerves, I marvel again at how magnificent the city looks from up here, my mind drifting back to the perfection of our first date.

Looking down at my watch, I notice it's 7:15. It's not like him to be late. My feet are pacing the platform, rose petals blowing in the cool breeze. Tick tock. Another few minutes go by and I pull out my phone. Brad's phone rings and rings, then finally goes into voicemail. Texting him doesn't elicit a response either. What the hell? Has he changed his mind? No, he hasn't. I trust him. I trust the way he feels about me.

Another half hour goes by. I'm cold, and it's not from the temperature. Four voicemails and four texts with no response.

Something's wrong. My body feels prickly, and not in a good way. Worry is beginning to consume me. I can't stay here. Willing my legs to move, I head for the subway and make my way to The Brew House, only to find the "Closed" sign on the door. Dammit, where are you Brad? I continue to call him, but he doesn't answer, and tears are threatening. I run to the subway. My feet are having a hard time catching up to my mind. I need to get home. I need Fran.

Tears are crashing down my face and I push open the door with more force than I'd intended. Fran sees the look in my eyes. "What is it, Gabby? What's wrong?!"

"I called Brad and told him I wanted to see him. But he didn't show up."

"What do you mean? Why didn't he show up?"

My breathing is erratic. "I don't...know. We were...supposed to meet...and...I...can't reach him. Something's wrong, Fran, I just know it. I've called...him...several times and sent him texts, but he hasn't responded. I don't...know...who to call."

"You need to try and calm down, sweetie. Maybe he had to stay at the shop a bit longer."

I'm screaming now. "No, Fran! I went by there! He isn't there! He would have called me!" Falling to my knees, my cheeks course with salty tears as soft whimpers leave my mouth. "I've finally found the person I'm meant to be with and I can't freaking find him." I've got a sinking feeling in the pit of my stomach. Fran runs over and folds her arms around me. I let go, sobs pouring out from every crevice of my body.

Fran calls the police. Apparently you can't file a missing person's report for twenty-four hours. That's such bullshit.

The last time I looked at the clock it was 6:00am. Somewhere between sobbing uncontrollably and waiting, we fall asleep. When I open my eyes, Fran is hunched up beside me. My eyes are sore and I can barely see through the slits. Squinting, I peer over at the digital clock and think it reads 3:00pm. Oh my God, we slept the whole day. Recognition of last night washes over me and I frantically grab my phone off the coffee table. Dialing Brad's number, I'm silently willing him to answer. *Please pick up, please pick up, please pick up.* The moment I hear his voicemail, I fall apart. Slumping down to the soiled carpet, my face dampens from a fresh batch of tears. I recognize this feeling. Something's happened to him. Deep down I know it's true, even though I'm praying like hell it's not.

My phone buzzes and with shaky hands I knock it over. I nab it quickly, and when I see it's Brad, relief envelopes my whole body.

"Gabby?" The voice doesn't belong to Brad.

"Who is this?"

"Gabby, this is Brad's brother, Matt." No, please no.

"Where's Brad. Is he okay?"

"Something's happened, Gabby."

I fall to the ground, and my next words are but a whisper. "Is he alive?"

"Yes, but he's pretty badly hurt."

"Where is he?"

"He's at New York Presbyterian. He's in the Intensive Care Unit."

"I'll be right there." I hang up and drop to my knees. It's happening all over again. I have to get to him. Tears are streaming down my cheeks and they won't stop. Silently, I offer up healing prayers. *Please be okay, Brad. Please be okay. You have to be okay.* I love you.

Pushing on Fran's shoulder, I jolt her awake. "Fran, it's Brad."

Only tears break the silence.

$$\heartsuit \heartsuit \heartsuit$$

Fran and I run through the hospital doors like freaking lunatics. Out of breath, I try and get the words out to one of the three people sitting behind the desk. "Where...is...the Intensive Care Unit?"

A nurse with soft hazel eyes and a sweet wrinkled face replies, "it's on the third floor, dear."

"Thank you." Fran leads me by the hand to the elevators. She says nothing, but continues to hold my hand.

The elevator pings open and we see the sign pointing to the Intensive Care Unit. Sprinting down the hall, we finally make it to the nurse's station. "I'm looking for Brad Dixon."

"He's unconscious, and we're letting in very few visitors at this point. Are you family?"

I'm about to say something, when a deep voice calls out. "That's his wife."

Fran and I whip our heads around to the sound. Matt. It couldn't be more obvious. Except for darker hair and a slight variation in height, they're identical. Matt doesn't hesitate. He pulls me into a hug and my tears start anew.

Once I'm calm, I look over at Fran. "Matt, this is my best friend, Fran. Fran this is Brad's brother, Matt."

Fran can't help herself. She does her once over before she speaks. "Nice to meet you, Matt."

Matt gives Fran a second look. It's hard not to. "You, too," he says.

Fran looks over at me with kind eyes. "I'll be in the waiting room if you need me, sweetie, okay?"

"Thanks, Fran."

Matt leads me through the glass double doors. The moment I see Brad, my legs give out. His eyes are closed and he's laying on the bed with a bandage wrapped around his head. There are all sorts of tubes protruding from his body. His face is swollen and bruises cover his shoulders and arms. I can't move. *Brad.* My whole body feels cold, and an ill feeling washes over me as I look at him, helpless and bruised. Teardrops hit the floor and I feel like I can hear them.

Matt raises me off the floor and helps me to a chair. My body is shaking. "I'm so sorry to have to meet you under these circumstances, Gabby."

I'm gasping for a breath. "Is he going to be okay? Tell me what happened."

"I got a call around 9 last night, your time. Apparently, after Brad closed the shop, he was jumped from behind. They took his wallet and beat him up pretty badly. He has some bleeding to his brain, which is why he's unconscious."

Jesus. This is all my fault. If I hadn't called him to meet me, this would never have happened. "But he's going to wake up, right?" I ask with a jittery voice.

"Gabby, the doctors can't say for sure. He was hit pretty hard on the head several times with some sort of blunt instrument." Matt chokes up a little at that and I can't help but feel sorry for the guy. His mom, his sister, and now his brother?

My hands are quivering uncontrollably and my head falls into my lap. Matt strokes my hair with his fingers. He's kind, just like his brother.

I just want to be near Brad. Moving my chair next to the bed, I grab hold of his hand. It feels heavy and limp. Laying my cheek against his arm, I silently offer up more prayers. *Please, God, let him wake up. Please let him wake up. He has to wake up.* Don't do this to me again. Matt comes and sits by my side, his arm draped around my shoulder. I have no words right now, and don't feel like talking, unless it's to Brad.

After a few moments, Matt makes his way down to the cafeteria so I can have some time with Brad. I don't know if he can hear me, but I talk to him anyway. I tell him how worried I am, but mostly how much I miss hearing his laugh, seeing his smile, feeling his touch. "I love you, Brad," I say, resting my head on his limp arm.

Matt taps me on the shoulder, as I must have dozed off. I have no concept of time. He suggests I go home and get some rest, but I'm not going anywhere. Not without Brad. I've already let Robby know I need some time off. Work is the least of my concerns right now.

I'm so thankful Matt's here. Being near someone that Brad is close to makes me feel nearer to him. With his mom and sister gone, and his dad nonexistent, Matt is all he really has. Wait, that's not true anymore. Now he has *me*. I just need him to wake up so I can tell him. Tears are forcing their way to the surface again. Why won't he wake up?

I run my fingers gently across Brad's cheek. It's so swollen. Tears I'd been holding in fall down my cheeks.

Matt goes over to his bag and pulls something out. "Gabby, this was with Brad's things when they brought him in. It has your name on it."

I reach out with trembling hands and take the note. Opening the folded paper, I attempt to read the words through a blur of tears.

Dear Gabby,

From the moment I first saw you, I couldn't take my eyes off of you. You took my breath away. Your beauty captivated me, yes, but it was something more. Something about you grabbed hold of me and I didn't want to let go. When you looked up at me and your eyes met mine, it was as if they spoke to me. They told me you needed me. They told me to look inside and come find you, so I did.

As time went on, I found myself wanting to make you smile, wanting to feel your warmth, wanting to hold your hand, wanting to steal your heart. You awakened me. I was unfulfilled. I was lost. But somehow, when you walked into my shop that day, with your quiet confidence and your beautiful smile, you found me. And I found the one person who makes me feel alive. But mostly, I found the woman I've fallen in love with. The woman who makes me feel more emotion than I ever thought possible, so much that I sometimes feel as though my heart might float away and carry me along with it. And I'm willing to go, as long as it's with you.

He's in love with me. I lay my hand on his and stroke it gently, whispering, "I love you too, Brad. I love you. I love you."

A nurse walks in the room. "I need to make him a bit more comfortable so I'd like you to step out." I'm about to give her my best right hook when she says, "don't worry, you can come back in soon." She smiles and I feel okay leaving Brad with her, if only for a few minutes.

Walking out to the waiting room, I find Fran and Kyle sitting together, holding hands. Kyle's genuine eyes reach me and he walks over and hugs me tightly. "I'm so sorry, Gabby. Brad's strong, though, and he's gonna be okay."

"Thanks, Kyle. I appreciate you being here, and Brad would, too." We all find a place to sit and Fran sits next to me and rubs my back with her gentle hands while I sob quietly. It's so soothing. She finally pushes away and looks at my face. "Sweetie, you look like absolute shit."

I make a futile attempt at a smile.

"What are the doctors saying?" She asks tenderly.

"He's got bleeding in his brain. We just have to wait and see. They can't make any promises. He was struck on the head pretty hard, so they won't know anything until he wakes up" Then I take a deep breath. "If he wakes up."

She pats my hand and forces a smile. "Gabby. You have to keep the faith. He's going to wake up. He has to."

"God, Fran, he can't die. He just can't. It's like Clark all over again."

Fran's face grows serious. "NO it's not, Gabby. He's *not* Clark. Brad's going to be okay."

What would I ever do without Fran?

She looks at me, anger consuming her face. "Did they at least get the assholes who did this to him?"

I hang my head. "No, they got away, and there were no witnesses."

"Fuck," she says, gritting her teeth. Kyle keeps his hand in hers, steadying her.

I don't care about anything else as long as Brad wakes up. "I just want him to wake up, Fran."

Fran looks at me with hopeful eyes. "I know, sweetie, I know."

Taking the letter out of my bag, I hand it to Fran.

"What's this?" she asks.

I can't bear to look at it again, it hurts too much. "Just read it."

Fran takes a minute to read the note. Her eyes go wide and she puts her head on my shoulder. "Jesus, Gabby, he's so fucking poetic. And he's head over heels in love with you."

A tear drips slowly down my cheek. "And I with him."

We sit quietly for a few minutes. Kyle pipes up. "Gabby, you're really pale. I'm going to run down to the cafeteria to get you something to eat."

"I'm not hungry, Kyle," I protest.

"You have to eat, Gabby," he says with forceful concern.

"Kyle's right. You have to keep your strength up." Fran puts her hand on his back.

I feel myself getting worked up, and I'm starting to bite my nails. I never bite my nails. "Fran, where's Matt? Maybe he's trying to reach their dad. I haven't seen the doctors lately either. I wish someone would tell me what's going on."

Fran takes my face in her hands. "Gabby, you have to calm down. You're exhausted, you haven't eaten, and you're sick with worry. That's not a good combination."

Kyle comes back with a cheeseburger, a latte, and a bag of Swedish Fish. I almost smile; he's so well-trained, but I don't feel like eating any of it. "Thanks, Kyle."

He gives me a kiss on the cheek, sits down next to Fran, and laces his fingers through hers. I need Brad to hold *my* hand right now.

Fran leans over to me and whispers, "you need to keep your strength up. How else are you going to be able to show your hot piece of ass how much you love him if you're withering away?"

"I love you, Fran."

"I know, sweetie. Oh, I almost forgot, there was a message at home from someone named Edith Hanley."

"Yeah, that's the program director from Parsons. I decided to enroll for next year."

"Sweetie, that's fantastic!"

It should be, but right now I don't feel very excited. "Yeah, I guess."

Fran and Kyle stay with me a bit longer, but I finally kick them out when the nurse says I can go back in to sit with Brad.

Fran stands up and pulls me into her arms, enveloping me in one of her bear hugs. Tears start to trickle down my cheeks. "Let me know if you need anything at all, okay, sweetie?"

Kyle hugs me and gives me another kiss on the cheek. "Keep us posted, okay?"

"I will. Thanks, Kyle."

Fran takes my hand and kisses it. "You need me, I'm here. It's as simple as that. I love you."

"I love you, too."

We embrace each other one last time, and then they're gone. As I think about Fran, I'm reminded of how important she is to me. She's my family. The real family that loves and accepts unconditionally. She does that for me. Now I have someone else who does that for me, too. I just need the chance to tell him.

Chapter Thirty-Four

It's been three days and no change. The doctors come in and speak with Matt and me about Brad's prognosis. "While he's been unconscious for a while, he hasn't gotten any worse, and that's actually a good sign. And he's still breathing on his own, which is great." When they say the word coma, though, I tune them out. He's not slipping away from me. I won't let him. Not this time.

Matt hasn't left his side. His clothes are wrinkled, his face is sagging, and his eyes are lifeless, but all I see is the love he has for his brother. Matt comes over to sit next to me and holds my hand. "Brad's told me so much about you, Gabby. I feel like I already know you." I just nod my head. "He's been in love with you for a long time." God, I'm such an idiot.

I brought a book with me today; I thought I could read some of the passages to Brad. I'm still not sure if he can hear me, but hold out hope that, somewhere deep down, my voice is reaching him. As I read the words, I'm silently praying he wakes up just like you see in the movies. After six chapters, he hasn't, and my brain clunks me over the head and reminds me that this is real life.

Brad has had several visitors over the past couple of days. Most of them I recognize from The Brew House. I didn't realize what a close knit group they all are, and how much they care about him. It warms my heart.

As the days trickle by, I'm starting to lose hope that I may ever look into Brad's eyes again. The eyes that love me. I have to stop myself, though. He just has to come back to me. Taking his hand, I keep it pressed to the slow, steady beat of my heart. Maybe he can feel my love. I hope so. *I love you, Brad.*

I'm so tired and I've cried so much. My face is tear-stained and blotchy and my eyes only allow in tiny slivers of light. As I stare at the same grey spot on the dingy hospital wall, the one I've been staring at for the past three days, I'm reminded of our kiss, and so desperately want us to go back to the kissing spot so we can do a lot more kissing. There are so many things I want to do with Brad. So much I want to say. Now I just pray I have a chance to do that.

A voice interrupts my thoughts. "Gabby."

I know that voice.

Looking over at Matt, I can see he heard it, too, as he immediately spins his head to the sound. We both move in closer and see Brad's eyes flicker. Oh my God. Another flicker. Then I see weary brown eyes and I hear singing, but there's no music. It must be my heart.

I stare into those loving eyes. I've never been so happy in my life. He starts to speak, but I quiet him. I don't want him to speak. I just want him to listen. "I love you, I love you, I love you," I say as I gently stroke the side of his cheek with my fingers. It comes out in the softest whisper, but I know he hears me. I see a single tear slide down his cheek. I lean forward and kiss it away.

Matt grabs his hand. "Hey, bro. You have no idea how glad I am to see you."

Brad squeezes his hand. "Hey, man," he barely whispers.

Matt runs out to get the doctors. I don't want Brad to talk yet, but he seems desperate. "I was trying to get to you," he says in a hoarse voice. "I tried to fight back, but I couldn't. Before I blacked out...the last thing I saw was you."

I'm crying again and I can't stop. "Shhhhh...babe, we can talk later. You need to rest now."

Two doctors walk in with Matt following close behind. One of the doctors addresses us. "We'd like you both to step out for a few minutes so we can examine him and take him down for a scan."

I lean down and lightly kiss Brad's hand. "We'll be right outside, babe."

"Okay, baby."

I melt at his words. He's alive and he's going to be okay. My whole world smiles.

Matt and I stand in the hallway in shock for a few minutes after they wheel Brad away. He finally pulls me into a hug and completely breaks down. It's his turn to cry and I hold him, stroking his hair, thinking how scared he must've been, must still be. Eventually, he pulls away to get us some celebratory coffee while we wait.

I call and update Fran, who's on her way, and keep checking my watch as we wait with our nasty hospital coffee for Brad to come back. It seems to take forever. How long can a scan take? Another half hour goes by and we finally see him being rolled down the hall. I stand up and hold his hand, walking with him as the nurses wheel him back into the room.

I kiss his cheek gently. "I'll be right back, babe, I want to talk to the doctors."

I walk back outside and join Matt.

"The scan was clear. There's no more bleeding and all of his vitals look good. We're going to move him up to a regular room in the morning. We just want to monitor him here overnight. He'll probably be in the hospital for a few more days, just to be on the safe side." Relief washes over me. He's really going to be okay.

Matt lets out a huge sigh of relief. I hug him and feel relieved not only for myself, but for him as well. "He's okay," I whisper in his ear.

Matt goes to make some calls. I don't actually think he has to call anyone, but just wants to give Brad and me some time alone. He's so thoughtful.

Walking back in to the hospital room, Brad cracks a smile. "Come here, baby."

Tears I've been holding in slide down from my eyes. I sit as close to Brad as possible, my head resting on his shoulder, and I feel him stroking my hair. I missed him so much. "I was so scared," I whisper. "I thought I'd lost you."

Ever so quietly, he says, "I'm not going anywhere. We superheroes are invincible."

I smile and I'm surprised I remember what it feels like. It's the first real one I've had in over a week. Brad's eyes begin to close. He looks so drained. We both fall asleep until I feel someone nudge me on the shoulder. It's Matt and he's smiling for the first time, too.

"He's really going to be okay, Gabby."

Chapter Thirty-Five

Brad's hospital room is an improvement from the Intensive Care Unit he was in until a few days ago. The nurse came in and removed all of his tubes and monitors, with the exception of the IV, so he's much more comfortable. He's still sleeping, so I take a moment to watch him. He looks so peaceful. Those long lashes fanning his face, that crinkle in his forehead, those soft lips. God, I love him. Leaning forward, I lay my face on his chest so I can feel his warmth again.

I must've fallen asleep, because when my eyes open, I feel Brad's fingers strumming my cheek. I sigh, relishing the feel of his hand, and look up. He looks so much better today. The bruises are finally fading and he looks more like himself. I've never been so happy to see him.

His eyes meet mine and I chuckle. "To think you were worried about me walking around the city by myself. Looks like you needed your own guardian angel."

Brad looks at me with such emotion I feel like my heart's going to burst. "I already have my guardian angel." He drops a kiss on my nose.

Matt pokes his head in to see if Brad's awake and joins us. He's heading back to Los Angeles today. I'm kind of sorry to see him go. It's been nice to have him here. "So listen, Bro, you better do exactly what the doctors tell you to do; no messing around."

"I will, man." Brad looks teary-eyed. It's hard to say goodbye to your family. Especially if you actually like them.

Matt gives Brad the biggest hug. I'm so glad they have each other. Then he walks around the bed and pulls me into one.

Brad scowls. "Hey, watch it! You've stolen enough of my girlfriends."

We both laugh, but not before Matt says quietly in my ear. "Take care of him, okay?"

With Matt gone, and the nurses no longer hovering, we're finally alone. My lips reach up and smother Brad's face with kisses. Mid-kiss, he stops me. "I don't know if that's such a good idea, baby."

My face contorts in my favorite eight year-old pout. "Why not? I feel rejected."

Brad points down at the bed with his index finger. "Let's just put it this way. This is a very thin hospital sheet, and I wouldn't want to give the nurses an eyeful."

I laugh. "Hmmm...true. But how about I lock the door, and you can give me an eyeful right now?"

He laughs. A rich, full laugh that I've missed and that reminds me why I love him. "Don't tempt me, baby."

Just then, Fran barges through the door. "Hey, lovebirds! I've come with an offering of coffee and..." she pauses and eyes Brad's crotch. "Whoa. If I'd known you'd be this happy to see me, I would've come sooner."

I throw an empty dishpan at her.

"Oh, and by the way Brad, your brother is freaking hot!" She ducks as my shoe flies past her.

Chapter Thirty-Six

Brad's coming home from the hospital today. After five days of crappy hospital food and a really uncomfortable bed, he's definitely ready. If we had trees in Manhattan, I'd say he'd be home just in time to see the fall foliage. The nurses are going to miss him, I've heard them giggling about him from time to time. It makes me laugh. He's certainly not an eyesore around here.

When I walk into his room, he's got a smile so big it makes my heart happy. He motions me over to the bed and I sit down by his side.

He takes my hand in his as he leans forward and reaches me with his lips. "Hi, baby."

I look up at his lovely face and I'm suddenly filled with guilt. "I'm so sorry."

"For what?"

"It's...my fault that you got hurt."

Brad raises my face up to look at him. "Gabby, listen to me. It's not your fault. Do you hear me? *It's not your fault.*"

"But..."

Brad takes me in his arms and cradles me against his chest, stroking my hair with his fingers. "No, baby. It's not your fault. It happened. It's over and I'm fine. That's all that matters."

I swipe at my wayward tears. Brad lifts my face to his and grazes his thumb over my bottom lip. "Gabby, you didn't hurt me, your love is what saved me."

Chapter Thirty-Seven

It's been a month since Brad left the hospital. He's fully recovered and back at The Brew House. Digging through my purse, I find the note that Brad made me promise not to read until I got to work.

Dear Gabby,

I can't wait to see you tonight, and show you with my body what I feel with my heart.

I love you.

Brad

I take a deep breath, running my fingers over the words *I love you*. I'm eternally grateful that I got another chance. It's a miracle to get two chances at love, especially love like this.

I'm so excited about our date tonight that it's hard to get through the day, especially after that note. I can't wait to see him. The accident is behind us now and we can finally move forward. Together.

It's really windy tonight, so I take a taxi to Brad's apartment. I don't want my hair plastered to my face when I get there. When the door to his apartment opens, I'm immediately warmed by the smooth trill of Jeff Buckley's voice playing softly in the background. I can't help but smile. It reminds me of our first dance.

I barely have a chance to get in the door when Brad grabs me. "Baby, dance with me."

As if I could ever refuse him anything. "Sure."

Brad pulls me to him, so close that I can feel his sweet breath massage my neck, the scent of him pulling me into a dizzying whirl. His fingers slowly brush my cheek as the warmth in his eyes wraps around my heart. He guides my hands to the back of his neck, the smooth strands of his dark hair tickling my fingertips. This moment here with Brad is like a dream, one I don't want to wake from. But as his lips find mine, I know I'm not dreaming. He folds his arms around my waist and slips his warm tongue into my mouth, gliding over my teeth and sucking gently. The thin fabric of his polo shirt presses against my tender breasts, inciting tiny sprinkles of electricity and sparking my desire, a desire that only needs the nearness of him to be ignited.

Untangling his wet lips from mine, his tongue brushes the delicate shell of my ear as he makes his way to the curve of my neck. I let my head fall back and the feel of his heavy breath on my skin causes my heart to pound rapidly. A soft moan slips out. "*Brad.*"

The oven timer alerts us that something is ready in the oven. He whispers a curse then pauses for a moment and looks up into my eyes. "Hungry?" he breathes.

There's only one thing I want right now, and food is definitely not it. "Not so much," I whisper.

He leaves me, but only for a moment, to walk over to the oven. When he returns, he threads his fingers through mine and leads me down the hallway to his bedroom. Before we step inside, I'm rewarded with his soft, warm lips. "Wait here, baby."

My anticipation builds and I'm suddenly grateful that I took Fran's advice and wore my brand new Victoria's Secret lacy black bra and matching underwear. I want to be sexy for him. In fact, I've never wanted anything more.

He sashays out of the bedroom, dreamy brown eyes alive with mischief, and motions for me to come in. When I enter, what I see takes my breath away. Candles alight the room. A trail of red rose petals lead to the bed, a single red rose on one of the pillows. Tears sting the back of my eyes at his thoughtfulness. It's so romantic and perfect, just like him.

He walks over to me and I sweep the hair off his brow, my eyes taking in his beautiful face, looking up at him in wonder. "I can't believe you did all this for me. Are you for real?"

He looks at me, a teasing smile playing on his lips. "Baby, I'm about to show you just how real I am." He grabs my hips, pulling me snugly against him, his erection pressing into my groin. His lips brush softly against mine. "Does that feel real to you? 'Cause that's what you do to me. You and only you."

I wrap my fingers around the curve of his neck, drawing him in. His mouth inches closer to mine while his hands wander lazily down my skin, which is now burning for his touch. As his fingers begin to ease the bunched silk of my blouse up, our mouths find one another. His tongue traces the curve of my bottom lip, capturing it, sucking me into his mouth. I open my tender lips and he presses me more tightly against his toned body.

I pull my blouse over my head and feel the ridges of his defined chest press against the thin lace of my bra, unruly breaths leaking out as he pulls me hard against him. I can feel every inch of his arousal. Small moans escape my lips and I hear him gasp as he whispers, "I love you, Gabby." The air leaves his mouth and bounces off my skin, continuing to taunt me, my nipples tightening deliciously. Slowly, he moves behind me and lifts the silky hair away from my bare shoulder, spreading soft, tender kisses across each delicate blade. His fingers make their way to the clasp of my bra, unhooking it, and I arch back against him as he reaches around and squeezes my full breasts and rolls his fingers over my nipples, which harden against his touch. He glides his hands down to unzip my skirt and it slides down my legs, leaving me covered only by the thin lace of my panties. Before I know it, I'm facing him, trying to control my now uncontrollable breaths.

Brad is staring at me, admiring me, loving me. "God, you're so beautiful."

I move closer to him and gently tug at his polo shirt so I can lift it over his head. His chest is smooth and muscular and I move my fingernails slowly across it, a sexy groan leaving his hot mouth. Bending down on my knees, I pull off his jeans, noticing he's practically bursting out of his boxers.

He moves his mouth over mine tenderly before he slides his tongue inside and grabs me with his desire. Without ever leaving my lips, he walks with me until the back of my knees are touching his bed, then lowers me down gently. Never taking his eyes off mine, he eases my lace panties down my legs and I'm exposed, but not embarrassed. I want him to see me. All of me. Standing back up, Brad rids himself of the last bit of fabric covering his manhood. For the first time, I take my eyes off of his and glance down at his arousal, stirring the pot of desire deep in my belly. God, he's so beautiful, inside and out.

He crawls onto the bed, pushing me back onto the pillows, and lifts himself over me as his tongue skims over my body setting me on fire. His wet lips surround my nipple, sucking gently as his fingers tease my other nipple and tiny whimpers fall from my lips. His tongue dives back into my mouth, our bodies pressed together like two intricate pieces of a puzzle. The feel of his heated skin against mine, coupled with his familiar scent and his warm, rapid breaths makes me ache for him. "I want to taste you," he whispers. His words make me swollen and wet. He rolls his tongue down the dips of my neck. Trailing featherlight kisses from my breasts to my belly button, he moves lower and my hips arch into his warm mouth as I let out a strangled moan. His tongue flicks back and forth over my dampness, causing my eyelids to flutter closed and my head to fall back against the pillow. When he comes back up, his lips are glistening with my desire, his eyes filled with heat. Raising himself over me, he takes in the length of my body before returning to my face. "I love you, Gabby. Pull me inside you." His voice is hoarse and full of emotion and I grab his erection and lead him into the deepest part of me.

I'm completely surrounded by his heat, by the feelings that seep through his veins. It's like an infusion; he fills me with his love, and I'm lost.

He continues to push inside me, rocking his hips back and forth, back and forth. Brad whispers, "I love you, Gabby. I love you," over and over again, his voice broken from passion.

I inhale the scent of our bodies loving one another. His lips find mine again, our tongues gently twisting in a motion that brings peace to our erratic heartbeats. We hold onto one another so tightly it's almost painful, silently begging the other to never let go, until are bodies betray our desires and we orgasm together.

It's amazing what the body can feel when accompanied by the heart. It's like a perfect symphony of feeling, of emotion, of a love you thought was impossible; until suddenly the impossible becomes inevitable.

Our breathing calms, and my mind opens to the depth of this moment for me. Brad leans in and kisses my face again, and again, and again. The wetness on my cheeks causes him to look up at me with concern. "You're crying, baby. Did I hurt you?"

The words don't come right away, only the tears. "I'm fine. It's just that...I almost lost you...and I love you, Brad...I love you so much."

His joy-filled brown eyes surround me as he brings his fingers up to caress my cheek. "I love you, too, Gabby. Fate led me to you. It will always be you."

I lay awake and listen as Brad's breathing slows and lulls him into a peaceful sleep. I don't sleep, though. I don't want to close my eyes for fear that this is all a dream. I push up on my elbows and watch him. I love him so much, and feel so grateful that he somehow managed to find his way through...through all the clutter, all the disappointment, all the pain, to finally find *me*. The real me. He loves me. Not who he wants me to be, not who he expects me to be. Just me, and that's all I've ever wanted.

I'm thankful now for every moment that has led me to this point. For all my life lessons, and the people who taught me them along the way. Without them, I would never have walked down this gravelly, uneven road. The road that led me here, to Brad. This is where I'm supposed to be, and my heart knows it because I can *finally* feel it.

Epilogue

BRAD

One Year Later

"Are we really doing this?" Gabby asks me anxiously as we make our way to the top.

"What do you mean? Of course we are. It's on your list."

I grab hold of Gabby's hand. As much as she wanted to do this, she seems extremely nervous now that we're here. We're making our way up in the elevator at ten miles per hour, and were told by the guide that the trip takes all of 41 seconds. Wild. I'm pretty excited because I've never done anything like this before, but even more excited that I'm doing it with my girl.

When we arrive at the top and step out, I'm in awe. The pictures and movies I've seen about the Space Needle don't compare to how absolutely breathtaking it really is. You can see everything. The downtown Seattle skyline, the Olympic and Cascade Mountains, Mount Rainier, Mount Baker, even Elliott Bay.

Gabby seems completely dazzled. She looks over at me. "Wow, babe. This is simply amazing. I never imagined it would be so extraordinary."

While Gabby goes back to admiring the view, I take a moment to admire *her*. She's so beautiful. Her shiny chestnut hair reflects the sunlight, blowing gently off her shoulders with the light summer breeze. Her blue eyes penetrate my soul. The curve of her neck so subtly connects itself to the rest of her sculptured body. Her spirit is so full of life. The life she fills me with every day.

I walk over to her and wrap my arms around her slim waist. She instantly leans back so I can cradle her head under mine. Contentment is the only thing I feel.

Gabby tilts her head back and I stare into those gorgeous blue eyes, then move in to grab a little slice of heaven from her lips. After, she settles again under the warmth of my chin.

I have to shake myself because I can hardly believe I'm here with this girl. The girl who stepped out of my dreams and into my heart. I don't remember ever smiling so much, feeling so much, or loving so much. She took everything I ever thought about love and turned it inside out. She turned me inside out.

"So I've been wondering something," I say nervously.

"Hmmm...mmmm."

"About your list."

"Yeah. What about it?" she asks curiously.

"Is marrying the man of your dreams on there?"

She whips her head around, her eyes as wide and blue as the sky. I take Gabby's delicate hand in mine as I lower myself to one knee. The tears are already beginning to form in the sweetness of her eyes.

"Gabby. Before I met you, the air surrounding me was stale; I was gasping for something...anything. But then you crashed into me and I swallowed a big gulp of life. You helped me breathe again....You made me *want* to breathe again. That moment you spilled your coffee in my shop, and you looked up at me with those embarrassed blue eyes, something inside me clicked. You awakened my heart. You got it beating again, so I could really feel it. I love the way it feels. I love the way *you* make me feel. You're the most beautiful person I've ever met, not just on the outside, but on the inside, where it counts. I want to spend every single moment of my life making you happy, making you smile. Gabrielle Willis...will you do me the honor of marrying me and spending the rest of your life with me?"

Tears run slowly down Gabby's cheeks as she stares into my eyes. Her lips move, but I don't hear anything, so I lean in closer. The word "yes" squeaks out in a whisper through her tears. I slip the engagement ring onto her finger and she pulls me to her. The only place I want to be.

She leans back and smoothes the hair from my eyes. "Thank you," she says.

"For what?"

Gabby takes my hand and lays it on her chest, her heart beating rapidly. "For being the one to hold my heart."

Her lips find mine and her sweet breath fills my lungs, our tongues dancing together tenderly. Wrapping my arms around her neck, I trail a path of sweet kisses from the corner of her full lips to the curve of her throat and smile as a soft moan escapes. I come back to her lips and slide my tongue inside, tasting her, breathing her. Time stands still until we pull back, lost of breath, but full of life.

The End

Acknowledgements

The journey to writing this novel has been such an amazing one for me. I feel so blessed and grateful to be in this place and have so many wonderful people to thank.

To my husband for inspiring me every day to live passionately and for supporting me unconditionally in whatever I decide to do in my life. For helping me to see that I could really do this, and, that I can do anything I set my mind to; because, well, when I set my mind to something, I do it. For picking up the slack through this entire process of a messy house and a completely scattered brain, all the while trying to finish up his own novel too. I love you deeply.

To my two amazing children who have been my joys since the day they were born. For inspiring me to tell and write stories, just so I can see their smiles and hear their giggles that take me to a happy place. I love my family and sharing this with them is what it's all about for me.

To Stephanie and Smokey for helping me find my sense of direction in New York and for always showing me so much love and support. I love you both.

To Lisa Deeds for being an amazing friend and support, and for all the constructive feedback regarding my novel. You are unique and special and I love you.

To Colleen Webley, Nikki Groom, Sherrie Cannitello-Fahey, Lisa Wrobel, Susan Carbine, Damien & Sally Connolly, David & Quynh Rodriguez, Jennifer Chrysadakis, Angel Sylvia, Jennifer

Zamuda, Angie Julious, Cristina Haithwaite, Amie Steelman, Marissa Terifay, and Suzanne Graceffa for being so incredibly supportive and showing me an overabundance of love, excitement and support. You all rock and I love you!

To my friends and fellow authors Devon Herrera, Monica James, L. Chapman, Tracey Manning, L.M. Augustine, Laura Howard, Colleen Albert, MR Joseph, Wendy Ferraro, and all of the other authors who have supported me and cheered me on, I am beyond grateful and feel humbled to be in the presence of such truly remarkable individuals.

To Cheryl McIntyre for all your kind words of encouragement, your enthusiasm for my novel, and for telling stories that I not only love to read, but that inspire me.

To E.L. James for making me fall in love with Christian and Ana, and for rekindling my love of reading that had gotten lost somewhere along the way. I have no doubt that I would not be in this place had I not decided to explore the world of Fifty Shades.

To Colleen Hoover and Jessica Park for your brilliance, for inspiring me with your words, and for making me feel so much.

To all the wonderful bloggers who have supported me throughout this process with never-ending enthusiasm. To Natalie Catalano from Love Between the Sheets for all of her hard work and efforts to organize my Blog Tour, Vilma's Book Blog, Tessa's Take, Mary Elizabeth's Crazy Book Obsession, Bookaholics Blog, The Blushing Reader, Chris's Book Blog Emporium, Book Addict Mumma, Can't Read Just One, Amber's Reading Room, T's Bookish Moments of Escape, The Phantom Paragrapher, Book Nerds Anonymous, Bridger Bitches Book Blog, Candy Coated Book Blog, Sarah's Book Blog, Hooked On Books, Angie's Dreamy Reads, Pretty in Pink Books and Reviews, Love N Books, Rude Girl Book

Blog, TheSecretBookBrat, Maria's Book Blog, Romance Addict Book Blog, Book Reader Chronicles, Winding Stairs Book Blog, Smardy Pants Book Blog, Naughty and Nice Book Blog, Wine Relaxation and My Kindle, A Love Affair WIth Books, The Book Enthusiast, Scandalous Book Blog, The Girl In A Cafe, Shh Mom's Reading, Romantic Reading Escapes, Kindle Crack Book Reviews, Mystical World of Books, Anna Reads Romance, Writing Belle, Tamara's One Stop Indie Shop, CherryOBlossoms Blog Spot, A Page Away...and to all of the other bloggers and those of you who have taken the time to read my novel and review it, I am beyond appreciative.

To my editor, Erin Roth, for coming along at just the right time, for believing in my story, and for helping me to grow and become a better writer. I feel very blessed!

To Angela McLaurin at Fictional Formats for taking my novel and making it look beautiful. You are amazing!

Lastly, but certainly not least...to my readers. Thank you for taking the time to read my story. I was a reader long before I became a writer, so I know what it means to read a book that makes your spirit soar and your heart happy. I hope my novel does that for you.

About the Author

I am a wife, a mom, an author, and a lover of all things chocolate, well, anything sweet really. While stuffing chocolate in my face, I enjoy reading young adult and new adult novels furiously, and spending time with my husband and two adorable children who keep me on my peppermint pink painted toes. Those same children who inspire me to tell silly stories that cause hysterical giggles to tumble from their bellies.

I love to laugh and love to have a good cry, especially after reading a novel that stretches my soul, one that makes me feel, and lingers in the corner of my heart.

I'm a hopeless romantic and a happily ever after fanatic, and I love to write about LOVE.

I began writing when I was in middle school, penning anything from short stories, to poetry, and then later moved on to write children's books. I have now endeavored into New Adult and Contemporary Romance novels and am loving every minute of it. *Love Love* is my first published novel.

I would love to hear from you, so please feel free
to reach out to me:

Email: beth@bethmichele.com

Website: http://www.bethmichele.com

Twitter: http://www.twitter.com/bethmichele8

Facebook: https://www.facebook.com/pages/Beth-Michele-Author/198619836947212?fref=ts